RAVES FOR **THE CAMINO CLUB**

IR

"Kevin Craig's *The Camino Club* is an intricately woven story of laughter and heartbreak, loss and love. In it, six troubled teens take a journey through the heart of Spain alongside their court-assigned counselors, finding their way through the issues that brought them together. Funny and poignant, this story of friendship and falling in love will remind you that our paths are not defined by our pasts, but the choices we make each day."

—DANIKA STONE, author of *All the Feels*,
Internet Famous and *Switchback*

"A beautiful book filled with heart. THE CAMINO CLUB takes readers on a pilgrimage along the Camino de Santiago in Spain with six delinquent teens. Not only do they find themselves along the way, but they also discover they're all worthy of love. I laughed, I cried, I couldn't put it down. "

—KIP WILSON, YA author of *White Rose*

"Often hilarious and always heartfelt, THE CAMINO CLUB is an uplifting story about six mismatched teens on the journey of a lifetime, who learn that the only way to get over the past and head for the future is to live in the moment."

—TOM RYAN, author of *Keep This to Yourself*
and *I Hope You're Listening*

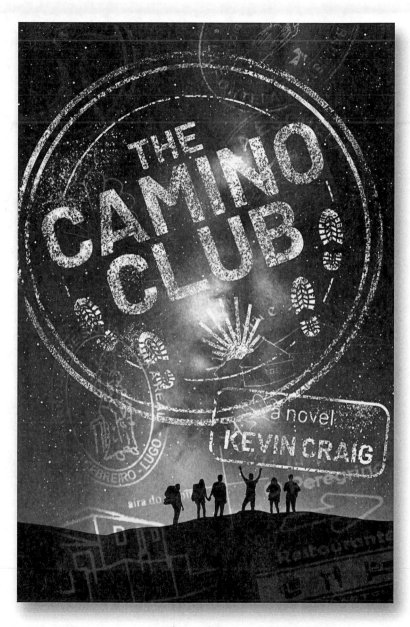

interlude ✦ press • new york

interlude press • new york

In Memory of Davida, who raised me, Connie Grisley, who walked with me in 2014, and Deborah, who followed along from home in 2019.

"I believe in the good things coming."

—Nahko Bear

CHAPTER 1

DIEGO NELSON

IT ALL STARTED WITH FIRE. I wanted to show Sabrina Vincent I'd do anything for her. Naturally, I set fire to the garbage in the first floor washroom, strategically near a sensitive smoke detector. Now I'm forced into The Walk, and Sabrina still doesn't even know I'm alive. Well, she may know the name of the guy who gave everyone a free period. But, I mean, she doesn't *know me* know me. Unrequited love's a drag.

I still think it might have been worth it. I mean, I *did* get my name on the map of her universe, right? Maybe now she wants to know more about Diego Nelson. Maybe she's intrigued. Who knows? Maybe I'm now a satellite in her night sky. I just have to wait for her to turn her telescope on me.

I know one thing for sure. The first part of the summer is not mine. The Walk Youth Diversion Program owns my ass, and there isn't a damn thing I can do about it. If your one and only slipup is a big one, your leverage gets taken away from you. Juvenile detention or The Walk.

This Gilbert dude who runs the program sounds like a total douchebag, too. My life is over. First of all, who the hell is called Gilbert, and why wouldn't they change their name if they could? Clearly his parents had it in for him. A week and a half with him, and I'll be ready for death. Hell, I was ready for it after fifteen minutes with him in the meeting with Moms, Principal Peters, and that lawyer. Dude is about as interesting and relevant as a dead cat. I might die of boredom before exhaustion ever even takes place.

But I guess The Walk is known for exhausting people. I don't even know how it's legal to take a kid out of his own country and force him to walk a gazillion miles in the hot sun over mountains and shit in a foreign country. I mean, you've *got* to be kidding me.

By the time I get back, summer will be almost over, and I will have missed any and every opportunity I would have had to keep myself in Sabrina's universe. I'll fade from her sky, probably forever.

Slight exaggeration, I know. A week and a half does not a summer make. But the beginning of summer is the most important time for setting things up socially. Hell, even my best friends will forget who I am by the time I come back from Spain.

Lesson learned? Don't set fires for people who will never appreciate the gesture even if you're mad crushing on them and desperate to get them to notice you. Dude, it just ain't worth it.

Now I find myself—me, Diego Nelson—packing a backpack with all this random crap, preparing for a flight across the frigging Atlantic Ocean. I mean, I've never been on a plane before. I've never even been outside Toronto.

Moms must totally hate me. Why else would she send her one and only child into the jaws of death just for setting a little fire at school? No matter how much my abuelita thinks it's a great idea.

I still remember the day the ultimatum came down. Moms freaking out all the way home on the subway, ranting about not having money for the program. "Look at all these things, Diego. Look at them—the backpack alone. I cannot afford this. What have you done?"

"I'm sorry, Moms." I pleaded with her to calm down. People around us were staring, listening in. "We won't do it. I'll take the other one. I have to."

"And have a record? Be with those bad boys? I'll never get you back. You've ruined everything. Everything your grandmother and I worked so hard for, Diego, paving the way for your success. It's gone."

She stormed off the subway at our stop. Didn't even look back to see if I followed.

When we got home it was even worse. She told my abuelita everything. Watching my grandmother's face sink as she learned of her grandson's crime? It felt like a piece of me died as that look of disappointment washed over her. I was mad. Mad at myself for being so stupid. Mad at Moms for telling her after she said she couldn't, after she said she wanted to spare her the shame and the hurt.

When Moms brought up the alternative to juvenile detention, though? The second she told my abuelita about the diversion program—about the Camino de Santiago—the look on her face changed instantly.

As Moms cried in desperation because we couldn't choose the costly diversion program, my grandmother took Moms's hands in hers, looked her in the eyes, and said, "He must go."

"Mami, he can't. I cannot do this. I can't afford these things," Moms said, tossing down the crumpled list she pulled from her purse.

My grandmother picked it up, glanced at the long list of random crap, set it back down, and said, "He goes. Ana, it is the Camino de Santiago. The pilgrim's path, the way of St. James. Pilgrims have been walking the Camino for hundreds and hundreds of years. Since before the Middle Ages. They walk to the bones of the apostle St. James that rest in the cathedral in Santiago de Compostela. They walk to find themselves. He goes, Ana. That is all. You tell them. Make the arrangements. It will be his penance. He is a good Catholic boy."

So not only have I totally disgraced and humiliated the two most important women in my life, I'm also going to the Camino de Santiago on my poor abuelita's dime, her cherished savings.

"Ma?" I yell as I continue to scroll down the *Things to Bring* list. "What's a spork?"

"It's a spoon and a fork in one."

I barely hear this. She's in the kitchen. I know what she's doing. The same thing she does every morning when I'm getting ready for school and she's getting ready for work. She's standing at the kitchen counter having her cup of instant coffee and her one slice of slightly burned toast with a light spreading of cottage cheese. Ack.

This morning isn't a schoolday or workday, though. This morning is the day of my flight. The bad kids' field trip begins.

"Why do I have to bring a *spork*, anyway?"

"Because Gilbert told you to, Diego." I can hear her walking down the hall. Coming to lecture me again. Just one more time. Again.

"Starting today, that man is your boss," she says as she arrives at my bedroom door, spork in hand. "You do *what* he says, *when* he says. If that includes carrying this spork on your nose across Spain, then you will do it. Do you understand me, mister?"

She tosses the spork onto the bed.

"Yeah, but—"

"Don't *yeah but* me, Diego Nelson. You will listen to him, young man. I didn't raise an arsonist. Do you understand me?"

"Yes, ma'am."

Moms has been on high octane ever since the incident. She's a tough cookie at the best of times. I don't blame her, really. She has all these dreams for me—university and a career—and she's seen how close I came to destroying it all. I'm such a loser.

"You're almost done packing, Dee. Just finish that list and come to the kitchen and eat your breakfast. You need to eat before we head to the airport. Breakfast is the most—"

"*Important meal of the day*," I say, finishing her once-a-day-repeated mantra on the importance of breakfast. Even though she herself lives on her daily piece of toast. "Yeah, Ma. I know. Almost finished."

"Roll, Diego." She pulls the three single, solitary T-shirts I'm allowed to bring out of my backpack and unfolds them so she can roll them up instead. "Rolling is better than folding when you're packing. Even for a backpack." She hugs my shirts. "Oh my God, I'm sending my baby across the world with nothing but the clothes on his back. I'm a terrible mother. Oh my God, Diego."

She's losing it. She said she wasn't going to lose it. She promised.

"Moms, it's okay. It's like you're sending me on an adventure. It'll be amazing, right? Like Gran says. Summer camp in a whole new country. Remember how happy Abuelita was when she found out, Moms? It'll be good. My abuelita is never wrong, Moms."

I smile and I hope it looks sincere enough to pass off the lie and not as fake as it feels. I think she buys it. When she looks at me, though, I can tell she knows this walk is the last thing in the world I want to do. But she plays along with me.

"Roll, Diego. Less wrinkles." She gives my shirts one last hug before sending them into the backpack to join the assorted randomness inside. I have a toothbrush, a flashlight, a notebook, a spork, Q-tips, Kleenex, wet wipes, a flattened roll of toilet paper, a towel, a water bottle, diaper pins, hiking socks, etc., etc., etc. "Looks like you're ready to go, my baby."

She grabs me and hugs me tight. She has coffee breath. I love that smell. I don't drink coffee. It's disgusting. But when I smell Ma's coffee breath, it smells so good. So... *home*. Yeah. I hug her back.

When I feel like she might snap me in half, I try to step out of the hug. But she holds on a little longer. I let her. I know she's crying. How could I do this to her? I'm, like, the worst son in the universe.

"Come, puppy," she says when she finally lets me go. "Breakfast before we leave."

CHAPTER 2

SHANIA REYNOLDS

Saturday, June 29th – Suckage Day 1 – The Summer that Never Happened

> *I hate my life.*
>
> *What a fitting way to start this stupid journal I'm being forced against my will to write*—It's part of the program, Shania. Mandatory. You have to keep a journal and you have to write in it every day of the trip—*What a bunch of crap.*
>
> *In the beginning, Shania declared her profound angsty disgust for the entirety of the universe and everything in it... including the journal in which she writes.*
>
> *They can force me into this nightmare program, but they can't make me like it. I still think I should have been able to pick my punishment myself. Dad left no room for discussion on that one. My choice? I'll take Juvenile Detention for two hundred, Alex.*
>
> *But no. Steal one car and suddenly I find myself in this program from hell with Captain Dweebhat running the show. Please, oh great Captain Dweebhat... please save me from a life of crimes and misdemeanors.*
>
> *Gawd!*
>
> *I hate my life.*

I close my journal and squeeze it into the side pocket on my backpack. I'm so ready to blow this popstand.

So, yeah. Bye, Mom. Bye, Dad. Thanks for *not* being here to see me off. I know you're sad I'm leaving, even though you're not even here on the day I leave the continent for a whole week and a half. That's *if* I don't contract a deadly disease or have a tragic unavoidable accident with a bull or a mountaintop. I love you too.

I hope this Gilbert guy isn't a perv or something. Don't they have to at least screen people who work with kids? Even the bad kids? Sorry, *troubled youth*.

And I better not get blisters. Who thinks walking across an entire country is a good idea, anyway? What a bunch of granola-eating, soy milk-sipping freaks. I so entirely hate this.

"You almost ready?" Dillon asks from my bedroom doorway. "Bus leaves in five."

"You know, Dill, you don't have to drive me to the airport."

"Oh, so how you getting there? Gonna hotwire the Wilsons' car?"

"Very funny," I say. "I can just take off and spend the time around here. You can tell the parentals you did your duty. I can stay at Veronica's place. Nobody needs to know."

"Come on, Shania," Dillon says. "Don't be stupid. Of course they'll know. You don't think this program is monitored like Fort Knox? Hello. Delinquent much?"

"Yeah, yeah," I say. I flip him the bird as he heads downstairs. "Whatever."

I put my backpack over my shoulder. I can't believe I'm going to carry this for a thousand million miles up a frigging mountain. I'm crazy. Gilbert's crazy. This program is crazy. And Mom and Dad are crazy.

I will puke daisies if I get one single solitary blister. Everyone will pay. They will know my outrage. Anarchy will occur.

I walk downstairs and already I can feel how impossibly heavy this bag is. Unfriggingbelievable!

"Say goodbye, Flibber. You might not see me ever again." I shed my backpack and curl up on the floor with my Newfoundland. He licks me all over my face like he usually does, but this time I don't yell at him or call him gross. This time, I like it. For real, I'll miss him. He's the only one here most of the time. Mom and Dad are always out there living their über-important lives, and Dillon is so whipped by Hattie he might as well be enslaved to her. Pathetic boyfriend extraordinaire.

"I love you, boy," I whisper into Flibber's ear. I look around to make sure Dillon has already left the house before I kiss Flibber on that amazingly soft spot between his eyes.

Flibber gives a little whine. He knows.

At the door, I turn back and look at the house as though I will never see the living room again or the umbrella stand in the corner of the front foyer or the stain on the carpet across the third step where Dillon spilled a slushy and almost died trying to get the blue out before Mom came home or the gorgeous Newfoundland looking back at me with drool hanging halfway to the floor. I am having all the feels.

"Bye, boy." I shut the door and turn to walk to the car. Great. Speaking of Hattie, there she is. Again. Shotgun. Can't he do anything without her by his side? His chain is so tight, I bet she holds it for him when he pees.

I hate my life.

CHAPTER 3

TROY SINCLAIR

WHEN I WOKE UP THIS morning, I couldn't even. I mean, Spain. I'm going to Spain. Like, in five hours I will be on the plane. On it. Going to Spain. Madrid, to be exact. Wow. This is a dream come true. I can't even breathe, I'm so excited!

The only thing that would be better is if Robbie Tremont suddenly came out of the closet and asked me to prom. What? It could happen. If wishes were kisses... well, he'd be covered in them by now. It'll never happen. He's as straight as a board.

The Camino de Santiago will have to do. Who knew when I pulled off that phenomenally stupid meltdown that my punishment would be a walk on the Camino? *The Way*? I only watched that movie a dozen times, imagining myself hiking the amazing pilgrimage route each time. If I had known this diversion program existed, I would have begun my accidental life of crime a lot sooner. Blowing a gasket certainly paid off this time.

"Troy." Dad comes to my door and waits for me to invite him in. My parents are all about boundaries. "Mind if I have a little talk with you while you finish packing?"

"Veuillez entrer, mon père," I say.

"Shouldn't you be honing your Spanish and Galician?" He sits on the bed. "French, Troy? Really?"

"Mi error. Introduzca."

"Better." Everything is a teaching moment with my parents.

"I'm so excited, I can hardly breathe."

"I know, sweetie. Remember, though, this *is* a punishment. Keep that in mind. Your mother and I want you to have the time of your life. We really do. But it's a little difficult seeing you treat this as a reward. Bad actions aren't rewarded, no matter the logic or reasoning behind them. This trip is a great opportunity for you. I hope you use it to reflect upon what you've done. You can't allow other people to influence you into bad choices, Troy."

"I know. And I will." I feel the blush enter my cheeks. It's true. I have been a bad boy. Very bad. "Almost ready. Where's Mom?"

"She's just walking Winston," he says. He's squirming a bit, and I get a bad feeling. He has something to say to me and he's finding it difficult to begin. I sense a lecture coming on. "I wanted some time alone with you, anyway. I wanted to go over a few ground rules."

"Dad," I say. Really!? He's going to attempt to micromanage me from across the Atlantic. "I made one mistake. You know I'm not stupid. I'm not gonna rob any banks while I'm there or beat up any old ladies."

"Ha. No, no. I have every faith in you, Troy. Seriously, I do. And in all honesty, I can't even be all that angry with you for what you *did* do to get to this place. I just… I wanted to talk to you about, you know… other stuff."

My own father attempts to kill me with embarrassment. Out of nowhere, he pulls out a stack of condoms. It's an eerie and offensive display of magic. He allows the strip to unfold until it dangles a good three feet from his hand. Not just a couple of condoms for this guy. No, no. Troy Sinclair, in fact, needs a truckload of them. Oh. My. God. I have to put up with this sort of thing every day. My parents are off the charts and out of their trees.

"Dad," I say, in my shrieky *I can't believe you're doing this to me* voice. "Oh my God. Please put those away."

"No. Your mother and I had a talk. We think it's only right that you pack protection for this trip. You never know what's going to happen and you don't want to be caught without protection."

They were bad enough in the *before I came out* days. Now, they're unbearable. All they talk about is safe sex and the fact that homosexuals can adopt. Talk about focus. Can't I have normal *don't want to talk about it* parents like other gays?

"Dad," I begin, shoving my first aid kit into a side pocket in my backpack. "I promise you; I will not need those. I refuse to take them."

"Can you please humor an old man? I've been there. Young and foolish and on a road trip. It gets wild in Europe. Just take them. You don't have to use them. Just have them on you. It will make both your mother and I happy. You'll actually be saving me. Because you have no idea how happy it would make her to know that you're holding."

"Holding? Really? How very drug culture of you."

I shake my head and sigh, a sure sign of defeat. Gah. Dad holds out the condoms, then folds them into a single pile before attempting to hand them to me.

"Just stick them in that pocket there, would you? If I don't have to touch them, it'll be less painful."

"Oh, Troy, you're like an old woman sometimes. I swear. They're just rubbers."

"Daaaad."

He laughs, stashes the condoms in the pocket I pointed to, and leaves me alone to feel the weight of my extreme shame. As if I'm gonna traipse across Spain having sex with every Pablo, Sergio, and Carlos I come across. Are those Spanish names?

From downstairs, I hear Mom return with Winston. Before she even has the door closed, I hear Winston crash full-tilt-boogie up the stairs. I'm gonna miss him. I told Avery he better give him extra love while I'm gone. As usual, I only got a few *whatevers* and a couple *yeahs* during that whole conversation. And one big *NO* when I asked Avery to sleep in my bed with Winston because it would make Winston less sad. The no came with a "You must think you're pretty special. Winston won't give a crap, bro."

This is what I live with: hysterically politically correct parents who are grooming me to be the vehicle for their impending grandparenthood, and a total douchenozzle brother. I'm sometimes ashamed to share a face with him.

Winston barrels into my room and bolts onto my bed. Nobody tells Winston he can't get up on the furniture. He's a golden retriever lapdog. I scoot in beside him and give him a big body hug. Winston is my people. He *gets* me. He kept my secret back when I still thought I had a secret to keep and a need to keep it.

"I'm gonna miss you, boy," I whisper into his ear as I squeeze harder and inhale his damp earthy Backyard-Winston smell. I love him.

"Troyboy," Mom calls from the front hall. "Time to go. Avery, come get ready to say goodbye to your brother. You're coming to the airport with us."

"Coming." I hear Avery in his bedroom next door. He doesn't even sound annoyed, which is pretty miraculous. Then he stops at my door before heading downstairs. "Hey, douche. Don't forget your nightlight. How you gonna hide the fact you're afraid of the dark from everyone? That's gonna be a tricky one in a hostel."

"Do me a favor and shut it," I say. Great comeback. I throw my pillow at him, but he's already gone.

Well, this is it. I'm leaving for frigging Spain. I get off the bed, pick up my backpack, and strap it over one shoulder. I look around the room in a panic. But if I forgot anything, too bad. I'm only gone for a week and a half.

"Come on, boy," I say to Winston. He jumps down, and together we make the long walk to the front door. He already knows I'm leaving him. He's been weird for a couple of days now. Dogs *know*. Poor Winston has already formed a hate relationship with my backpack. I'm sure I'll agree with his judgment once I carry it across Spain, but right now I'm too excited.

At the door, I break down and cry for the first time. Kissing Winston's furry face, I try to regain my composure before I have to sit beside my judge and jury in the backseat. Avery thinks everyone should show the same amount of emotion he shows: exactly zero. If he notices I've been crying, he'll call me out on it.

"Bye, boy," I say one last time. "Be good. Okay. Avery's a jerk, but if you need a hug, I'm sure he'll give it to you. Love you, my good boy."

I swear to God, Winston moans. And in the moan, I hear, "*How can you leave me here alone with these people?*"

DIEGO NELSON

MOMS. SHE TOTALLY LOST IT when I had to go through the gate and leave her behind. For someone who said she wasn't going to lose it, she had an epic meltdown. She acted like I was seven and I wouldn't be able to go through security on my own.

I kind of wish my abuelita was able to make it today. I felt awful leaving Moms standing there all alone. Abuelita would have known the right words to comfort her. She always does.

Moms didn't like that Gilbert wasn't waiting, ready to hold my hand and walk me through the rest of the airport. I don't know what she thought was going to happen, like the dude would walk me through big, bad customs or something.

She nearly killed me when she hugged me too. It felt good, though, despite the fact everybody in the entire airport turned to look at us when she began to wail.

Turns out Customs *is* kinda scary. Would have been nice to go through with someone else. They made me feel like a thug. Freaky being pulled aside with everyone else looking as they walked on through. I had to stand in a body scan machine. *Terminator* shit.

Anyway, I'm walking toward my gate. You know how, when you try to look like you know what you're doing and you don't, you keep making these foolish moves that tell the entire world you're new? Yeah, well… that. I almost died on the moving walkway. Long story.

I can see Gilbert before I get there. He looks like a total dork. No change there. He's such a hippie. I don't know how he convinced the authorities he could supervise children. He looks like he can't even dress himself.

"Diego," he says while I'm still about six miles away. He says it like we're lifelong friends. His face breaks into this crazy, annoying smile. "You're here. Good to see you. You must be so excited!"

His backpack is on the floor beside him, and he's kind of on his tiptoes, bouncing around like he can't wait for our adventure to begin. I can tell by the looks on the faces of the two kids sitting behind him that they're fellow inmates. They look the way I feel.

"Hey," I say as I finally reach Gilbert. He holds his hand out, and I take it. He practically shakes my hand right off my arm.

"We're here," he says. If he smiles like this for the rest of the trip, I may eventually pop him one. "Diego, meet two of your fellow peregrinos, Shania and Manfred. Guys, meet Diego."

His enthusiasm is *not* infectious. At all.

"Ha. Like the Twain chick." I can tell right away that was the worst thing I could have said. This girl is hot. But in a bad girl way: long blonde hair, too much makeup she doesn't even need. She's trying to be edgy, but she looks like one of those spoiled rich kids I see at the mall. I probably shouldn't mess with her before I even know her.

"Um, no," she says. She glances up from her phone screen, just long enough to sneer at me. "Not at *all* like the Twain chick. *Nothing* like the Twain chick, in fact."

"Oops. Sorry. Hi, guys." Too late. I can tell I already lost Twain. I mean Shania. "Hey, Manfred."

I will not laugh at his name. I will not laugh at his name.

"Please. Call me Manny. Everybody does." He stands and offers his hand. A much better name than Manfred. A slightly warmer greeting than hot angry girl's. "Hey, Diego."

I shake his hand, move to the free chair beside him, and plop myself down.

"Hey, man. We're shaping up to be the most badass *Breakfast Club* ever." I think, *Latino hood, sport jock, and angry, white, poor little rich girl.* I don't say it out loud. Oh, and our overly-excited hipster sidekick who is nothing like the dweeb vice-principal in the movie. I wonder who else is going to show up. We're still missing the trippy, messed-up girl and the mad genius computer nerd.

"What's that?" Shania asks.

"What's what?" I ask.

"*The Breakfast Club*?"

I look at her like she's crazy, because, seriously, she must be. Just as I open my mouth to rip her a new one, Manny steps in.

"Wait." He leans forward in his chair with a comically shocked expression. "You never heard of *The Breakfast Club*? What planet? That's a sad life you're living. Google is—"

"—your friend," I say, finishing his sentence. "Best angsty teen movie ever." We high-five. I'm gonna like this Manny guy.

"Whatever," Shania says. She rolls her eyes.

"Only," Manny says. His face lights up as he has an aha moment. "We're the Camino Club."

"Nice one." That deserves another high five.

"Where's the rest, though," Manny says. "Because you don't look like a jock, and I'm pretty sure you're no genius."

"Nice," I say. But he's laughing, just ribbing me. "I took you for the jock?"

"So, anyway," Gilbert says. "We're waiting for four more. Maybe you'll find your genius among them. We're on two flights. You three are with me. My lovely co-leader, Meagan, will have the other three kids."

"Two cops for six juvenile delinquents? That sounds a bit dangerous. You sure you can handle us?"

"We're not cops, Shania. We're both highly trained. We're stealth ninja warriors. But we are *not* cops. Nothing you can do can distract us from the focus of the mission. Don't even try me."

He says this all smiles and joking, but something tells me he'd tase our asses in a second if he had to. He's not messing around.

"Not like we could do anything. What are we gonna do, asshole? Walk away?" She laughs when she says this, but it's not a *haha* laugh. More like an *I hate you* laugh. This girl must have been born hostile.

It actually makes me a little sad when I see Gilbert deflate a bit. She doesn't have to be so nasty. It's not his fault.

"Just wanted to check." Gilbert is doing his best to bring himself back to his previous level of excitement. Shania, it seems, might be really good at bursting balloons. "Did everyone get their peregrino packages? Peregrino means pilgrim. Your patches? Your guidebooks? Your credencials?"

"Yep," I say. "I did." I tap the patch on the back of my backpack, which sits at my feet. It has a scallop shell and a Canadian flag on it. My abuelita helped me to stitch it in place.

"What's a credencial?" Shania says.

"Got it," Manny says. He holds up his own credencial, which he's been flipping through.

"Camino passport," Gilbert says to Shania. "This little green booklet. For your stamps."

"Oh, right. Yep. It's in my bag. You'll have to believe me, because I'm not digging it out." She folds her arms and rests back against her seat.

"No problem," Gil says. "As long as you all have them. You'll need them for the journey. Now, on to a few ground rules. Phones away. I need your full attention."

Shania moans and slumps in her seat.

"Sorry, princess," Gil says. I snicker and look to Manny, who also smiles. "You all heard the drill, how important it is to pass this program. It's the only way you get to walk away clean on the other side. The rules include daily journal entries, completing the walk all the way to Santiago de Compostela without breaking any laws, and, of course, one solid mandatory hour of check-in and discussion every day while we're out there."

"So much fun," Shania says. "I can't wait."

"Attitude, I should remind you, is also important. Meagan and I don't need any bad attitude during our group discussions. It's unproductive.

"Now, these discussion periods will be different every day. Some days we'll have them while we walk, some days at the breakfast table, and others we'll have at the end of our walks at that day's albergue. It will depend on us all being together and being able to find space to go off and be alone together.

"Because it's also important that we have privacy. There's going to be some pretty frank discussion happening. You've all been given an incredible opportunity to come away from this relatively unscathed. A new lease on life, if you will.

"But it requires your complete cooperation. Do you understand this part? How integral your cooperation is with every stage of this program?"

Gilbert asks this last question of all of us, but stops his gaze directly on Shania.

"Yes, sir," Manny says. "Loud and clear."

"Absolutely," I say.

"You're the boss-man," Shania says. "Are we done here?"

"We're just getting started, Shania," Gilbert says. "I hope you don't have any crazy ideas about testing us. That would be a bad move on your part."

"Yes, sir. No, sir," Shania says. She gives him a great big phony smile. This should be interesting.

We sit quietly. I watch the departure board and notice that our flight leaves in forty minutes. My first time flying. I wish I wasn't so scared, but I am. I hope I sit next to Manny. He seems less insane than Shania.

"Your first time?" Manny asks. He sounds a bit shaky. "Because it's my first. How do they even keep those things in the air? They're big steel bullets with wings. Something that big ain't supposed to leave the ground. I don't get it, man."

Okay, so maybe he's a bit insane. At least he's not grumpy.

"Yeah. First time. And I agree. It's beyond freaky. At least *someone* knows what they're doing, though, right?" It seems like I'm consoling him. Which kinda makes me feel better about it myself.

"Wait," Shania butts in. She leans forward in her chair so she can look at both of us. "You mean neither of you girls have ever been on a plane before? Like, ever? What the fu—"

"Words!" Gilbert interrupts. "Same rules apply here as in school. No swearing. Like I said, you need to pass this program in order to avoid detention, Shania… not just show up. I'd step off the cursing if I were you."

Yep. I knew he was badass. Mr. Nice Guy is gonna work us like a drill sergeant. I'm thinking Twain brings out the worst in him.

"Sorry, what the *hell*?" She's still looking at us, completely miffed that we haven't flown before. Either she's showing off or she's just more of a bitch than I thought she was. Either way, it's obvious I pegged her right. I can smell a rich girl a mile away. "How does that even happen?"

"I don't know where you come from, Shania," Manny says, "but where I live... I'm probably the first one in my neighborhood to even see an airport up close. Doesn't make you special you were on a plane before, princess."

We're bonding. Nice.

"I'm just saying." She frowns, falls back in her seat, and returns to her phone screen. "Don't have to be an asshole about it."

"Shania, words. We're gonna have to drop the profanities. Seriously."

"Yes, sir," she says, without looking away from her screen.

"It'll be fine," I say to Manny. I kind of like him more now. Anyone who can trash-talk an angry white girl gets extra points in my book. "They go up and down every day. Hardly ever crash."

"LOL. That's reassuring, dude." He playfully punches my shoulder. "What are you in for, anyway?"

"Not yet, Manny," Gilbert says. He's still bouncing. His excitement is palpable. Unless maybe he's nervous about flying too. "Let's not talk about why we're here quite yet. How about we keep questions to *getting to know you* stuff for now. You know, siblings, parents, grade, age, favorite music. Stuff like that. Once you get to know each other a bit, you can share your tales of delinquency. This is something we'll delve into during our group discussions once we're all together. Fair enough?"

"Sure thing, dude," Manny says. He makes this crazy face only I pick up on. It makes me laugh. Yeah. He's okay. "So, Diego. What's your story?"

"No brothers. No sisters. Live with my mom. Just me, Moms, and my abuelita—my gran. Three musketeers. No daddy. I go to St. Mark's. Just turned seventeen last month."

"Catholic boy. Ooh. That's nasty," he says. But he laughs, like it's okay with him. Like I haven't offended him *too* much. "Chapel Hill High right here. Born and raised. Chapel Hill, represent."

He does a fist pump and winks. We share smirks as I ask, "Any brothers or sisters?"

I see Shania is paying attention now. She's leaning toward us, like she wants to be a part of the conversation. But also like she's too cool for school.

"Do I!" Manny laughs. "Mama and Papa were busy. I have three older brothers, two younger sisters, and a younger brother. Oldest is twenty-three and the youngest is seven. Me? I'm seventeen too."

"Cool," I say.

"Oh, and also no dad. He passed." He looks beyond me to Shania. "How about you, sweets?"

"Seven kids? Holy crap. That's some real shit. And call me sweets again, and I'll throat-punch you. Without warning."

"Shania. Enough. Last warning."

"Oops. Aye, aye, captain."

"Sorry about your dad," I say. Manny offers a shy smile.

Our flight gets called and everybody around us jumps up and heads for our gate, even though they only called for certain rows. So that's how it is.

"That's us, kiddos," Gilbert says. He waves his Canadian passport, with his boarding pass tucked into one of its pages. "Get your passports out and put the boarding pass in the page where your ID photo is. Let's do this."

We all get up, but only Shania speaks.

"Are you always gonna be such a perky cheerleader?"

"Only until you no longer need a cheerleader, dearie." He points the way with his passport and smiles that too-big smile at us as we file past him.

"I. Don't. Need. A. Cheerleader," Shania says.

"That's what they all say. You'll see. Just let your guard down a bit and you'll start to have fun, Shania. I'm not kidding you."

"Yes, sir."

We join the crowd at the gate and make our way to the front of the line. After a thousand years.

I'm right behind Shania, so I hear the attendant say, "Seat 24C. Enjoy your flight, Ms. Reynolds."

I glance at my ticket. Yep. I get to sit beside angry white chick for, like, twelve hours. Kill me now.

CHAPTER 5

SHANIA REYNOLDS

Sunday, June 30th – *Suckage Day 2* – *The Boy Who Hates Me and Why I Hate Myself*

I hate my life. I had to sit next to a boy named Diego on the plane. I'm in Madrid. Spain. Big fine whoop. I'd be happier if I hadn't completely alienated a hot boy before I was forced to sit beside him for a thousand hours on a flight over the ocean. I couldn't even be nice to him when we hit turbulence, and he clearly thought he was going to die. I mean, his seat was shaking so much, I kind of think he might have been the reason for the turbulence.

Every single time he tried to talk to me, I bit his head off. This boy with amazing dark skin and gorgeous huge brown eyes like a puppy dog. I don't kick puppies; I don't know why I felt the need to kick him. I mean, even his name is hot. Diego. I hate myself so much sometimes. Even the other guy with us, Manny, leaned over and told me to cut the guy some slack. Jesus! Clearly I'm a monster. And Diego and Manny were like instant friends. Now they'll be against me for the whole trip. I hate my life.

I swear, I'm so tired I can't even think. I'm somewhere in Madrid and we're taking a bus in the morning to someplace called Ponferrada. That's where the real hell will begin. The endless walk to Santiago de Compostela. I can understand people doing this a million years ago, but today? It's just insane. I don't get it. They're called cars, people.

Not to mention, we have to be downstairs in the hotel lobby at six in the morning. Not get up at six, be downstairs and ready to board the bus at six. This is child abuse.

I bet if I took the juvie, I wouldn't have to drag myself out of bed before seven or eight. Like Dad would have allowed me to do that. He pulled huge strings to get me here. I didn't have a choice.

I hope to God some of the other delinquents are more bearable than the two I'm stuck with so far. Diego and Manny both hate my guts. I pray for a sane, normal person to join us. I have three more chances, but who am I kidding… they'll be the same. Lemmings. Insufferable, intolerable lemmings.

At least I have my music. I'll just zone everyone out and walk. Thank God they didn't make us leave our phones at home. Miracle of miracles.

When the cops stopped me in that car, I thought for sure I was a goner. Like, isn't that grand theft auto? I don't know what my father even did to get me out of it, but I'm guessing it was my last Get Out of Jail Free card. I guess it pays to have a lawyer for a father. Still, I think he's laughing his ass off right now. This is practically worse than jail. Bad enough I have to hang out with some overachieving dweeb and some juvenile delinquents. But walking across an entire country with them? Not fun. Not funny.

I hate that Dillon knows me so well. All the way to the airport, he lectured me on not being myself. Apparently, I'm some kind of super-bitch or something. His lecture was insidious, though. Every time I caught myself snapping at Diego on the airplane, my brother's voice repeated, *"Just try to be nice, Shania. You chew people up and spit them out just for trying to have a conversation with you. It's not their fault you're angry. Do yourself a favor and leave yourself at home for this trip. Don't blow this opportunity."*

I'd like to punch Dillon in the throat, but he's a hundred percent right and more than a thousand miles away. And just seeing Diego's puppy dog eyes every time I ripped him a new one made me feel guilty. Damn Dillon. If he had kept his opinions to himself, I wouldn't feel so guilty right now.

I don't even know if I *can* take it down a notch. I mean, I'd like to. It's not my fault I'm raging mad. I'm a product of my environment.

One thing I *can't* do, though, is let Diego and Manny know I'm rich. They hate me enough already. I don't need them to hold privilege against me too.

TROY SINCLAIR

I'm sitting with Meagan, which is fine by me. The other kids seem a bit sketchy. Not that I'm judging, but Jesus. Claire would give drug dealers a run for their money. Not to mention, her life of crime seems to be the only thing she wants to talk about. Shoplifting seems to be her favorite pastime, though apparently not the thing that brought her here. So not my scene, girlfriend.

And Greg? Well, he's almost too hot. I always get uncomfortable around impossibly hot guys. Dimples, cheeks, hair. It's all working for him.

I can't sit in silence. That's a thing with me. I like to be where the conversation is. I like to *be* the conversation.

I yank on Meagan's earbuds. "Whatcha watching?"

"Hmmm?" she says, as though she wasn't watching anything but nodding off. "Oh. Just a rerun. *Will and Grace.*"

I already knew this, of course. I can see Jack on her screen, being his same old Jack-self.

"I love that show."

"Yeah," she says, removing her earbuds. "Me too."

She smiles and turns toward me.

"So, what makes Meagan want to deal with a boatload of badass kids? Who hurt you so badly?"

"Ha ha. Not hurt. I just want to make a difference in the lives of dirtbags, Troy." She winks.

"Nice one."

The drinks cart makes its way toward us again. Last time, the flight attendant attempted to remove my elbow with it. I'm not going to let that happen again. This time, I'm ready.

"I like working with kids. I used to be one, you know."

"I did *not* know that. You learn something new every day."

"Is this your first trip to Spain?"

"Yep. Dad took my brother and me to Paris last summer. That's the closest I've ever been to Spain. I already knew about the Camino, though. I read about it and watched every movie I could find. It's a bucket-list item for me. It actually begins in France. Did you know that?"

"Yep," she says. "I walked the entire route last summer. Probably around the same time you were in Paris with your folks."

"Not folks. Just my dad."

"Oh, I'm sorry your parents are split. That's always hard to—"

"Oh, no, no. They're not apart. They just think it's important we spend time with them individually. After Paris with Dad, we went to London with Mom. My brother Avery and I traveled from one place to the other together. So Dad had Paris with us and by himself and Mom had London to herself and then with us."

"Hmm. Interesting. Sorry, I just assumed. That actually sounds quite amazing."

Drinks cart attendant approaching. I try to remain aware. He's still a ways back. I have time to save myself.

"We like it. My brother and I, that is."

"So it's just the two of you? Older or younger?" Meagan asks.

"He's older. By three minutes. And he lords it over me every single day of our lives."

"Ooh, twins. Twins have always fascinated me."

"Trust me. We are anything but fascinating. No secret handshake. No eerie twin senses. We're as different as they come. I mean, he likes girls, Meagan. Ew. Just, ew."

"Hey, watch it, bucko. I happen to *be* a girl. I don't think we're all that bad."

"Oops. Sorry. But you know what I mean."

"Ha. Yeah. Oh, watch yourse—"

"Ow!" He got me again. Goddamn it.

"Oh, my goodness. I'm *so* sorry. I just can't stop hitting you today," the flight attendant says. "I'm usually a really good driver. Here, take an extra cookie, darling. Don't tell the pilot. He's just looking for a reason to throw me off this bus."

Now I'm giggling too much to worry about my elbow.

"That's okay. Didn't hurt. I'm good." I try to stop rubbing the pain away. I don't want him to feel bad or know I'm lying.

"What will you have, sweetie?" he asks.

"Ginger ale?"

"Sure thing," he says. "Coming right up."

"What am I, chopped liver?" Meagan asks. She's smiling like mad, though. The guy has an abundance of charm.

"Honey, please. I always talk to the handsome ones first. You'll wait your turn or you'll get tomato juice. Understand?"

"Fresh," Meagan says, as an admonishment.

"Girl, all my drinks are fresh. I promise you that. That's what keeps them coming back to my yard."

Now we all laugh, as do a few of the passengers around us. It's always this way on planes, isn't it? A camaraderie happens. It's kind of nice.

"Hello," comes a screechy little voice from the seats ahead of us. Did I mention Claire has streaks of wild color in her hair? Blue, pink.

Back at the airport I thought she might be interesting—before she opened her mouth. She didn't take Meagan's ground rules discussion too well. "You gonna entertain them all day or are you gonna move on and serve us? Sometime today?"

"Missy ma'am, I'm sorry. I didn't realize you were thirsting. Let me get this nice woman a drink first and I'll be right with you, shall I?" He says this with a nicety that is so filled with sarcasm, Meagan and I look at each other and laugh some more. Then the flight attendant winks at Meagan and asks, "What will you have, dear?"

"Just a Coke for me, please. Sorry about her. She's a bit on the edgy side. Those two are with me. I apologize."

"No need, dearie." He bends close to us, as though he's doing so to pass Meagan her drink and not to diss Claire. "We can't be accountable for the bad manners of others."

"Thank you," Meagan says.

The attendant moves on. My elbow is still intact. I like him too much to care about being smacked. It's probably my fault anyway.

"Finally," Claire says. I realize, not for the first time, that I want to smash her in the face. I already know I will not be girlfriends with this one. She's a bit too nasty for my blood. I hope to God there's a nice girl on this trip. It would suck to have to spend the entire walk with just guys. I don't really get along well with guys. Well, straight ones anyway. Even more especially, hot straight guys.

"Well, Troy," Meagan says. "We're about halfway there. I think I'm going to try to catch some rest. I suggest you do the same. It's tricky with the time difference. Jet lag. The first day or so is going to be a bit difficult adjusting, especially since we'll hit the ground running. If we sleep for a while now, we might beat the lag."

"Okay," I say. "I could probably sleep."

She leans forward and taps Greg on the top of the head. He pops his face over the back of his seat, pulls a hot pink earbud out of his ear, and looks at her quizzically.

His hair. Gah. Long, straight and blond. Typical beach bum surfer dude. One of the many looks that work for me. My God, the boy is more beautiful than a boy has a right to be. I try not to stare at him. Nothing makes a straight boy more nervous than being goggled at by the gays. I don't want to blow it with him before we know each other, but he's just so gorgeous.

"You should catch some shuteye," Meagan tells him. "To beat the jet lag."

"Sure thing, Meags." His Colgate smile blinds me. "Just listening to tunes. I was probably gonna crash anyway."

"Okay, tell Claire too, please."

"I'm not deaf. I can hear you. Everyone on the plane can hear you."

"Thank you, Claire," Meagan says. She looks from Greg to me and shrugs as if to say, *what did I do*? We all exchange knowing smiles as if to confirm to each other that Claire is a burden we'll agree to carry together. Or maybe I'm just making that up. Then Greg's beautiful face disappears.

Please, God, let there be a nice normal girl on this journey. One who is not homophobic and likes to talk. A lot. I need a bestie on this walk or I swear to God I'll die.

I put my earbuds in, turn on my music, and, before the first song is over, I drift off.

CHAPTER 7

DIEGO NELSON

HERE GOES NOTHING. TODAY WE take the bus from Madrid to Ponferrada, with stops along the way to check out a few things. I guess it's not all punishment.

Moms would kill me if she found out I skipped breakfast, so I'm the first one down here. We get on the bus at six. I couldn't sleep, so here I am. Four-thirty in the morning, showered, and ready for breakfast.

I skip the coffee and go straight for the orange juice. The machine they have to make orange juice? Whoa.

Moms would be happy with my breakfast choice. An apple, yogurt, and a baguette with some weird jelly I never heard of. And, of course, a Spanish omelette. I can't believe the hotel breakfast bar is open this early.

I'm sitting at my table in the corner with all my food before me when this guy walks in.

"Hey," he says. "Are you with Gilbert, by any chance?"

"Um, yeah." I tear the top off my yogurt, pick up my spoon, and start to shovel the yogurt into my mouth.

"Well, me too," he says. "My name's Troy. Mind if I sit with you?"

"Knock yourself out." I point to an empty chair across the table and continue to eat.

"Thanks, man. What you in for?"

"Too soon, Troy," I say. I smirk, but I kinda mean it too. I don't even know the guy and I'm trying to follow Gilbert's rules.

"Sorry. Guess you're right. Meagan told us that'll happen in *group*. Sorry. Forgot. I'm just gonna drop my bag here and grab something to eat."

"Knock—"

"Yourself out. Gotcha." He drops his bag on a chair and walks away. I watch him as I finish my yogurt cup and move on to my omelette. He gets the guy at the coffee station to make him a coffee. This seems to take a ridiculous amount of time. Then he grabs a croissant and butter and heads back to the table.

"The breakfast of champions." He proudly holds up his catch.

"That stuff'll kill you, dude." I nod toward the coffee. "And breakfast is the most important meal. You should eat something real."

"My word, is this croissant not real? What are they trying to pull, serving fake croissants? It's an outrage. I'll need to revolt." He moves his bag to the floor, pulls out the chair, and sits down. He smiles this goofy smile. I laugh. "And coffee is king. Sorry, what did you say your name was?"

"I didn't. Yet. Diego. Nelson."

"Which one is it? Diego or Nelson?" He takes a sip of his coffee and makes this face like he just experienced an orgasm or something. "Oh, my Lord God. This is the best coffee I have ever tasted. He called it café con leche. Remember that name. I need to get more of this. Must be a Spain thing."

"My name is Diego Nelson. First and last. And that just means coffee with cream, dude. I take it you don't know any Spanish?"

"Oh. Oops. I frigging knew that. I'm trying to learn Spanish. I don't know what I was thinking. Of course it means coffee with cream. My father would kill me. Still, it's way better than anything I've ever had."

"It's the way Moms makes coffee sometimes."

"You have two mothers?" Troy asks. I laugh.

"No, dude. It's what I call my mother. Moms. Anyway, they heat the milk here. Moms says it's way better, but I wouldn't know. Hate the stuff."

"You take those words back," Troy practically screams. He stops buttering his croissant and points his knife at me like he's going to stab me for insulting his drink of choice. Dude.

"You're kind of funny."

"I try, Diego Nelson. I try." He finishes and puts the knife down. "I'll let you live this time. Just, no more insulting the java bean please and thank you."

"Oh, boy," I say as Shania enters the room. It's probably my imagination that the lights dim. "Here comes trouble."

"One of us?" Troy says. "I hope she's nicer than the one I flew over with. Wait until you meet Claire. Real piece of work."

"Oh, great. Because Shania there is a real treasure. We should bury her."

"Shania? Like Twain?"

"Yeah. But no. Don't say that to her. She hates it."

"But I was hoping for a girlfriend on the walk. Don't tell me she's not a worthy candidate."

"You? A girlfriend. Really?"

"Hey. I resemble that remark, smarty. I don't mean like that. I mean, someone I can kiki with. A bestie. Someone to gossip with. You know."

"Kiki? No comprende? She's probably not what you're looking for, but yeah, I think I get it. I'm afraid she might not be the one, dude. She'd rather bite your head off than carry on an actual conversation."

She's almost at our table.

"Who else was with your group, then? Any other girls?"

"Nope. Just me, Shania, and a guy named Manny. Cool guy, but no other girls. Sorry, dude."

"Damn," he says. He kind of deflates right on the spot.

"Hey," Shania says. "Good morning, guys."

I try to hide my shock. The Twain speaks in non-screech. Who knew?

"Um," I say, just so she knows I picked up on the change. "Good morning?" Yes. It's a question.

"Hi there," Troy says. He stands and offers her his hand. "I'm Troy."

"Hey, Troy," Shania says. Then she shocks me by following with, "I hope Diego here hasn't informed you that I'm a bitch from hell yet. I hope Diego…" She turns to look at me as she shakes Troy's hand. "…can forgive a girl and understand that we all have bad days occasionally. Especially when one is being forced to do something against her will."

"Whoa, whoa." I won't let her off so easy. "Are you attempting to apologize? Because that doesn't quite sound like an apology. That sounds a bit more like a passive-aggressive *I'm sorry/not sorry*. You'll have to do better."

"You're nasty," Troy says. But he laughs. He's liking this. Twain cringes.

"Okay, Diego. Please forgive me for being a not-so-nice human being yesterday. I was having a really bad day and maybe I shouldn't have taken it out on you."

"Maybe?"

"Okay, okay," she says. "You drive a hard bargain. I should not have treated you like shit. I'm sorry."

"Better," I say. "An actual apology."

"Girl, you deserve a medal for that," Troy says. "Go reward yourself with this über-fine coffee. It will blow your mind. I promise."

Shania has what looks like an *aha* moment. She looks Troy up and down. I can almost see her realization dawning. She just picked up on the fact that Troy is gay. Or I'm guessing, anyway.

"I'm going to like you," she says to Troy.

"Café con leche, girlfriend. Go forth. You will thank me."

Shania smiles, and okay... it's a great smile. Her hard-ass self disintegrates in that smile. Hopefully, this is the Shania who joins us on the walk. I can deal with *this* Shania.

As I watch her walk away, Manny and Gilbert arrive and drop their backpacks. I notice another kid sit closer to the entrance. He's with some lady. I'm guessing it's another one of the kids and Gilbert's other half. I can't remember her name, but Troy confirms my suspicions when he waves at her and she returns it with a smile and a wave of her own.

"Hey, dude." Manny sits beside me. He puts his fist out and I bump it. "Sleep well?"

"Not bad," I say. "This is—"

"Troy," Gilbert interrupts. "Hello, Troy. I see you've met Diego. And this is Manfred."

"Dude," Manny says. "It's Manny. Please, stop calling me that. Nobody calls me Manfred."

"Sorry, right. Manny."

"Hey, Manny," Troy says. I can tell he's a bit gobsmacked by the way he says Manny's name. Troy might be insta-crushing on my man Manny. He's totally barking up the wrong tree if he thinks that's going to happen.

"Troy," Manny says as he nods hello. He's oblivious to Troy's attentions.

"Let's get some food before it's too late. Bus boards soon," Gilbert says. He leads Manny away to the omelette station.

Troy watches them walk away. His mouth kinda hangs open.

"Dude, just no."

"I know, I know. Story of my life. I'm used to it. A boy can dream, though, can't he?"

"You out?" I think I already know the answer.

"Yeah. My parents are insane about it, too. P.S. If you need any condoms during our trip, I happen to have a backpack full of them. Dad seems to think I'm capable of conquering *all* the Spaniards."

"Dude. Poor you. Ha ha. That's a good one. So sorry, dude. That must have been an awkward conversation."

"You have no idea, Diego. No idea."

*　　*　　*

WE'RE READY TO BOARD THE bus when Troy asks Meagan where Claire is. Claire is someone I haven't met yet, the one Troy bitched about earlier. Apparently, she's a monster. But who knows, yesterday I thought Shania was a monster. There's hope for this other girl still.

"Oh, shi—" Meagan begins, but catches herself. "Oh, no. I hadn't noticed. She must still be in her room. I'll be right back."

She runs out of the room toward the elevator. We all get up and half strap our backpacks over our shoulders. We move toward the hotel lobby where we stand and wait for Meagan to come down with Claire.

Gilbert starts to get fidgety. He keeps taking out his phone and looking at the time.

"We'll have to make our way to the bus without them. Sorry, guys; let's go." He leads us into the street. I look both ways, but there are no buses in sight. "We have to walk about a block to the station.

They can meet us there; Meagan knows where the station is. Come on, guys."

This is not going to end well. If this Claire girl is like this today, on day one, guaranteed it'll be a habit. Girl's gonna make us late every morning. I don't like non-morning people. I can't deal with them.

I look at our surroundings as we walk down the street. So much for seeing Madrid. In and out like thieves. Please, let there be air conditioning on this bus. A whole day on a bus is not my idea of a good time. Thinking I should try to sit with Manny. Or, hey, even Troy. He's not a bad guy. Makes me laugh.

CHAPTER 8

SHANIA REYNOLDS

Monday, July 1st – Day 3 – I Hate Myself and Why I Need to Punch Dillon in the Throat

I hate my life. There, I said it. Again. But today was bordering on okay. I mean, we did spend a good portion of the day on a bus. But I got to sit beside this guy, Troy. He's awesome. And more importantly, he doesn't want anything from me. He's gay, so I know he's not looking at my boobs or trying to play me to get into my pants. I don't even have to think about crap like that with him. The guy's a genius comedian too. I think I love him. I hope we get to walk together.

Damn, I sound almost like a happy person. Yuck. Which is why I want to punch Dillon in the throat. Ever have an older brother who is always (one thousand percent of the time) RIGHT!? Well, that's Dillon. He's right again. I tried really hard today. I was nice, and mostly nobody was douchebaggy to me. I do feel like Manny is trying to play me, though. He's smooth. And totally hot. But not my type. IF I were trying to be honest, I would say that Diego is more my type. But that ship sailed when I was nasty to him on the plane. Guys remember stuff like that. Burnt bridges and whatnot. Which is why I can say with complete honesty, I hate my life.

We're in a place called Ponferrada. I'm not shitting, there's a castle across the street from our hotel. And not just any castle, either. The thing belonged to the Templars. Castillo de los Templarios. I said I wasn't going to get caught up in this thing, but man. This guy lived there, the Grand Master of the Knights Templar. It's from, like the 1100s or something. How can I not get excited by that?

I feel like I'm failing as a pissed-off, angsty teen. Dillon would so throw this in my face. I hate him.

We had our meeting earlier. We picked a quiet corner near the castle and just stood around talking. Mostly, today was just about telling us what to expect when we start to walk tomorrow. And a list of *dos* and *don'ts* again. They're not even going to force us all to walk together. Main rule is that the shit hits the fan if we don't meet at the designated place when we make plans to eat lunch together, and, more importantly, we can consider ourselves out of the program if we don't show up at the designated albergue each night.

Tomorrow, we set out on foot for the first time. We will walk to the castle to say goodbye to it and then take off in the opposite direction. And walk all day long. Unbelievable. I'm so not ready for this. I should have just smashed some of Mom's stuff or something. Not like stealing a car got her attention anyway. She still doesn't know I exist. Maybe if I had smashed her precious shit she would have noticed me. But whatever.

Mother-daughter relationships are so overrated anyway, right? I mean, who needs them?

And now some nutjob is knocking on my door. Awesome.

"What the hell do you… Oh. It's you. Sorry."

"Caught yourself," Diego says, laughing. "Almost snapped there. Good save."

"Yeah, well. It *is* kind of late. What do you want, Diego?"

He looks at his feet. He shuffles a bit and it's adorable. "Well, I just, you know, wanted to thank you for the apology this morning. Didn't get to thank you earlier. There was always someone around, and we didn't get to sit near each other on the bus or in the piazza. So I just wanted to stop on my way to my room and say thank you."

"Um, well. Thank you back, I guess. It's no big deal. I just realized I was a little nasty to you. But I was in a serious bad mood, crap with my parents. Like I said, I shouldn't have taken it out on you. I'm sorry. Really."

"Thanks. You don't need to apologize again though. We're good. I just wanted to thank you. Moms is always saying that the hardest thing is to say sorry when you've been difficult for no reason. She lectures me on everything. She says I need to thank people brave enough to apologize for their actions."

"Wow." I leave the door open, but walk back to the bed so he feels free to enter the room. "You really sound like a momma's boy, Diego. Careful, you might get a reputation."

"That's one reputation I wouldn't be sorry to have, Shania. I am my mama's boy. You don't know Puerto Rican boys, do you? We live for our mamas. I'd kill for her if she'd let me."

He makes up the few steps between us and stands at my bedside. His smile is so amazing. *I will not like this boy. I will not like this boy.*

"Well, I guess that's a good thing. Thanks for stopping by. Really. It was hard, but I knew if I didn't say something this morning it would be too late and I'd have to walk this whole shitty thing alone and furious. It was apologize or suffer. Thanks for making it easy for me."

"No problem. You should go easier on yourself, though. You're not the big bad witch you try to be sometimes. I can tell."

Again with the smile.

"Well, thanks."

"No sweat."

We stand in awkward silence for what feels like hours, but I'm sure only half a minute passes.

"Well," he finally says. "I guess I should go. Just wanted to stop by. Tomorrow's a big day. I'm guessing we're all gonna need to be friends for this. Not going to be easy, I'm sure."

"No shit. If I get one blister, I'm revolting. I hope you're with me."

"Ha. Moms would skin me alive if I caused any crap on this walk. I already hurt her enough, thanks."

Wow. How hot is it that he thinks so highly of his mother? I never met anyone like this guy before in my life.

"Catch you later, Shania. Maybe we can eat breakfast together if we come down at the same time, eh?"

"Sounds good, Diego. Thanks."

"No sweat. You can chill. I'll shut the door on my way out. Goodnight."

He walks back to the door and as he's about to shut it, I call out, "Goodnight."

He pseudo-salutes as the door shuts behind him.

What a guy. Maybe I pegged him wrong before. He's so sweet.

I set out my hiking shoes, put my other shoes away in the bottom of my backpack, get ready for bed, and turn out the lights.

Lying here in the dark, I can hear people talking in the street. I know what it is. It's Camino pilgrims walking past the hotel, laughing and talking together. I saw some earlier when we sat in the plaza beside the castle eating pizza. I can almost imagine myself being one of them. Walking with my backpack, talking with the rest of the delinquents… maybe even laughing every now and then.

I almost can't wait to fall asleep, just so I can get out there and be one of them. I swear, I'm folding like a lawn chair. Thanks, Dillon. I can hear your *told you so* from here.

CHAPTER 9

TROY SINCLAIR

AND SO IT BEGINS. DAY one of my Camino walk. I had two showers. I woke up way too early just to have my first one. I'm a creature comforts sort of person. Who knows what the bathrooms will be like along the way? Gilbert already warned me this is the last normal hotel. He said we would even be staying in dorms sometimes, with bunk beds as far as the eye can see. Not looking forward to that.

It's like he's been trying to prepare us all for the worst.

I'm in the hotel breakfast area. When I first got here, I noticed this crazy contraption. It squeezes oranges, but it's this gigantic plastic thing, all orange and green and filled with gadgety cranks and gizmos. Total awesomeness. It makes me feel like I'm in Willy Wonka's chocolate factory. Obviously, I ordered orange juice. I Instagrammed that crap. Likes out the wazoo.

I was the first one down here. We're supposed to be on the road at six-thirty. I wanted to get something to eat and start writing in my journal before we leave. Plus, alone time. It's a thing, you know. And I, for one, like it.

After my orange juice, which was just as amazeballs as the contraption it came from, I get a magical café con leche and walk out to the outdoor patio. I take a seat and, okay, so I just stare straight ahead in awe for several minutes. Yeah. That's a castle in front of me. A frigging tenth-century castle, no less. I read all about it on Wiki. Truth? I even have a picture of it pinned to the corkboard above my desk at home. I'm a geek.

The oldest thing in my city is that lady on the corner of Yonge and Bloor who sings "Alouette, gentille alouette" for spare change.

There are ramparts and flags flying at the top of all the towers, even a drawbridge. And holes used by cannons and archers to defend the keep. Phenomenal. And I get to look at it while I sip nectar of the gods. I don't think it gets any better. All I need right now is for a gorgeous available boy to come sit down beside me and serenade me with a Kylie Minogue song.

Annnnnd, cue the clowns. Who should appear but Manny. His afro is delightful. And a tank top never looked so hot. Gray is his color. He's carrying a café con leche and a roll. And he looks terribly lost, poor thing. He drops his backpack on the patio stones beside the entrance and looks around until his eyes finally land on me. I smile. He returns my smile and walks over to my table, seemingly relieved. Yum.

"Why, hello, Manny," I say, attempting not to sound too coquettish. *Don't scare away the straight boy*. I swear this is going to have to be the mantra to my Camino. Why do all three of the boys have to be gorgeous and straight? It's just not fair in the least.

"Hey, dude." Manny takes the seat beside me. At first I think, *Oh my God, he's sitting* beside *me*. Then I realize he took that seat so he could see the castle. "Holy crap, that's amazing. Hard to believe stuff like that even exists. And we're sitting here in front of it. I mean, wow. How in the *hell* is this punishment, Troy?"

"Right?" I say. Lame. Ack. "Today's the big day. You ready?"

"I'm not too worried about walking. I jog every day so I'm used to pushing myself. This'll be nothing. So, yeah. Ready. What are you doing up so early, anyway?"

"Well, this may sound crazy, but I'm kind of spoiled. I don't do camping or roughing it back home."

"I never would have guessed." He laughs a bit, and I can't tell for sure but I think he just faked a gay tone. He's messing with me.

"Yeah, well. I heard the horror stories about the hostels, so I wanted to have two showers. Spoil myself a little."

"Ha, you're a little bit crazy, aren't you? You know you can't *store up* showers, right?"

"Very funny. I just needed one last morning of pampering. Don't tease the diva. It's not nice."

"Ha ha. You're okay, Troy. I think I like you."

Yeah. And I think I love you. Stop thinking these thoughts, Troy.

"I like you too, you big lug," I say in my best macho dude impersonation as I give his shoulder a small punch.

"Ha. Dude. Just, no. Don't even try. I like you for you. Don't go changing, yo."

He stares at the castle, picks up his coffee, and takes a sip. I'm content to smile and join him in taking in the scenery. This is going to be an amazing adventure. I always knew it would be. I wonder what evil deed I'd have to pull off to get this trip again next summer. I know, I know. That would never happen. I heard all the serious lectures that came along with the awesome opportunity. I'm not stupid. My life of crime is over.

After a few minutes, Meagan joins us.

"Good morning, gentlemen. You guys look eager and ready to walk. Could I be mistaken?"

"No, no," Manny says. "We are so ready. Right, Troy?"

"Ready as I'll ever be."

"Good to hear. I thought Gil and I would have to stare into the faces of six sourpusses this morning. It's a good sign that the first two I see are both smiling."

"I can't wait, Meagan."

"Excellent. We're going to have a meeting in…" She takes out her phone and looks at the time. "…twenty-five minutes. Just inside. Don't worry, you still have lots of time to castle-gaze. It's amazing, isn't it? Just wait. There are so many amazing sights along the way. Every town is going to fascinate you. We *do* begin at the castle in Ponferrada because of how cool it is, though. A glimpse at the potential of the Camino."

"Well, I'm sold," Manny says. He drains his café con leche.

"Me too," I say. "This is going to knock me out."

"You're both disappointing me profusely. You're supposed to be moaning about possible blisters and the hot sun and the stupidity of walking. You let me down."

"I'll try to be more miserable, Miss Meagan. I do solemnly swear I will."

"Thank you, Troy. That's promising. Don't let me down now."

"I will try my level best to be a miserable drama queen." I get up to leave. "Now, if you'll both excuse me, I was going to start my journal this morning. Court-mandated, remember. We must journal our experiences! I'm just going to go sit in the grass in front of the castle and write a page or two. That's a sentence you don't hear every day."

"Okay," Manny says. "I guess I should crack mine sometime soon. Not my favorite hobby, writing."

"That's too bad, because, me? Well, let's just say you're looking at a future Pulitzer Prize-winning author. It's okay, you don't need to fanboy over me just yet. I will be patient and await your future idolatry."

"Well, that's good," he says, laughing. "Because, yeah… so far, you don't impress me much."

Is he teasing me again?

"I'm off for brekkie, boys. As you were," Meagan says. "Don't forget to get out your credencials when you come back in. We'll get our first stamp when we check out of the hotel."

"Aye, aye. Ciao." I cross the narrow, cobbled street between the hotel and the castle. It feels like I'm on a movie set. At any second knights on horseback are going to come galloping out of the castle gates swinging some medieval weaponry at me. I'm too young to die.

I stretch out on the grass, open my journal, and pull out my pen to begin my first entry. I stare at the blank page, afraid to tarnish it with ink, afraid the words won't be the best I've ever written. I try to organize the words in my head before they fall onto the page. I hope to God they don't actually read these things. Gah.

CHAPTER 10

DIEGO NELSON

IF THAT WAS DAY ONE, then we did it. It actually wasn't half bad. I mean, it started out rocky. We had to wait for that Claire girl. Again. I'm tired of her already, and it's only been two days with her. She came down late for breakfast. We were all standing there with our backpacks on, ready to start walking, and she was like, "Well, duh, I *have* to eat, people. Seriously."

If it wasn't for Gilbert, she would have made all of us wait. As it was, Gilbert had to stay back with her. We started our walk without them.

This was okay, I guess. We didn't have to walk with her. But since there were five of us with only one supervisor, and they had wanted our first day on the Camino to be fully supervised, we needed to stay close together. All because this snot-faced girl with the wild hair slept in and didn't give a crap about the rest of us.

I don't care if it *is* ironic that I'm pissed about someone wasting my time. My principal would love the irony, though. Seriously. He'd be like, *I hope this drills home the lesson that you can't go around setting fires or pulling fire alarms and wasting everybody's time, Diego.*

So we walked together today. Greg, Manny, Troy, Shania, and me. And Meagan, of course. Our jail guard. I should drop that crap, though. She's cool. I guess she and Gilbert are only doing this because they believe in it. They believe there's hope for us derelicts, that we can be redeemed and rehabilitated. That *can't* make them bad people.

Anyway, day one wasn't that horrible. It was sunny and hot. I met, like, a zillion people, all ages, from all over the world. I fell in love with a girl from the Netherlands and then watched her walk away with her friends. Sophie. Even her name was sexy. But she came in and out of my life just like that. We walked together and talked for a couple of hours, and then she was gone. She knows things about me some of my closest friends don't know. How weird is this trip gonna be if people keep coming in and out of our lives, disappearing at will? Strange. But fun.

Tonight we'll sleep four to a room. Apparently, this is a good thing. Gilbert said there'll be days when there are twenty or thirty people in one room.

I'm crashed on my single bed, inside my mandatory sleeping bag, looking at day one's passport stamps in my credencial. *Your own sleeping bag* was at the top of the list of things to bring. It's not like my abuelita has money to throw around on stuff we won't use. Like I'll ever go camping again in my life. It was just another added expense to feel guilty about.

Moms tried to make me feel better by saying they'd save more than what they spent on the sleeping bag when they bought groceries for one less Diego while I'm away. Probably true. I try not to, but I eat like a pig.

We're still waiting for Gilbert and Claire, which pisses me off. I'm a growing boy, yo. I need my food when I need it. We're all waiting for them so we can eat together. I'm more than a little pissed. At least we got to choose our beds so we didn't have to share a room with her.

I kind of feel sorry for her, because clearly we all hate her and we're still at the beginning of the journey. There's no way she can redeem herself now, not like Shania did anyway.

I'm in a room with Manny, Troy, and Greg. I couldn't even believe Meagan allowed that breakdown. I thought there would have to be a supervisor in each room, but she said it didn't matter… not like we could go anywhere.

"Greg and I are going outside for a bit. You guys wanna come?" Manny says. I was *gonna* journal, but any excuse not to is a good one.

"Sure, I'm in." I knock on the bathroom door. We lucked out with en suites tonight. They're probably trying to ease us into roughing it. I'm okay with that. I'm not as bad as Troy, but I like comforts too. I've never been camping. I've actually never been out of the big city. "How about you, Troy? Coming?"

"Where?" he asks from behind the closed door. "What's up?"

"We're just going outside for a bit. Wanna come?"

"I'm in. Just give me a sec. Where the hell are we anyway? Ow, Jesus! Damn."

Troy got a blister already. First day. He was the one who was most excited about being here, too. He's in there staring at his blister and cursing. Clearly someone is going to have to actually do something about it. Not like he will.

"Leave it alone, dude," Manny says. "It's just a blister. Crying over it isn't going to take it away, diva."

I laugh. "Dude, take it easy on the kid."

"Nah," Manny says. "He loves me."

The door opens, and Troy comes out. "I heard that. You are *so* not my type, Manny." He pseudo-limps past us on his way out of the room. "Let's go, gentlemen. Is anybody going to answer my question?"

"What question was that?" Greg asks. Dude is quiet. Just when I think he must have taken a vow of silence he pops up again and says something. Own. Little. World. For sure. I make a mental note to try to get to know Greg better. Maybe he's just feeling out of his element or something.

"Where are we? What's this place called? Shouldn't we all write this down for our mandatory journal entries? *Dear Diary, tonight we stopped in the quaint little town of* fill-in-the-blank." He does a little *dot, dot, dot* with his finger. Weird that he doesn't know. His face practically lives in his guidebook.

"Cacabelos," Manny says, because Manny knows everything all the time. He's unbelievable. "We traveled just over sixteen kilometers today. Meagan said they started things easy to get us worked in. Apparently it worked for you, dude. You are *worked in*."

"Very funny." Troy continues out of the room. "May you never know the pain of a blister on *your* heel, dear Manny. May you never know it."

He flounces and is gone. Manny is right behind him.

"Follow the leader," I say to Greg.

"Hey," Greg says. "Wait up." He races out behind me.

"What's your story, anyway?" I ask him once he's caught up to me.

"I really don't have one. I did some lame-ass thing, just like everyone else here. Not a lot to tell."

"Nah, dude," I say. "Not what I meant. Besides, Gilbert has this thing. He doesn't want us talking about our *crimes* yet."

We both laugh.

"I'm just some guy, Diego. I kind of just want to keep to myself. I have a lot to think about. I have a lot of crap on my mind. Hey, where'd they go? How'd they disappear so fast?"

"Other way, genius. If you don't want to talk, I'm cool with that." We walk away from the albergue to join Manny and Troy. "Wait up, guys."

"Listen, I'm sorry, man. It's nothing personal," Greg says. "I really don't have much of a story. I just wanna walk and get this over with. I have someone waiting for me back home. Someone who needs me."

"Dude, I totally understand. No worries."

"Did you guys get a load of this church?" Troy calls to us. "What is it with churches here? They're everywhere. And they're beautiful."

Manny and Troy sit down on the church steps. It's only then I realize Troy brought his journal. He begins to write.

"Scoot over, dude." I shove him a bit as I sit. Greg hovers in front of us. Now that he's told me he doesn't have a story, all I want to know is his story. And who's waiting for him. "Have you noticed they all look kind of the same? There's like three different kinds. Replicated over and over again. This one looks a bit like the one we're walking to."

"What is? What looks the same?" Troy asks.

"Dude, Troy," Manny says, laughing. "You are easily distracted. You *just* mentioned the churches. Diego's talking about the churches. You're one of those squirrel people, aren't you?"

"Huh? No. Just tired. Long day. Blister."

We sit taking in the view. I look up at the windows of our albergue room. Wrought iron grates bar most of the windows, and I can see a pair of underpants hanging from the grate outside our washroom.

"Please tell me you didn't hang your skivvies out our bathroom window, Troyboy."

"What the—" Greg says as he follows my sightline. "Man, Troy, that's messed up."

"Troy wears boxer briefs?" Manny asks. "I never would have thunk it. I saw you as a bikini bottom kind of guy."

We burst out laughing as Troy turns a dozen shades of red, drops his journal to the cobbles, and buries his head in his hands.

"Oh my God, Manny," Troy says. "I can never look you in the eye again. Don't do this to me, guys. A boy's undies are private. I mean, Jesus."

"Private doesn't wave in the breeze for everyone to see, dude," I say. "What the hell were you thinking?"

"We all got the handout, Diego. It said to wash our underwear in the sink and hang them to dry." He's pretty much pleading with us now. This only makes us laugh harder, which is only making him turn deeper shades of red. "Don't talk about my underwear. Please, show mercy."

"It's a particularly flattering shade of green," Manny says. He jumps off the steps to avoid Troy's punch.

"I just died. I'm dead," Troy says. "Manny, stop."

"I would call that mint green." Greg puts on a lisp as he says, "Or maybe a nice pistachio. Gay couture. Better accentuates the swishing."

As much as I don't want to laugh, I do. Manny loses it. It's not until I look back at Troy that I realize we might have gone too far. He's so red now, but also totally deflated. I think we may have stepped over that line and bullied him. Totally didn't mean to.

Troy picks his journal up from the cobbles and starts to head back to the albergue.

"Ah, come on, Troy," I say through my laughter. "You know we're only kidding. It's okay. It's all good. Come on back."

"Yeah, sorry, Troy," Manny says. "No harm, little dude. Come on. Don't be a spoilsport."

Greg goes quiet and stares at his feet. I run after Troy, who's already across the street and almost back to the albergue. As I reach him, I grab for his shoulder. Still laughing, I pull him toward me, and he turns a bit in my direction.

It's only then I *know* we've gone too far. But come on, dude. What was he thinking, sticking his underwear out the window? Of course we're gonna taunt him and go off on him.

Tears stream down his face.

"Dude," I say. "Come on."

I let go of his shoulder and he quickly swings away. I look at Manny and Greg. They've settled down on the steps of the church and look too afraid to join us.

Without facing me, he says, "No, Diego. *You* come on. Go to hell."

Totally short fuse.

We're at the entrance of the albergue. Troy steps inside, and I follow him.

"Bud, please. I'm sorry. I didn't realize you were *actually* upset. I thought you thought it was funny too. I'm sorry. We were just being stupid. It's underwear, dude. Underwear's funny."

Clearly frustrated, he turns to face me as he wipes at his eyes.

"Would it have been funny if we were out there joking about Manny being Black, Diego? Or about Shania being a bitch? Or your *Moms.*"

"What?"

"You guys were clearly joking about me being a fag. It was funny for about the first second when you pointed out my underwear.

"After that, it just got all gay and mean and everyone thought it was okay to take potshots at me. Do you know how hard it is for me to be around guys? Especially good-looking ones who are all being so nice to me. It's messed up. Did you *all* have to be hot *and* nice? I mean, seriously."

"I'm sorry. I didn't—"

"Then you toss out a couple homo jokes and bam. Everything's ruined."

"Oh, man, dude," I say. "I'm sure it wasn't like that. We were just joking about your gotchies, man. Not about that. We've been cool about that, Troy. Haven't we? There's no way any of us would make fun of that."

"Bikini bottom. *Pistachio*," he says, complete with Greg's affected lisp. He looks at me like I'm crazy, and I begin to see his point. "Yeah. They weren't teasing the gay, trying to make him uncomfortable."

"Shit," I say as Gilbert and Claire come storming through the door, laughing. Troy quickly looks away. He darts back to our room before they can get a look at him. I think I'm still the only one who saw that he was crying, so I might be able to save this. But damn.

"Hey, Diego," Gilbert says, all bubbly, as though he didn't just come in over an hour late dragging the pain in the ass behind him. "How was your first day of walking? Everything I promised it would be?"

"And more." I turn to go. "Sorry, sir. I have to go talk to Troy."

"Sir? Seriously, Diego. No. I'm not okay with *sir*. First names only, please."

"Right, yeah," I mumble, but I'm already mostly gone, trying to catch up to Troy before he locks himself in the bathroom or something.

I can fix this.

CHAPTER 11

SHANIA REYNOLDS

Tuesday, July 2nd – Day 4 – Walking with Diego

What is there to like? It was hard to get time alone with Diego. It was like everyone was out to ruin it for me, I swear. We'd be there, just the two of us, laughing about something silly, and then I'd see a shadow and bam… next thing I know I'm walking with three boys instead of one. Then this girl from the Netherlands butts in, and they hit it off. I couldn't get a break. I hate my life.

I like that Diego is always trying to make me laugh, though. His smile is so… but I can't take all the interruptions. How could they not know we were trying to have a private conversation? Especially that Sophie girl.

It felt like we kept going more and more uphill, too. I wonder if that was just my imagination or what? Meagan says the next couple of days are going to be way harder. I can't imagine harder than what we did today.

It was beautiful. Rolling hills and flowers everywhere. Old buildings. These little towns. It even smells better here than back home. If it wasn't for all the climbing, it would be awesome.

I manage to get the chair beside Diego at supper. We're in a large dining room, and all the albergue guests sit together at one huge wooden table that looks about a million years old.

As soon as I sit down I know something is off. The energy in the room is bad, and it feels like I'm back at the beginning with Diego.

Everyone seems miserable. Maybe the walking just made them all tired today. No, there's something else going on. I'm almost positive. The undercurrent stings. Too many sidelong glances and too much intentional silence.

Claire doesn't count, because she's always a hot mess of anger. And besides, she was with Gil all day.

I attempt to make eye contact with Troy, but he's stubbornly looking down at his empty water glass as if it's the most important thing in the goddamned world. His vibes are anger. Something I never see from Troy.

Nobody's talking, and it's almost painful. What the hell? It's like being at the dinner table at home. If Mom and Dad were giving off these vibes, Dillon would say something like, "My Spidey-senses are tingling." On those miraculous occasions when we actually have dinner together, that is. Dad's usually at the office every waking hour and Mom is always out spending his money and being all debutante diva. They really are ghosts in our lives.

I tap Diego's leg under the table with my foot to get his attention. Because everyone is looking everywhere but at each other. He startles and gives me a dirty look. There's a slight shake of his head as if he's telling me to leave it alone, to drop the subject I haven't even had a chance to bring up.

When I don't look away, his face slowly softens. There's no outright smile, but his dimples appear as his mouth softens. He *wants* to smile. That's a start. So it isn't me. Thank God.

"You have to give me something here, Diego."

"Huh?"

"*What* is going on? It's like everyone's mad or something. It was a tough day, but it wasn't that bad. I need to talk if I want to decompress. This silence is killing me."

"Sorry, Shania," Diego says. "It's not you. I don't know how to fix this."

"I'm actually a pretty good listener." I pass him the basket of bread and, as he holds it, I take a small piece for myself.

He turns to me and shrugs. Then he nods toward the hallway just outside the dining room, gets up, and leaves the room. When I get there, he turns to face me and gives me these big puppy dog eyes.

"You gotta save me," he says. "You gotta save all of us. We did a crappy thing, and I don't know how to fix it."

Diego's face is now Twizzler red, and he looks like the hunter who murdered Bambi's mother in the meadow.

"What did you do?" It's kind of obvious he did something. Guilt wafts off of him in waves.

"We may have teased Troy about his being gay. On accident."

"*By* accident, Diego? Really? Just how does a shitty thing like that happen, anyway?" I kick his foot and give him the dirtiest look I can muster.

"I know, I know," Diego says. "It just happened. Trust me."

Diego tells me this cockamamie story about Troy's underwear and the boys teasing him about it flapping out their bathroom window.

"I swear to you, Shania, we were totally only joking around about his underwear. He's too sensitive. It's stupid that he—"

"No," I interrupt. "You don't get to decide that. You're not the gay one here. You're not, *right*?"

"Very funny. Obviously not."

"Nothing's obvious, loser." I smirk to show that I'm at least halfway joking. "But you don't get to decide if he's being sensitive or not, Diego. For reals. That's his decision to make. He was in a group of straight guys making fun of him. If he felt like it was poking at his sexuality, then it was."

"Okay, Dr. Phil. Settle down. I wasn't asking for a lecture. Can you help us out of it here? I feel like a dirtbag. So do the other guys. But he won't even look at us now. He's so stubborn."

"Stop. Again, you're making it his problem. His fault."

"Shania," Diego says, now totally flustered. "Come on. Okay. I get it. What can we do?"

"I'm trying not to be *Nasty Shania* right now, but you're making it very difficult. You guys need lessons in how to be compassionate human beings. Seriously. Have you tried apologizing in a way that doesn't sound like a non-apology?"

"What do you mean?"

"Shania? Diego?" Gil calls from the dining room. "Why don't you join us before your dinner gets cold? You gotta try this Galician soup."

"Sorry, Gil," I say. "Coming." I start to walk away.

"What do you mean?" Diego says, pulling me back.

"Diego, it's really easy. I just mean don't apologize for how he *feels* about what happened. That's making him own what happened, not you guys. Apologize for doing what you did. Tell him you won't do it again. I'm guessing if you already apologized it went something like, *I'm sorry you feel that way?*"

He gives me this goofy grin that answers my question perfectly. Their apology wasn't an apology at all. Kudos to Troy for holding out for a real one.

"Come on, guys," Gil says from the table.

"You may have a point," Diego says. I shake my head, and we head back together before Gil bursts a vessel or something. "Thanks."

"Don't mention it." I pull out my chair, and we both sit down. The soup smells freaking amazing. Worth today's walk.

CHAPTER 12

TROY SINCLAIR

I MAY HAVE OVERREACTED. BUT I doubt it. It's hard when you have crushes on everybody you're hanging around with. I know I'm being overly sensitive, but I can't help it. I can't even look at them.

Diego, even? He's such a stand-up guy. At least *he* apologized. Finally. The right way the second time around. Greg's the ass. He's the one who made it ugly. Now I have to wonder for the rest of the trip if that was him showing his true colors. I hate when I feel like I can't be myself.

Greg went too gay too fast in that skit he pulled off at my expense. Like he had been dying to make fun of me, waiting for the right moment to pounce.

Even though Manny was right in there, saying all those cringeworthy things, I can tell he just thought he was being funny. His teasing was friendly. He may even have a non-gay crush on me. Which would totally be okay, because Manny.

I can just barely make out his face in the dark right now. The blinds on the other side of the room are only half closed, and the moon must be full or something because it's completely filling the room with light. I could get used to staring at Manny's face like this. Even though that's probably stalkerish. Nah. It *totally* is. No probably about it.

All the guys are sleeping. Diego puffs out little pops of air every once in a while, but doesn't snore. Manny looks angelic with his hair halo and his perfect chin. His chest rises and falls so slowly I stop breathing to focus on it, to make sure he's still alive. And his one eye is slightly open, like he's watching me watching him. Even though I know he's asleep.

It's Greg the jerk who's snoring. I want to throw my pillow at him or kick his bed. But I'm so mad I might just keep kicking until there's nothing left. I was kind of hoping crap like this wouldn't follow me here.

Instead of attacking Greg in his sleep, I get up and leave the dorm. I shut the door behind me and tiptoe downstairs. Once outside, I'm relieved to finally stop tiptoeing. As the front door of the albergue snaps shut with a pop, I turn to make my way across the street to the church steps.

That's when I see Claire. Claire, who has said maybe ten words in total to the lot of us. Aloof Claire, who is always late, elusive, and miserable.

"Oh, hi," I say as I approach the church steps where she sits looking up at the night sky.

"Come out to howl at the moon?" she says, pointing at the sky.

"Huh?" I turn to look. It *is* a full moon or close to it. It lights up the entire night for us. It's beautiful. All the surrounding hills are visible in its light.

"Werewolves. Full moon. Howl." She shrugs, reaches into her hoodie pocket, and pulls out a bag of Skittles. "Want some?"

"Sure." I sit beside her and hold out my hand. She shakes some of the candy into my cupped palm. "And I'm not a werewolf."

"These Skittles are the only thing between me and madness. They're my lifeline."

"If I had known that, I would have said no." My mouth is full of lifesaving rainbow.

"Ha, ha. No. You're okay," she says. "I have enough to see me through this trying time. I made priority space for them in my backpack. No hiking shoes for me."

I look at her feet and for the first time I realize she's wearing Crocs. Before I bestow upon her my eternal respect and undying love for bucking the system, I have to ask, "Are those the *only* shoes you brought with you? On the Camino?"

"I wouldn't really call them shoes. But yeah."

"You're a goddess. I bow to your awesomeness."

"Calm down, cowboy." She stands, folds up what's left of her bag of Skittles, and puts it in her pocket. "This might sound a little crazy to you, Troy, but do you want to go for a walk?"

Crazy? Maybe. But a walk out here in the beautiful Spanish countryside on a night when the moon is illuminating everything in a magical light I'll probably never see again in my lifetime? How could I refuse?

"Sure," I say. "Why not? Yes."

"Cool."

I stand and bow. "Show me the way, O Captain, my Captain."

She rolls her eyes, nods for me to follow her. "Walt Whitman? Okay. Anyway, there was a cool-looking statue at a church we passed. Just a couple minutes away. I couldn't stop, though. Gilbert was anxious to get here."

"Well, let's go see it now." We start walking. "Mind if I ask about the whole Skittles thing?"

"They're just this little secret thing my girlfriend and I have going on. Skittles are our *I love you*s. You know, incognito like. We trade them back and forth in class or when she's at my place. Each color represents something different. Skittles are our language. I swear, sometimes we have whole conversations in silence... just handing Skittles back and forth. And now I'm here and she's there. And I have mad love for her and I can't pass her a single solitary Skittle. So now

I'm popping them like druggies pop Oxy because I just want to tell her I love her."

We've been walking the dirt path back the way we came into town. Claire stops. She kicks the dirt with one of her unbelievably Croced feet, takes out the Skittles, and pops a few. She puts the bag back in her pocket. I guess I was lucky to get one taste of the rainbow. It will have to do me.

"Wow," I say. She just unloaded a pile of information on me. During our first real conversation. The girl who doesn't talk has so much to say.

"Sorry. TMI?"

"No, no. It's all good. Love is complicated."

"Ha," she says. "We have to cross the little footbridge to get to the other side of the river. The church is over there."

I look to where she points, and the church is aglow under the moon's white stare. It literally looks like there's a spotlight illuminating it.

"Cool," I say. "But tell me, Claire, what's so special about that one? Really, I feel like I've seen seventy-three churches exactly like it on the way here today."

"Oh, Troy. That may be so. You probably have. But you have not seen the Creepy Jesus this particular one has. Even from afar I knew that thing was outrageous and worthy of closer inspection. Creepy Jesus has been calling me. I was afraid I wouldn't get to see him, because to tell you the truth I was a little afraid to get closer to him without backup."

She laughs, and I join her but I'm a bit horror-movie leery now. We step onto the bridge, and the church looms closer. Is its shadow reaching for us? This girl has my geese all bumped up.

"Creepy Jesus, eh? Isn't that sacrilege or something?"

"When you see Creepy Jesus, you'll think the church is the only one being sacrilegious here, my friend."

"I'm sure." We stop at the center of the bridge and look out across the water. The river is extremely narrow. I'm sure even *I* could swim across if I had to.

I search the rocks about my feet and bend to pick up a skinny one. I skip it across the water, but even under the light of the moon I lose visual before it hits the water. I hear a soft plunk, and a ripple appears a few feet out.

"That is *not* how you skip a rock," Claire says, laughing.

"I suck at stuff like that. Guy stuff."

"Shut your face. That's not guy stuff." She picks up a rock and skips it. This one I see because it skips to catch the light a few times before it disappears into the depths of the river. "Girl Power."

She walks off, and I rush to catch up with her. "My bad," I say as I come up beside her.

"Number one," Claire says as we leave the bridge. "That's the last time *my bad* comes out of your mouth. Number two, prepare to meet *The Creepy Jesus of Cacabelos.*"

"You're freaking me out." We're almost at the church. As we step into its small courtyard, I stop to ask, "So how long have you and your girlfriend been together? Are you out? At home? At school? Do you—"

"Whoa. Too many questions, Troy. Zoe and I have been together for... seven months. I'm out, mostly at school. I'm *so* not out at home. I was. But not anymore. Why do you think I need to communicate with my *friend* in a secret language?" She strikes air-quotes around the word *friend*. "And I'm not out yet on the Camino. Unless I count you."

"I count." I smile. "What's with the *used to be out, not out*? How's that even a thing?"

"Well, Troy. That's a very long and troubling story. Maybe one day I'll tell you about it. Time will tell. Then again, maybe I won't. I only know today is not the day."

"Fair enough. Sorry if I put you on the spot. My friends tell me I talk too much and ask too many questions. I'll back off now."

"We're good. I'm just not ready to go there tonight. It really *is* a long story. Are you out?"

"Yep. I'm the trophy son. My parents are these weird *we-have-a-gay-son* people."

"Buddy, don't complain. My mom cried for a week because she thought she lost her chance to be a grandmother. Not to mention how she cried for my soul because I'm destined for hell. And that was just the beginning."

"My mom says she's counting on me to give her her first grandchild, because she doubts my straight brother will ever have any kids."

"That's cool. Hey. Here it is. Okay, wait!" I turn to look up. "Don't look yet." She physically tears me away before I get a chance to look at this Jesus guy.

"Whoa. It's so wild. Creepy Jesus." She holds me back, but I see the horror in her expression as she inspects the face of the statue. Her nose wrinkles, and her eyes bulge. I begin to think I may turn to stone or something if I look into the face of Creepy Jesus. "Okay, are you ready for this? You can't unsee it once you look. I'm cool if you don't want this one in your memory bank. I'm just glad you were here with me when I saw it up close."

She's only half kidding. I can see this look of awe in her face. And maybe fear.

I laugh and push Claire aside. "Come on. It can't be that bad, psycho."

I'm standing in front of the most hideous statue of Jesus I have ever seen. It's out of Stephen King. Mary? Yeah, it's gotta be Mary holding him. *It?* Mary's holding *it.* He's man Jesus, but he's only the size of a baby in her hands. He's got these long thin arms, and she's holding him sideways, but his hair is straight down his front, and there's seventy-eight kinds of wrong with this Creepy Jesus. Even Mary looks disgusted to be holding the thing.

"Argh," I mumble. "You're right. Please make me unsee it."

"Cannot be done, my man. That's in there for life." She taps my noggin, and I swear I hate her right now. But, all the same, I pull out my phone and take a few pics.

"I was minding my own business. I just came out for some fresh air. I was going to pace a bit and then go back inside the albergue. This. Will. Never. Ever. Leave. Me."

"Ha ha," she says. "I win the day." She puts up her hand for a high five, and I reluctantly give it to her. She deserves it. Impressive.

Claire takes some pictures, too, and then we get in for a selfie with Creepy Jesus and his reluctant mother in the background. Sweet. I can't wait to show this thing to Tommy when I get home. Maybe even Dad.

"Let's go back before Meagan or Gilbert wake up, notice we're missing, and send out a search party."

"Or Creepy Jesus here gets down out of his mommy's arms and slays us both," she says. I can't even tell if she's joking, because I'm not quite sure what Creepy Jesus is actually capable of doing. I mean, besides filling our hearts with terror.

DIEGO NELSON

WHEN I COME DOWN TO breakfast, Troy's here first. I'm glad when he smiles at me instead of giving me an *unh-uh, keep walking* expression. I guess he really did accept my second apology. The one I practised with Shania.

"Good morning, sunshine," Troy says as I sit down across from him. "Ready to greet the day?"

"Ready as I'll ever be. What's for breakfast? I could eat a house."

"I think you mean horse." He laughs and passes me a bite-sized muffin. "Here. Nosh on this for now. The line is too long."

I turn to look, and the hallway leading into the albergue's kitchen is filled with peregrinos. Looks like everyone got up before me. Except Greg and Manny. When I left the room, Greg was snoring, and Manny was lost somewhere inside his own hair.

I turn back, thank him for the muffin, peel the paper off, and pop it in my mouth. As I begin to eat—and realize it's carrot, my favorite—he looks at me and says, "So."

"So, what?" He's smirking like he has something big to dish.

"I hung out with Claire last night."

"You what, now? How?" Last I saw Troy last night, he was in bed trying not to look like he was checking out my man Manny.

"I couldn't sleep. We saw this crazy stuff last night, Diego. A thing of nightmares. On a full moon night, too."

"More importantly, Claire. Is she nice? Or is she the thing of nightmares of which you speak?"

"No, she's okay. She's pretty awesome. I thought maybe I would walk with her today. You know, maybe give you more space to walk with, you know…"

"No. What? Who?"

"Come on, Diego." He takes a large swig of his coffee. "It's glaringly obvious. You have a thing for Shania. You gave me a look yesterday, back in that little town with all the dogs, like you were going to kill me if I didn't disappear. Remember, when I lost my footing walking that little garden wall and stepped in that huge puddle and got stuck with a wet sock for the rest of the afternoon?"

"Okay. Maybe you have a point. But do you think *she* knows?"

"Diego, I think Mother Teresa knows. And she's been dead for decades."

"I don't know, Troy. I mean, at first she terrified me. She was so nasty. You wouldn't believe it."

"We're delinquents." Troy leans closer. "We're here against our will—some of us, anyway—maybe she was just having a bad day. To me, this whole Camino de Santiago thing is a goddamned Mardi Gras. What crime do I have to commit next year in order to do it again? Let me know; sign me up. But maybe it sucks bags for our friend Miss Twain."

"I hear you." He's totally right, too. "I'm gonna hit up the breakfast line now. Kinda died down some. Yo, maybe I *will* walk with her today. Thanks, man."

Troy picks up his Camino passport and glances through it. I make my way to the line. The faint smell of eggs and syrup grows stronger as I near the kitchen. My stomach growls.

I can't believe who I see coming down the stairs—Claire. She's not going to make us wait today. Maybe she just needed to break the ice with someone in order to get on track. My man Troy, he's a good head.

*   *   *

"Oh my God, Gil wasn't kidding. This is killing me." Shania is just ahead of me and she's been moaning for a good five minutes. Trust me, I'm moaning just as loudly.

"When is this going to end? I need a break. Ay," I say between heavy breaths. "I did not sign up for this."

There's a light drizzle, but after two hours every single drop feels like a punch. We've walked uphill almost since we left the albergue. Though Shania started to moan and complain first, I'm not very far behind her. This is unreal.

"There was a sign about a mile back that promised café con leche up ahead," she says, turning back to offer me a slight smile. "Maybe Troy was right about that crap, and it'll give us some magical powers to keep us going. We still have over ten miles to go before tonight's albergue."

"Buen Camino," an elderly couple says in tandem as they come up alongside me, pass me, and repeat their greeting to Shania before they pass her too. I return the greeting, but then I stop for a breather at a slippery rock with enough surface for me to place both feet on it.

"Yo, Shan," I say. She stops climbing. "Hold up. I just need to stop for a second." She comes back down beside me. "For real, did those grandparent-y people just breeze on by us? Or did I imagine them?"

"No. They were real, and seconds away from skipping. You didn't imagine it, my friend. They looked happy about this rain too. I hate people."

"Nah, they're okay. We're just not ready for this kind of intense workout. We were too busy committing crimes while those old folks were training for the Camino. They have a jump on us."

"Ha. Yeah." She looks up at where we have to go. It's all uphill. "Well, shall we go? Must be something coming up soon. The signs can't lie, right?"

"Keep telling yourself that," I say. "Let's go."

So we start to climb again. I gotta say, I feel like I'm cheating by walking behind Shania. I get to watch her. I'm falling for this girl, for real.

She starts to hum a song, and I put one foot in front of the other and watch her while I attempt to figure out what song she's humming. Just as the lyrics come to me and I start to sing them out loud, my foot slips on a slick rock and I go down hard. I'm so lost in my head, I don't have time to put my hands out to break my fall.

I fall face-first into mud, and my forehead hits a rock. I see stars, but then I slide downhill and thunk against trees and rocks. Somewhere along the way, I manage to scream, and the desperation in my voice annoys me.

"Diego!" Shania screeches as I finally come to a halt against something hard and unmoving. A tree?

I watch Shania run down as carefully as she can without landing on her own ass. As I try to stand, I grab for the tree trunk that stopped me. That's when I realize it's a leg.

"Oh," I say, as I look up into the friendliest face I ever saw, except for Moms and my abuelita. "I'm sorry. I didn't know you were a person."

"Haha. It's okay, my friend. Bastien Mercier, at your service." He leans a walking stick against a nearby tree and offers me his hand. Shania arrives at my side. Bastien is an old man with a gray beard and white hair. He looks grizzled but capable. More capable than me, anyway. "Are you okay, my friend? Your head, it bleeds."

"Huh?" I say, as he helps me to my feet. I put a hand to my forehead and bring it away. Yep. My fingers are smeared red. "Oh. Yeah. I guess. It doesn't really hurt all that much."

"Shit, Diego. You're gonna need stitches."

"It's okay, my friend. In two miles or so, the hôpital. Just on top the hill and in the town ahead."

"We need to get you there, Diego," Shania says. The look on her face is almost comical. She's terrified, as though I'm gonna drop dead any minute from this small cut that doesn't even hurt all that much.

"Nah, nah. I'm fine, Shan, really." But as I start to walk, I lose my footing and fall back into the stranger who helped me up. Like my feet aren't my own. "Oh, man. Dude, I'm sorry."

"It is not a problem, my friend." He holds me upright while Shania examines the cut. "Like I say, I am Bastien. Bastien Mercier. Let us help you up this hill."

"I'm fine," I say, but I wobble when I try to break free of him. It's not happening. I actually *do* need his help. And maybe Shania's too.

"It's okay to need help," Bastien says. He puts his arm around me and looks up the hill. With his other hand, he retrieves his walking stick. "Let's go, my friend."

Shania gets on my other side. She won't stop looking at me like I'm dying. It makes me nervous.

We start out slowly, one foot in front of the other, careful about where our feet land on the uneven rocky ground. After a few steps, the rain stops.

"Thank God," Shania says. She smiles, but it fades and turns into a frown when she glances at me. "Jesus, Diego. You're a total mess."

I look down at myself and I'm mud and crap from head to toe. Every inch of me is caked with it. Even my leg hair is matted with thick clumps of mud. And under the mud, I see blood in a few spots. Obviously my legs got cut on the rocks and shifting gravel.

As if seeing the blood triggers something inside me, I begin to feel the burn of the scrapes up and down my legs.

"We're almost there. The top is soon. This is my third Camino. The town above is lovely. They will help you. Maybe even a shower, no?" He laughs, entertained by the mess, as he takes in the state of me.

"Thanks. I'm glad I made your day."

"No, no, Diego. I laugh because I have been here. Days ago—a week and a half maybe—back in Burgos. Another lifetime, it seems. I tripped my way up the cathedral stairs. Blood, it was everywhere. I did not need to shower the mud away, but blood. Mais oui, I was a wreck. It happens on the Camino. Someone helped me that day. Many someones. Now, I help you. I'm sorry I laugh. It just reminds me of the Camino's way. Expect, how you say, the unexpected."

Only now do I notice the scab across the bridge of his nose and a scrape along the side of his face. War wounds from his own tumble.

We walk in silence as we attempt to focus on the slick rocks and ground cover at our feet. The trees all around us drip with rain water, even though it has stopped raining. Everything is so incredibly green. I look up into the sky, but mostly just see the thick canopy above us.

"We're almost there, Diego." Shania breaks the silence. "We'll have that café con leche *after* we get you fixed up. I'll sacrifice myself for your gushing head wound. See what kind of friend I am?"

"Sweet," I say, my voice filled with sarcasm. But, for real, I'm so glad she's leaving her home crap behind. I never would have guessed this was the same person I met at the airport. "I'm touched."

"Yeah, you are," Shania says. "In the head."

"Ha ha."

We make our way to the top of the hill, gingerly stepping from one stone to another and one flat foothold to another. At the top, the town opens up to us. The road goes in two directions as we come into a clearing. The house across the street has a great big arrow made of scallop shells that are painted yellow—one of the ever-present yellow arrows that show us the way to Compostela—and cemented directly into the wall. It points left.

"We go right," Bastien says. He offers me a small smile and points the way opposite the arrow. It seems wrong to ignore the arrow.

"What about Gilbert?" I say to Shania, reluctant to go off the beaten path. "He's just ahead of us." I turn to Bastien. "He's our leader. Our counselor. We're supposed to stay close to him and Meagan."

"Stay close and lose your life's blood, Diego," he says. "You're bleeding. In town, they will help you. Then, on your way, no? You can catch up to your Gilbert after. Your health, it matters."

He has a point, even though his English is broken and I have to concentrate to put it all together. I sigh, defeated. I just worry because I don't want to do anything on this walk to disappoint Moms.

"Okay," I say.

"Dude," Shania says. She places a hand on my shoulder. "It'll be fine. He'd want you to do this, jackass. You need medical help. You're bleeding like a stuck pig."

"Yeah, I guess." Sometimes I think trouble has a way of finding me. "I should have been more careful on those rocks." I'm pissed, but only at myself.

"Save the self-loathing drama for later," she says. We reach a cobbled sidewalk and walk on, turning our backs on the scallop shells. "Let's get you fixed before it's too late."

"Too late?"

"You bleed out and leave me holding the corpse."

"Very funny," I say.

"Come," Bastien says. His walking stick begins to make a steady click-click-click sound along the cobbles. "I will show you the way."

They stay close on either side of me, and just as I'm about to say I'm okay—that I don't need them to crowd me—I change my mind. The fog in my head has me feeling more than a little loopy. I think about what Moms is going to say when she sees I picked up a new scar along the Camino. The way she'll shake her head—and maybe even her fist—and say, "*Mijo, oh, my baby.*" The way that'll make me feel both like she's babying me and like it's the best thing ever. And she'll hug me and say it makes me more handsome or some shit like that.

CHAPTER 14

SHANIA REYNOLDS

WEDNESDAY, JULY 3RD – *Day 5 – So Much Blood*

It feels so weird to sit here in some stranger's kitchen. Somewhere in rural ass-kiss Spain. But that's what I'm doing. It took only ten minutes for Diego to get in to see a doctor and get his head stitched up. Back home, it would have taken hours. Next thing we knew, we walked with this lady from the clinic to her house.

Bastien is in the living room speaking to the lady. They're speaking flawless Spanish, so I have no idea what they're saying. I mean, he's obviously French. He told us he's from this place called Toulouse. But he speaks perfect Spanish. Freaky. Seems everyone over here can speak so many languages.

Diego's upstairs—in this stranger's house—having a shower. And his clothes are in the washing machine. This lady from the doctor's office just totally opened up her home to us. Back on the path, when Bastien said he'd be able to have a shower, I did not picture it being in a random house. Crazy. I'm starting to love this place. I mean, I know it's bad that Diego split his noggin open, but look at this. I'm in Spain, sitting in this nice lady's home, having a café con leche, chilling. Stuff happens out here.

As I finish up today's impromptu journal entry, I hear Diego's heavy feet on the stairs. He comes into the kitchen rubbing a towel gingerly through his hair. A second towel is wrapped around his waist. I try not to look at his belly and chest, even though it's almost impossible not to stare at them. Because they're perfect, just like I imagined.

"Really, Diego," I say. "Walking down a flight of stairs with your eyes covered by a towel after suffering a massive head wound? What is wrong with you?"

"What can I say? I'm a daredevil."

"Or a jackass," I say, hoping I'm not blushing as much as it feels like I am. He looks at me and suddenly becomes more embarrassed himself. He takes the towel from his head and wraps it around his shoulders.

I shy-smile, like I wasn't just staring at his body. "You didn't get that wet, did you?"

"No, Mom. It's good. See. Dry." He taps the bandage.

"Diego," Bastien says. He must have heard Diego's elephant feet on the stairs. "You're all fresh. Must feel good."

"Seriously, a thousand percent better."

"Luciana just went to put the clothes of yours in the dryer," he says. "Soon, we go."

"You don't have to wait for us, Bastien," Diego says. "That's cool. You've helped so much already."

"It's what we do on the Camino, my friend. We are peregrinos together. We help each other. We go, we meet with your *leader*."

"Thank you," I interject on Diego's behalf when his expression warns me he is going to continue arguing against being helped. "We appreciate it, Bastien. We might not be able to find our own way back to the arrows. We're glad to have you with us. Aren't we, Diego?"

I give him my *agree-with-me-right-now-or-else* stare. And he switches gears to comply. Maybe he's still a little afraid of me.

"Um, oh. Yeah. Sure. Thank you. I really do appreciate everything you've done. Thank you."

"It is nothing, my friend."

Bastien goes to the sink and sets down his mug. Diego sits opposite me, and Bastien joins us at the table. Diego's looking a little shy, being the only one in towels, and I'm kinda tripping on his obvious embarrassment. I can tell he's praying to the gods that the dryer doesn't take much longer. He wants his clothes back big time. And I want the dryer to take forever.

CHAPTER 15

TROY SINCLAIR

WE'VE BEEN LOST FOR OVER an hour. The way Claire is so chill about it, I'm beginning to think she doesn't much care. She might have had something to do with us taking the wrong turns in the first place.

We were only a city block or so ahead of Meagan. Every once in a while, I would slow our pace so she was always able to catch glimpses of us. And Manny and Greg walked just slightly ahead of us. They sped up, and, as soon as we lost sight of them, bam. Everything fell apart.

The rain didn't help. We're soaked through. At least it's stopped. Hopefully it stays this way. I need to either dry off or find my way back to the path before I go mad. I can't be wet *and* lost. But here we are, drenched, on this quiet street with no peregrinos anywhere in sight. We have lost our way. And I kept letting Claire lead me in the wrong direction, because I assumed she was trying to find her way back to the yellow arrows.

Clearly, not a good idea. Not an arrow in sight. I should have just kept walking with Manny and Greg. Even Gil disappeared at the albergue after he realized Claire finally had a new walking partner.

Last night may have been a one-off, though. She seemed nice enough at the time, but I think today's Claire may have gone rogue. I'm almost positive. Maybe she's possessed by Cacabelos Jesus.

"I give up." I stop in front of a small grocery. "I'm asking for directions."

"No, don't. It's more fun this way. Can't we just wander around and figure things out for ourselves? Where's your sense of adventure?"

"You know what I think? I think you *want* to be lost. I think you did this to us on purpose. I don't want to be drawn into any of your plans to screw this up. You're sabotaging me."

I walk into the grocery. I let the door close on Claire, shutting down her ability to respond. I hope they can point me in the right direction. I don't care if she follows me or not. I'd rather she didn't.

I have my phone out, getting directions from the lady behind the counter, when Claire finally enters the store. We're struggling through the language barrier, but the woman understands Camino and is able to show me on Google Maps where I have to go to get back on the path. Claire stands behind me, skulking noisily. After I have the directions, I buy a couple apples that happen to sit in a basket on the counter.

I turn to Claire and give her a dirty look as I put one of the apples into a side pocket in my backpack. I bite into the other and say, "Come on. Let's go." I hold up my phone to show her I know where I'm going.

"Nah," she says. She pops a handful of Skittles. It was cute at first, but those little candies are beginning to annoy me. "I think I'll sit this one out."

"What does that even mean?"

Claire heads for the door without saying another word. I thank the woman behind the counter again before I leave. She says *Buen Camino*, and I wave as I leave her store.

"What is your problem?" I ask Claire when I catch up to her. She just shrugs and keeps walking in the opposite direction we need to go in order to get back to the yellow arrows. "Come on, Claire. You're going the wrong way. You can't just get lost in Spain. Are you nuts, girl? What is wrong with you? I thought we bonded last night. I thought—"

"Oh, what?" She pivots, cutting me off mid-sentence. "You think because we spent half an hour together we're best friends now? What about the day before that? Or on the plane? You know, when you didn't say two words to me?"

"I just want to get back to the Camino, Claire. I don't want to fight with you."

"What are you even in for, anyway?" She walks over to where I stand waiting for her.

"You don't want to know."

"Give it a shot. Hit me. Diego's in for setting his school ablaze. Manny told me this morning he's in for some kind of weapons offense, and Shania is in for grand theft auto. That one's pretty hot, actually. I don't know how she was ever able to get her sentence lowered on that one. You think if some chick jacks a car, she's going to have to spend time in jail. Or at least juvie."

"Her dad's a—" I stop myself. If Shania didn't tell her her dad's a lawyer, she didn't want her to know. "It's none of your business. What does it matter? What's going on here, anyway? Are you coming back to the path with me or not?"

"That remains to be seen," she says. "Maybe I'll—"

"Wait." I cut her off. "What did you just say about Manny? Weapons offense? Seriously? Manny?"

"What was it you said about Shania? Oh yeah. *It's none of your business.*"

"Grow up. Her father's a lawyer. There. Now you know."

"You cave easily when you want something. Did you ever notice that about yourself?" She smiles. She's liking this day way too much.

"Just tell me what you're talking about already. Weapon? Really? Manny seems like such a good guy. You're destroying my image of him."

"It's true. I swear," she says. She motions to the stoop of an abandoned storefront beside the grocery, and we sit down. "There's a big story behind it, believe me. You can keep his image untarnished. The boy's a saint. He took the fall for a cousin."

"That sounds more like Manny."

"Yeah, right? Apparently, he was standing by his locker minding his own business and his cousin gets called to the office. Next thing, the guy's running up to Manny all panicked and telling him to hide a bag in his locker. He tosses it to Manny like it's a hot potato and then he bolts. Right out of the school."

"And there's a gun in the bag? And Manny gets caught in possession, and his cousin is free and clear and doesn't own up?"

"Almost. You're good," Claire says. "The cops were on Manny right away. Guilt by association. Then they found the gun. Then Manny did that noble thing all broken superheroes who don't know what they're doing do. He takes the fall for his cousin by refusing to rat on him."

"Jesus. Man. I don't know if he's a loser or really really awesome."

"Maybe both." Claire laughs, but there's no humor in it. "The only reason he got off so easy? He's an honor student with a squeaky clean record. Like, top student in his school. Everyone knew it wasn't his gun. Manny wouldn't steal a pencil or punch a fly. He's like untouchable at his school. They moved mountains to get him in *The Walk*."

"Wow."

"Yeah. So back to you, Troy. What are you in for? Have you been a naughty boy?"

"Stop. Wherever the new attitude is coming from, you can stop anytime." I get up from the stoop, take a bite of my browning apple, and wait for her to join me.

"I'm just tryna have a conversation with you." Claire stands up.

I walk off in the direction of the yellow arrows and I'm relieved when she falls in beside me. I wouldn't want to have to tell Gilbert or Meagan one of their charges has flown the coop.

"I don't like this new you. Can we go back to the girl I met last night? I can't believe I'm saying this, but I miss Creepy Jesus."

"Ha," she says, smacking my shoulder. "Good one. Here's a heads-up for you, Troy. I think I'm gonna bolt sooner or later, but maybe I shouldn't do it while I'm with you. You're okay. Other than the cold shoulder at first. Wouldn't want to get you in trouble."

"Mighty big of you," I say. She stops again and my long sigh is out before I have a chance to stop it. "What now?"

"I'm just taking my Crocs off." She sits on the sidewalk, removes them, and stuffs them into her overstuffed backpack. She pops back up, now barefoot, and says, "Okay. Let's go. All ready."

"Yeah, ready to cut your feet to bits on glass and gravel."

"Nah. I'm good. I go barefoot all the time. It's good for you."

"Whatever." I'm still angry. I'm having a hard time hiding it. "Tell me something, Claire. Were you *trying* to get us lost, or did it just look that way?"

"Guilty. I'm sorry. But when I saw your face back there at the grocery, I figured it was time to stop. I'm an ass most of the time, Troy. That would be good for you to know and remember."

"What was your plan, lady? To get us both lost and ruin everyone's holiday? For what? And what's your deal at home, anyway? You try to make it sound like this big mystery."

"In case you forgot, this isn't supposed to be a holiday," she says. "And my *deal* at home is none of your business. Yes, I was going to screw off. And take you with me. I thought that was obvious. To mess with them, you know."

"Listen." I make her look at me. "Let's make a pact, shall we? We walk into Santiago de Compostela together. You stay on the path and don't screw this up for *all* of us."

"You know I can't promise that, Troy." She deliberately steps into a puddle in the gutter along the side of the road and walks in it. She attempts to splash me, but I jump back. "I don't foresee myself making it to Santiago. Ooh. Maybe I should have asked the Creepy Jesus of Cacabelos to tell me my future. Maybe *he* knows how all this will play out."

"Funny. Let's go find those arrows."

"Yes, sir." She reaches into her pocket for more Skittles. She's come to a wide section in the never-ending puddle and attempts to splash me again, this time successfully.

"Gee, thanks."

"My pleasure," she says.

"If we ever catch up to the guys, we can walk with them. You'll see, they're okay. If you give them half a chance."

"You didn't look too happy with them last night."

"Yeah, well. They're asses. But they're okay."

"Come on. Let's see the directions. I've got a good memory. If I can just see the map, you can put your phone away, and we can move faster."

"Yeah, and I'm going to believe you're not gonna get us lost again? Fat chance."

She grabs my phone and runs ahead, just out of reach. Once she's a good distance away, she concentrates on the screen. "I promise. I've had a change of heart. Girl Scout's honor."

"How am I supposed to believe you? Like you've ever in your life been a Girl Scout."

"I guess it's a chance you'll have to take."

When I catch up to her, she hands me back my phone and taps the top of her head. "It's all in here, now, bub. Let's go. You up for a run?"

"You're barefooted. You'll kill—"

"I'll be fine. Really. I'm used to it. Let's go."

I liked Claire better when she slept in and walked with Gilbert.

"Okay," I say, worn down and hopeful. "Let's go."

CHAPTER 16

DIEGO NELSON

I HAVE NEVER FELT THIS loopy in my life. Bastien and Shania have stayed close ever since we left Luciana's house. And by close I mean they're practically carrying me. One on either side, both propping up an arm. I think I'm okay, just a little wiped out. I doubt it's a concussion or anything.

The sun's been out since we hit the road, and the sky has cleared up some. With any luck it'll stay this way until we get to our next albergue. I'm not up to walking in the rain anymore.

"I still can't believe how nice she was," I say. "Letting a stranger into her house like that. Into her shower. I probably left mud everywhere."

"On the Camino, it is the way most times," Bastien says. "Not everybody love the peregrinos, but they do as they can. There is respect for pilgrims."

"They might not respect these particular pilgrims if they knew why we walk," Shania says. I give her a dirty look, but she waves me off. "Come on, Diego. We both know Bastien's okay."

"What is it I miss?" he says.

"What Shania is trying to say is, we are here because we have to be."

"What is it for?" Bastien says. I stop walking, and they both come to a halt, holding firm to my upper arms as though they're afraid I'll fall if they let go. If Moms could see me now, she'd flip her lid. "I do not understand, Diego? *Have* to? On the Camino, nobody *has* to. We are *called* to the Camino de Santiago."

"Some, actually, are court-mandated," I say. "I think I'm okay. You can let go. Just stay close by."

They release their holds on me, and I take a step back and give my arms a shake and wriggle around a bit to test the waters. I don't fall flat on my face, so there's that.

"Remember we said we were walking with guides? Leaders?" I continue. "Well, they're counselors. There are six of us kids. And then two counselors, Gilbert and Meagan."

As I explain, Bastien nods steadily to let me know he grasps my words. We walk on. As we round another corner, it's clear we're leaving the town. Up ahead, there are open fields on either side of the road. Across the road, I can see a yellow arrow pointing to a dirt path that leads up the middle of one of the fields. The path is lined with trees, and there's a mile marker at its entrance with tons of stuff hanging from it and from the trees around it.

"Well, we all did something bad," I say. "Something we could have been punished for by going to a juvenile detention center. I'm not sure what they're called in France."

"We have the same, almost, to you. I understand." We get to the place in the road where we need to cross, and Bastien puts his arms out for us to stop. He looks both ways, to make sure it's safe, and then waves us across.

"Okay, so we made some bonehead moves, but not really, *really* bad." I can no longer read the look on his face, but I'm pretty sure it's not fear. "We were given the option to walk a portion of the Camino over custody or some other punishment."

"Sorry to interrupt," Shania says, handing me her phone. "But could you *please* take my picture in front of this marker? Instagram shot." She smiles apologetically, runs over to lean against the marker, and drapes herself in some of the cloth streamers hanging down from the branches above it. I snap a couple shots, and she runs back and grabs her phone.

"Sorry," she says. "As you were."

Shania walks just ahead of us as we enter the canopy made by the trees on either side of the path.

"In ancient times, the criminals, they walked," Bastien says. "A thousand years ago, under this same sky. This is not new, Diego. Remember, no judging on the Camino. Sometimes the call, it comes in ways we don't understand. But still it comes."

"What now?" Shania starts to walk backward so she faces us. "Criminals? On the Camino? For real?"

"Yes, yes. It is true. There have always been prisoners on the Camino de Santiago. For to get pardons if they finish their walk. I think in Belgium it is, they still allow one prisoner—like the chocolate factory, no—the Golden Ticket. It is believed they will meet a spiritual life and turn over the leaf."

"A new leaf," Shania says. She turns around and keeps walking ahead of us. "That is so cool. We're not the first. Whaddaya know."

"Oh, no," Bastien says. He laughs. "No. For hundreds of years. Maybe the first Americans, no?"

"Whoa, whoa," I say. "We're from Canada. We're Canadians." I step ahead of him and pat my backpack to point out the Canadian pilgrim patch my abuelita helped me to sew in place. "See."

"Oh yes. Canadians. Yes. Oui. I knew; I knew. First Canadian prisoners."

"Prisoners," Shania says. She guffaws. She doesn't turn around to face us, but keeps walking. "That's a good one."

"All pilgrims are pilgrims," Bastien says, clearly his final words on the subject. Probably to let us know he doesn't care he is walking with a couple of juvenile delinquents. "Whatever the reason."

"Thanks, Bastien," I say.

We walk in silence. I feel a little less shaky and loopy now that I'm some distance away from my boneheaded fall. I'll probably survive another day. Still, I'm a little worried about telling Moms tonight when I talk to her. She'll worry about me. Even more than she probably already does.

"Where are you walking to today?" Bastien asks, breaking the silence. We are back in the sunshine, walking on a narrow dirt path surrounded by tall grass. We need to walk single file, it's so narrow. With Bastien in the middle and me behind him. The view to my left is endless: rolling hills and fields. And the sky is filled with small, puffy, white clouds and endless blue.

"Um, Trad—Trem Tradelco—"

"Not even close, loser," Shania says from the front of our little pack. She laughs. "Tradello."

Now it's Bastien's turn to laugh, but it's not like *his* outburst is malicious. He giggles at Shania's butchering of the language.

"Trabedelo. It is not far ahead. Not bad." He points into the vista beside and just ahead of us. "That town there. See."

Sure. It *looks* close. But I've been fooled before. I know how it works. Something looks minutes away, but it'll be another hour or two before we even get close to it.

"Oops. Yeah. That's what I meant. Trabedelo."

"Yeah," I say. "Not even close, loser." We all laugh.

Then we disappear into the silence and the walking. All I can hear is our feet on the ground, the swishing of the tall grass around us, and the occasional thunk of Bastien's stick as it connects with the wet and drying earth. I can get used to this. Head gash and leg wounds aside, I feel like there's this ball of something inside my chest, this tight fist that is waking up and slowly unclenching. I know it sounds crazy, but the more I walk, the more I feel it. Something is happening.

CHAPTER 17

SHANIA REYNOLDS

***Wednesday, July 3rd** – Day 5 – Shania Writes Two Entries!*

Yep. You read that right. Two entries. I think this one is because I want to, not because I have to. What is happening to me?

We just ate that kick-ass soup again. I can't get enough. The bread always rocks too. Too bad about the wine, it's everywhere… but in my glass.

Everyone loves Bastien. He stopped for the night at the same albergue as us. He said he wanted to talk to our prison guards, to make sure we wouldn't be in trouble. He's such a great guy.

We're all just sitting around talking. This albergue is quite big. They have this huge table where some of us are sitting. And little tables they brought in for other pilgrims too. I don't know if these places ever turn people away. They find room.

Little conversations everywhere, and everyone is laughing. Even the old lady with the totally sick blister on her heel. They have volunteer women in the neighborhood who go from albergue to albergue just to fix people's blisters. For free. They come in with their medical bags and sit on the floor washing feet and bandaging blisters. It's unreal. That just would not happen at home. There's totally an audience watching this woman attend to the pilgrim lady's blister. It's that sick. It makes the one Troy had look like nothing. Phones are out snapping pictures to send back home.

We went to our rooms to put our backpacks on our beds earlier, and, when I got there, I realized we have a room for eight tonight. Four sets of bunk beds. All in the same room. I almost died. Diego and I looked at each other, and I think we were both thinking the same thing.

No, not anything romantic or sexy or hot. Trust me! We were thinking about farting, snoring, and sleepwalking. And sleep-talking. And anything else that could cause embarrassment. I hate my life. Seriously.

On the bright side, though—and I do want to try finishing these journal entries on the bright side from now on—there's an awesome seating area outside the albergue. Stone-walled, with little bistro tables under umbrellas. Pretty. Troy said we should all sit out there later.

Troy says, with tonight's clear sky, we'll be able to see the Milky Way perfectly. From his vast Camino knowledge bank, he told me about the Milky Way pointing the way to Santiago de Compostela in the olden days, and how the route was once called Voie Lactée. It just means Milky Way. Anyway, I thought that was so pretty… that a galaxy would be interested enough in a pilgrim's journey to light the night for them to find The Way. That's bright side, right?!

I won't even think about farting.

"Are you gonna write in that thing all night?" Claire asks me. I finish my sentence and close my journal with a little slam.

"I wondered when you'd get around to speaking to me again," I say. Harsh words, but I try to say them nicely.

"Sorry." She sips from her coffee cup and sits in the abandoned chair beside me. Diego left the room to have some face time with his mother. "I've been kind of hiding from everyone. I'm antisocial back home, not gonna lie. Coping mechanism for survival, actually."

"Deep." I smile to let her know I'm willing to give her a second chance. It's obvious she's trying. Which is also kind of pathetic.

"I thought I may have broken Troy today, but after seeing Diego tonight maybe I shouldn't be so hard on myself. You were harder on your guy."

"Ha. Right?"

"Let me guess. That crazy steep mountainside with all the rocks and trees?" She takes out a bag of Skittles and pops a few. She offers the bag to me, but I pass.

"That's the one," I say, raising a finger in victory. "Two stitches. He went down that mountain hard."

Just as I'm about to ask her if she heard us telling the story to Gil and Meagan, a voice rises from across the table.

"No, no, ladies," Bastien says. He breaks his own conversation with the lady beside him to interject into ours. "*That* was no mountain. Tomorrow, we *begin* the uphill climb. Today, an incline perhaps."

"What?" I almost screech. That cannot be possible. Claire looks at me like she may cry, and I'm pretty sure I return the expression.

"It is true. The way to O Cebreiro is long and it is up, up, up. It will be a big day. Maybe not as long as today, even, but much much longer."

"Gil *did* say it's a hard day," Claire says. "Uphill."

"We're dead," I say.

"I said to your Gilbert, it's the next day, the day after O Cebreiro," Bastien begins. He says this louder, in a little bit of a mocking and scolding tone. Loud enough for Gilbert to hear. "Is the day that brings the tears." He traces his fingers down his face to show Gilbert where his tears will fall. Gilbert laughs.

Gilbert and Meagan leave their table and join us. It's a night of musical chairs at this albergue.

"I know, I know," Gil says. "You told me. We should have split up the walk differently and taken on more tomorrow so we would have less the next day. I know."

"Our little villains, they will be, what is the Galician? Esgotado?"

"Hey," Troy says from a couch behind us. "I know that word. I just used it in a text to my dad."

I give him a *what-the-hell* look.

"Everything is a teaching-slash-learning opportunity with my father, Shania. Everything. He's grilling me on my Spanish. And, yeah…" He scowls at Claire. "…I'm exhausted right now. Right, *Claire*? That's what esgotado means."

Claire gives him an evil smile and winks at him. "Shhhh. Our little secret."

"Yeah, right."

"That's very good, Troy. You're right," Gil says.

"Yes," Bastien agrees. "You all will be exhausted tomorrow once you start up to O Cebreiro. But the real mountain, it's after O Cebreiro. The tears will not come tomorrow. They will be saved for another day."

"Now you're just scaring them, Bastien," Meagan says. "That's just cruel."

"Ha ha, yes," Bastien says as he picks up his wineglass and swigs down what is left. He rises and bows toward Claire and me. "Well, mes petits méchants. This old man must go to his nighty night place."

Claire and I both say goodnight to Bastien.

"Will we see you in the morning, Bastien?" Meagan asks. She has this pleading look on her face, and I feel exactly like that look. We all wait for him to answer her.

"Mais oui, Mademoiselle Meagan." His smile lights the room, just like Troy keeps talking about the Milky Way lighting up The Way. "I will walk with the Canadians tomorrow. If you will have me."

"We'd be honored, Bastien," Gilbert says. I feel relief, and it's ridiculous.

"Bonne nuit and buenas noches and boas noites, my friends," he says to all. The room bursts into a round of goodnights in different languages. He hasn't only endeared himself to us. "See you in the tomorrow and onward to O Cebreiro."

As Bastien walks across the room to go to his bunk, Diego enters. I see him say goodnight to Bastien and I nod in their direction to get Claire to notice.

"What's up? Is he okay?" Claire asks. But it's such a large room, so many people are talking at once, I can't hear what they're saying. I only see that Diego is wiping away tears.

I get up to make my way over to them, but I'm only halfway there when Bastien takes Diego in his arms and holds him to his chest. The room slowly goes quiet as people become aware something is happening. Before I get to them, I can see Diego's sides shaking. He's crying uncontrollably into Bastien's shoulder.

CHAPTER 18

TROY SINCLAIR

By the time I reach them, Bastien has gently passed Diego to Shania. He went from crumbling against Bastien to falling into Shania's arms. I still don't know what's wrong with him. I'm not sure anyone does.

"Diego, Diego," Shania whispers into his ear as he continues to slump into her like a rag doll. "What is it? Diego?"

"Is he okay? What's wrong?" I put a hand on Diego's back and pat him. He's inconsolable.

"I don't know. Where's Gilbert? Where's Meagan? Diego. What's wrong?"

Bastien pulls me gently aside as Diego, unable to speak, continues to cry into Shania's shoulder.

"His abuelita is gone, son. He has lost her," Bastien whispers to me, sorrow in his expression. I wrack my brain. Dad would be so pissed at me right now for not knowing the word.

"I don't understand." I also think Diego may have heard Bastien's words, because he slumps farther down on Shania. Just as Bastien opens his mouth to speak, the word's meaning comes seeping up from the fog. "Oh my God, his gramma? His gramma's dead?"

Diego moans, and it's a sound unlike anything a human being should ever be capable of making. He slips from Shania's arms and makes a slow descent to the floor at her feet, and there is nothing she can do to stop him. I hate myself for thinking out loud. My words have sliced him open and made his nightmare more real than it already was.

"Yes," Bastien says. It is the first time I've seen him look anything but beatific. He looks as though he could punch me, and I don't blame him.

"I'm sorry," I say to Bastien. Then I slip to the floor beside Diego and put a protective arm around him. "I'm sorry, Diego. I'm so sorry."

He slinks into me and puts his head in my lap and continues to cry uncontrollably. Shania and Manny join us. I see feet all around us, but concentrate on Diego. I don't know what to do, so I just pat his shoulder.

"Oh, Diego," Gil says, leaning close to Diego's ear. "I'm so sorry. You poor child. I'm so sorry. What happened?"

He brings his head up out of my lap and attempts to speak, but it's just an ugly struggle of hitches and tears and mucus and wails. He's completely destroyed.

"She had an attack," Bastien says. He waves his arms. He is a man capable of crowd control. "Please, please, s'il vous plait. Can everyone give space? Por favor, haz espacio."

The crowd begins to disperse; everyone talks amongst themselves, saying how bad they feel for Diego. Some give their condolences as they leave to make room, but I'm sure he hears nothing.

"She had a heart attack, Troy," Bastien says. Every time we speak, an animalian squeal of pain comes from somewhere deep inside Diego. It hurts just to be here, inside this thing that's happening to him.

"Diego," Gil says. He puts a firm hand on Diego's shoulder. "Come. Up we get. Come sit down on the couch. We'll talk there."

"I can't, I can't, I can't," Diego says. He is breathless from the effort. "My abuelita is gone." He looks up into Gil's face with those big dripping brown eyes, and it's the end of me. I can't help myself. I start to cry. I know we only just met, but he's so nice and he loves his mama and his gramma. It's the sweetest thing about him.

"Oh, Diego," Meagan says. I hadn't seen her. She's been hovering behind me, just as lost as the rest of us. Big unfallen tears shimmer in her eyes.

"I know it hurts, Diego," Gil says. He takes on this authoritarian voice I haven't yet heard, not even during his few attempts to be stern with us. "But we have to get you up off the floor. We're blocking the doorway. The peregrinos will need to get by to get to their rooms. Come on now, son. Up."

The voice is what finally spurs Diego into action. He struggles to his feet with Shania, Gil, and me helping him regain his legs. Bastien shadows us all the way as we walk Diego slowly to one of the couches along the sides of the room.

Our hostess comes over with a glass of water. She looks sick with worry. "For your friend," she says to me in a whisper before she hands me the glass and disappears into the kitchen, almost as though she's afraid of catching the sadness.

By now, the eight of us surround Diego in a cocoon of protection. The others slowly go back to what they were doing before everything fell apart. I catch Greg staring at me and I give him a *what the hell* look in return. He just looks away.

"What happened, Diego," Meagan finally says. We all lean in as Diego tries to get his crying under control and catch his breath.

He sits up with his back straight and his hands on his knees and takes a big breath. I feel so bad for him.

"I was talking to Moms onscreen and I could see there was something she wasn't telling me. Something wrong. Like she was trying to be strong. At first, I thought she just missed me."

"I'm sorry, Dude," Manny says. He looks so uncomfortable, like he doesn't know how to deal with situations like this one at all. Who does?

Diego's face crumples, but he regains composure almost instantly. Gil sits beside him and puts an arm around him and pulls him back down into the couch beside him. Diego just melts, giving up the rigid position. With his back against the cushions, he kind of nestles into Gil and continues.

"She tried to keep it together. To not tell me. But I knew. I know Moms. It's just the three of us. I know how to read her. The two of us. When I asked her what was wrong, she tried to hold off. But she fell apart and I knew it was something… something bad."

"Aw, hun," Meagan says. She sits on his other side and takes his hand in hers. But I don't think he even notices. "I'm so sorry for your loss. Your grandmother. You poor boy."

He breaks down again, but only for a few seconds before he fights to regain hold of his emotions.

"I can't go home," he says. Claire opens her mouth in a look of surprise. "I need to finish the pilgrimage. Don't make me leave." He stares rigidly into Gil's eyes. "I need to finish. For my abuelita. I told Moms I would finish for her mother."

He just barely gets this out before he buries his face in Gil's shoulder. Gil pats Diego on one side, while Meagan holds his hand and strokes his arm on the other. They look at each other, and, I swear, it looks like they're trying to keep it together. And it scares me that the two adults looking out for us look so fragile.

"It's okay, Diego. You don't have to do anything you don't want—"

"No. I want to. I want to walk. I told my mother I would."

"And you will," Meagan says.

I look at Shania and realize she's practically crying her eyes out. I step past Greg to offer her a hug, and she falls into my arms. As we embrace, she says, "No, no. I'm okay. I just feel so bad for him. I'm okay. Just emotional."

"I know," I say. "I just really needed a hug." She pulls back and smiles at me.

"Thank you, Troy," she says. I return her smile and squeeze tighter.

"You're okay, Troyboy," Manny says. He pats me on the back.

"Diego, of course you can continue. It's completely up to you. I meant you don't have to *stop* walking."

"Okay." He gasps for a steady breath he can't seem to find. "Okay, Gil."

We all go silent while Diego tries to adjust to his new world, one without his grandmother.

*   *   *

AFTER MOST OF THE OTHER peregrinos have gone to their rooms for the night, Shania stirs in her seat, like she wants to say something. We've been sitting in utter silence for quite some time, and it's making me edgy. All I feel is defeat.

We all brought chairs from one of the tables before the hostess stored them away for the night. We have surrounded the couch Diego shares with Gil and Meagan. We sit in a semicircle in front of them, first row seating for the still life of a boy destroyed.

"I have an idea," Shania says. Greg jerks in his chair. I'm pretty sure he nodded off. I'm trying to like him, I swear.

Shania has everyone's attention. Even Diego's. He's holding wads of Kleenex in his fists, and seems angry with himself for needing them. Other than that, he's pretty calm. He's at least breathing properly.

"Actually," Shania says, looking at me. "It's Troy's idea. It was just postponed a bit."

"Huh," I say. I have no idea what she's talking about. "You'll have to remind me."

"Voie Lactée," she says, with this *ta da* look on her face. Oh yeah. I forgot all about that. "The sky is perfectly clear tonight. And the patio out front looked so pretty."

I'm pretty sure Bastien is the only one who knows what she's talking about. But all the others want to know. I can tell by the looks on their faces.

"The Milky Way," I say, and Bastien offers me one of his golden smiles that make you feel as though you've won something priceless.

"Ah, yes. Tonight is a night of magic stars. They shine maybe for Diego's abuelita alone, no?"

Diego looks questioningly to Bastien and then to me.

"Earlier I told Shania we should go out and look for the Milky Way tonight. When I read about the pilgrimage back home, I discovered they used to call it Voie Lactée. Because when the sky is clear, the Milky Way points the way to Compostela for the peregrinos who walk through the night. They followed the Voie Lactée—the Milky Way—and named the path after the galaxy."

"How do you know so much, you little freak?" Diego says. At first I don't know what to make of his words, but then his broken face cracks such a tiny smile it breaks my heart. I go over to him and reach down and hug him. I don't care.

We all have this collective moment, and I can hear held breath releasing and little sighs escaping. There's a lot more to come, but for now we can all exhale just knowing that Diego has.

"I say we do it, my man," Diego says to me as I release him. He puts his hand up for a high five, and I give it to him. "I think my grandmother would like that very much."

"Yes," Bastien says. "To have the stars shine for you is a great honor. She would like, Diego. Come, we go."

And with Bastien's announcement we all move. In a flurry of scraping chair legs and activity, we are on our feet and heading for the front door of the albergue.

CHAPTER 19

DIEGO NELSON

MY LEGS FEEL WEIGHTED DOWN with cement, but as soon as I heard Shania's idea I knew we had to do it. Especially after what Bastien and Troy said about it.

The more I feel like being alone, the more I know I shouldn't be. Moms was so worried for me. That's probably what finally made her break. I can't believe she wasn't going to tell me. She's always trying to protect me from the hard stuff, but this is different. This is my abuelita, my life.

As we step outside, I can already see the light given off by the night sky. We're on the main drag of this little town, and a bunch of tables are set out with umbrellas over some of them. The air is filled with the smell of freshly cut wood, and I remember the massive pile of logs by the side of the road just up from the albergue. It towered over our heads. Our last selfie stop of the day before reaching the albergue. It now fills the night air with fragrance.

There are not many lights on in the street, but the sky is bright. We step past the cobbled patio and stand in the center of the road beyond.

No one speaks.

We all turn our faces to the heavens at the same time. Even Claire.

I see Manny's mouth form a silent *wow* as he takes it in. I agree. It's almost too vast to believe. We don't get this kind of sky in Toronto. The city lights kill the stars.

It's beautiful. My breath catches in my throat as I stare up into the bowl of stars. I swear I can see her. My sweet abuelita with her crooked little smile and her wild hair. She approved of what I'm doing here, even though she was furious about the reason I had to do it. She was the only one of the three of us who had ever heard of the Camino. As I stare into the bowl of stars, I remember how her face lit up when she learned I would soon walk the pilgrim's path. Her anger vanished, and she exploded with Catholic pride.

I don't think anyone wants to brave breaking the silence. It feels too sacred, but I'm not surprised when it's Bastien who does so. I take my eyes off the Milky Way when he clears his throat, steps away from the others, and turns his gaze upon me.

"Guard these your children who, for love of your Name, make a pilgrimage to Compostela," he begins. As though he was a galaxy more spectacular than the one above us, the others all bring their gazes back to earth and look to Bastien. Before he continues, he turns *his* gaze to the stars. I let the tears fall freely as I prepare for the rest of his words.

"Be their companion on the way, their guide at the crossroads, their strength in weariness, their defense in dangers, their shelter on the path, their shade in the heat, their light in darkness, their comfort in discouragement."

Bastien pauses. *Comfort in discouragement*, I think to myself. I let the words sink in because I'm an absolute wreck. My grandmother would love this.

Shania offers her hand, and I take it. I'm not sure who makes the next move, but eventually we're a circle of near-strangers all linked by our hands, orbiting the planet of our new friend who came out of the blue to save me this afternoon. He's saving me still.

"And the firmness of their intentions…" He continues. "…that through your guidance they may arrive safely at the end of their journey and, enriched with grace and virtue, may return to their homes filled with salutary and lasting joy."

When he stops reciting this gift he has given us, we return to silence. Inside the silence, I hear sniffling. I look over to see that Greg is crying. As I look about me, I see only sadness. I can't help but feel responsible.

"That was beautiful, Bastien," Claire says. I'm pretty sure these are the first words she has spoken to him, but in them I can see she's as mad about him as the rest of us are.

"These are not my words, ma chère. These are words of prayer from the books of the Codex Calixtinus. From the twelfth century. The first pilgrims' guide to the Camino de Santiago. *Tonight,* they are our words. Tonight, we pay our respects to the abuelita of our new friend Diego."

We are all standing in the Church of Bastien. This guy. I fell into the right person today. I can't believe that was only today. It feels like a lifetime ago.

"Please, to continue holding hands," Bastien says. "We pray for the bones of…"

He looks to me and I somehow know he wants my grandmother's name.

"Isabel. Isabel Maritza Correa." He nods his thanks.

"Tonight we pray for the bones of Isabel Maritza Correa. Maritza—the star of the sea—like the stars that shine above us."

I'm not surprised he knows the meaning of her middle name.

"That these bones may be at rest, that she may be free of weariness. That she may be home. She looks down on us, peregrinos of The Way. Now our guardian angel. We pray for her grandson. Diego…"

"Epifanio Nelson." This time it's even more obvious what he wants. I feel the heat in my face as I share my middle name, afraid the others may say something. I especially don't want to see Shania laugh. It's not like I picked it out myself. Nobody moves a muscle, though. They're all completely focused on Bastien's prayer.

"We pray for her grandson, Diego Epifanio Nelson. Epifanio, *he who shines brightly*. It had to be so. We pray for he who shines brightly below this Milky Way. Below this Voie Lactée, which guides our way to the cathedral. We pray for her family, her little girl back home in *Canada*." Bastien winks at me as he says this, and I recall my little freak-out at being mistaken for an American. "And her little grandson here on the Camino. May he find peace in The Way."

There is only silence now. When Bastien looks away from us and up into the Milky Way, we slowly follow his gaze. We all look again to the endless gathering of stars above us. Only the sounds of the night around us remain.

"Amen," Bastien eventually whispers. We repeat the word in unison. And I'm crying again. Bastien comes forward and hugs me. I don't know what to make of his kiss on my forehead, but I think I like it. When he is finished, he steps back.

Everyone hugs me in turn. This ritual is one of the greatest things that has ever happened to me. Even if it came from losing my one and only abuelita.

"That was beautiful, Bastien," Gil says. His words help to break the spell.

"Yes. Thank you, Bastien," Meagan says. "We needed that."

Bastien takes a deep bow; his white hair glows in the darkness. When he rises, his smile is as real as the sorrow in his eyes.

"We need to hit the sheets now, gang," Gil says. "I think we can forego a discussion group tonight. You've all earned that at least. Tomorrow, new rule. We walk together. At least for the one day."

Nobody moans or complains. Not outwardly, anyway.

"This is a good idea, I think," Bastien says.

"I'm good with it," Shania says.

"Me too," says Troy. But he gives Claire a dirty look after he says it. Something's going on there, but I don't know what it is.

"That was some spectacular stuff you did here, Bastien," Greg says. "Magic. Thank you, man."

"But of course," Bastien says. Greg walks silently past him, but nods to him in appreciation.

"Let's go, children," Meagan says. "Sleep beckons."

We head into the albergue and, despite how I feel, I know I'll sleep like a rock. I can't wait to get into my bunk and pass out. Longest. Day. Of. My. Life.

CHAPTER 20

SHANIA REYNOLDS

Thursday, July 4th – Day 6 – I Hate This SO Much!

*Today, we walk together. Everyone already got their passports
stamped at the front desk. We're just waiting for, you guessed it, Claire.
It's not like she slept in, though. We all made sure of that. I'd be lying if
I said I didn't laugh when Troy put his feet on the bunk above him and
shook the crap out of it to wake her up. Serves her right. She claimed
to need to go to the washroom as we were heading out the door. She
still hasn't come down, ten minutes later.*

*Gil's about to blow. And Troy is cursing under his breath. Manny
is trying to stuff more food into his mouth before either it disappears
or we do.*

*Diego stands by the door staring off into space. He cried off and on
all night. I'm sure we all heard him. We were all restless, lying helplessly
in the dark and feeling useless. I think we'll have to physically guide
his every move today. He's like an automaton. Just point him in the
right direction, and he'll walk. He's broken. His brain is back home
in Toronto with his mother.*

*Meagan stomps up the stairs, and it sounds like her feet are going
to go through them. The tension mounts. Enough words for now. I
don't want to be the one to keep us waiting, ever. I would so hate that.
Bright side—gotta remember to add this at the end of my entries.
Today's bright side is Bastien. Nuff said.*

And we're off. Finally.

"Thanks for joining us, princess," Troy says to Claire as she stomps down the stairs ahead of Meagan. "Do you think we might be able to go now?"

"I don't know, smartass," Claire says. "You can give it a try."

"Yeah." He pivots and heads out the door. "Whatever."

Once we're out in the road, Gil says, "Remember, kiddos, this is going to be an uphill day. Tomorrow's going to be the hardest, but that doesn't mean today'll be a picnic."

"Man. The more you talk about tomorrow, the more I want to just turn around and walk back to Ponferrada. You guys are killing me." Everyone stops what they're doing to look at Greg. It's the most he's ever said at one time. In the silence that follows, I burst out laughing. Then I feel guilty for laughing because Diego's grandmother died.

But then everyone else, including Diego, laughs. Maybe we needed to. Maybe Greg knew it.

"Goodbye, Trabedelo. Been nice knowing you," Greg says, now more than doubling his word count since boarding the plane. "You kicked our asses, but you also gave us the stars. So, yeah, thanks."

"Okay, kids," Gil says. "Let's go. The sooner, the better. It's gonna be a scorcher today. Did everyone sunscreen?"

"Oops," Claire says. "Let me just—"

"No," Manny says. "Not havin' it. Just, no. Lady, you keep us waiting any more, I'll snap. Enough is enough. You're worse than my sisters."

"Hear, hear," Troy says, and I could dance, it makes me so happy. This girl needs to get with the program.

I look around, and everyone's smiling except for Diego. I want to hug him, because I'm pretty sure he's thinking about his mother. I wonder if he feels like he's walking away from her or toward her. Poor Diego.

"Here, Claire," Meagan says, taking her tube of sunscreen out of the side pocket of her backpack. "Come on. Walk with me. I'll help you slather up while we walk. The peasants are revolting."

"Tally-ho," Bastien says. He turns in the direction we need to walk and stamps his walking stick against the road for emphasis. With his words, we set out. I move alongside Manny, because I see that Troy has just buddied up with Diego.

Gil and Bastien lead the pack. Bastien doesn't need a map, since it's his third time doing this thing. Three days ago, if someone had told me it was their third time walking the Camino, I may have just hauled off and hit them. Today? I get it. There's just something about this place that makes you forget all the crap back home. The people and the beauty here soften everything.

"Hey, Manny," I say, after we walk a few minutes in silence.

"Um, *hey*?"

"You gonna make this difficult on me, eh?"

"Girl, what are you talking about?"

"Conversation."

Greg passes us, shuffling his feet as he goes. "Coming through."

"Nah," Manny says to me, ignoring Greg. "We're good. Whatcha wanna talk about?"

"For starters, what did you and Greg even talk about yesterday? He's so weird."

"Nope," he says. "You read him wrong, Shania. He's cool. Just gotta get to know him some. He's a pretty funny guy. Some people are like that. All inside themselves at first. He's cool. He's just carrying stuff. A *lot* of stuff. He's got heavy things happening at home."

"Yeah." I laugh. "Like Claire."

"I don't know about that. I'll reserve judgement. I don't know much about her. She's a good listener, though. I told her about some of my stuff. She's okay." He raises an eyebrow comically and grins like he has a secret. Manny could be a model. He has the most perfectly straight white teeth I've ever seen. And his hair.

"I wonder how Troy would answer that one."

"Not sure I know what you mean." He kicks through the stones as we move from beaten asphalt to gravel. As we leave the town, the path narrows before we make our way to a road and walk the shoulder alongside it.

"I don't know. It just seems like there's something going on between them. Like they're pissed at each other."

"Wouldn't know. Oh, we're getting the wave." He signals up ahead.

Bastien and Gil wave us all across the road to walk on the other side, so we cross. Greg passes Diego and Troy and moves up beside Gil. I can see that he slips himself easily into their conversation. So he does talk regularly. Just not so much to me, yet. Okay.

I can hear Meagan and Claire's conversation behind us. They've moved on from sunscreen to granola bars. Apparently we all moved too fast this morning for princess to get a chance to have a proper breakfast. Funny, I saw her eating.

"Too bad about my boy Diego's nana." Manny shakes his head and makes a little tsk tsk sound with his lips.

"Yeah," I say. "He totally doesn't deserve it. I mean, I guess no one does. But, Manny, he's just so sweet."

"Right!" he says. "I don't know what I'd do. My nana? Man, she is everything, Shania. Sometimes, when the noise is just out of this world insane back home and I'm about to pull my hair out or kill one of them… I just pack up a knapsack, head across town, and flop at Nana's for a night or two."

"Are you kidding me?"

"What?"

"It just seems so wholesome. Damn. Between you and Diego, I don't know which one of you is more unreal."

"Hey, watch what you say," he says. But he's laughing. "For us boys, there's one person we stop the world for. That's our nana. Or, what is it Diego calls his, his abuel..."

"Lita." I say as he stumbles over the word.

"Right. Anyways. You don't make fun of a boy and his nana. Besides, *you* try living in a house with five brothers and sisters. It's insane. You don't get to turn that shit off, girl. My nana is my safe place. My island. I'm staying with her in two years when I go to university. She's closer to campus. I'll get to escape the nuthouse long-term."

"Whoa. Hold on. Go back. I thought you said there were seven of you. Five plus one is six. Suddenly there's only six? Did I just catch you in a lie?"

"Yep. Seven. That's right."

"You don't have six brothers and sisters. What are their names, then? Prove it."

"One of us doesn't live at home, Sherlock. You really that slow?" *Oops.* My brain is mush today. "Steven lives with his girlfriend Deandra in Scarborough, Darren and David—not Dave—share a bedroom."

He's counting off each name on his fingers, all wild-eyed, like I'm going to be in trouble when he's finished. I try not to giggle. Claire and Meagan have caught up to us and listen in, all smiles.

"Maya and Angel share a room. Last, but not least, Manny—not Manfred—and Tavish share a room. Sometimes, the last one on the list is affectionately referred to as Tav. And Pita, the cat, and Fred and Trixie, the two dogs, sleep wherever they want to. And, of course, there's Mom."

"Wait a minute; wait a minute," Claire says. She waves her hand to get his attention.

The four of us are all together now, and I can see that up ahead Bastien, Gil, Diego, Greg, and Troy are all walking in a pack. I'm glad Diego is surrounded by so many people today.

"What?" Manny asks her. "What's your freak, girl?"

"You have a brother named Tav and a cat named Pita? I'm not even going to *ask* about Fred."

We're all laughing, except for Manny, who looks at us suspiciously.

"Fred is the name Angel gave her. And, yes, Fred's a girl. A Chihuahua. Nobody questions Angel. It's just one of those things. Pita, that's Tav's fault. My boy just loves his pita bread. So much that he christened the latest orphan after it. And he's the baby of the family, so that was that.

"I just figure if the cat's stupid enough to come when he's called Pita, it serves him right."

Up ahead, the guys head off the road into a gully or something. They're following the arrows. We've started to walk beside a bunch of trees and the farther along we go, the thicker they get until it's almost all forest beside the road. The opening they entered comes up for us too.

"Okay," Meagan says. She's getting right into it. "What about Tavish?"

"Why am I getting grilled? What's this, Twenty Questions with Manny Johnston? Enough, now." He's so totally kidding. I can see he's loving the attention.

"Come on," Claire says. "We know you wanna."

"I doubt it, ladies. Wanna get up there with the guys before I lose my mind back here with you all asking me silly questions about my family, more like."

But Manny can't fool me. He's walking with swagger now. Like he owns the world. As we enter the forest, Claire points out a tree filled with ribbons. Manny runs over and pulls off a bright yellow one.

"What are you doing?" Claire asks, like he just stole the Mona Lisa from the Louvre.

"They say things. They have little sayings on them. We're *supposed* to take them. Why else are they here?"

He returns to the group, clears his throat, and makes a big production of reading the writing on it. "*One step, Camino. Two steps, your life*. What the what does that even mean?"

"Actually, I love it. Can I have it?"

"Sure, Claire. Whatever." Manny streams the long yellow ribbon out behind him as he turns his back to us and keeps walking. Claire snaps it out of his outstretched hand and ties it into her hair. The yellow almost disappears among the other colors.

"Thanks, bud," she says. And when she offers him a smile, it looks like the first genuine one she's given this whole week. Too bad Manny doesn't see it. But Meagan does, and it makes her smile.

"It sounds like Bastien is holding court up there," I say. His voice can be heard booming above the others. And they've slowed down, shortening the gap between us. They're probably too wrapped up in what he's saying to walk any faster. His voice carries across the quiet morning.

I pick up the pace, and the others in my group follow suit. We narrow the gap between ourselves and Bastien's group.

"Tavish was named after a great-great-uncle," Manny says out of the blue.

"Oh?" Meagan says. "Well, that sounds interesting."

"Yeah, well, I wanted you all to know it was a family name. He came from the South a zillion years ago or something. Someone in my mom's family always gets the name."

"Huh," Claire says. "It's a cool name. Tav. Tav sounds like he'd be a cool guy."

"Are you kidding me." Manny laughs. We're just behind the guys now, and I can just barely hear their conversation. Bastien is telling them about a place coming up called Las Herrias. "My Tavs boy is about the coolest thing since Popsicles. For a seven-year-old, he's got this brain. Wow. He's everything, girl."

Manny's face lights up and becomes even more expressive when he talks about his baby brother. It's obvious he has a case of hero worship.

"The first Tavish brought his girl to Nova Scotia. That's where Mom's from. She moved to Toronto just before she met my dad. But I have, like, a thousand cousins, aunts, and uncles down there."

"Wow," Meagan says. "That's amazing, Manny."

He shrugs. "Yeah, I guess. And I have two of them. Tavishes, that is. Mom's brother. Uncle Tavish too." He smiles. "He's still in Nova Scotia."

"Tavish," Claire says, once again. "I like it."

"You join us," Bastien says as the two groups merge into one. "I just told these boys to get ready. Soon comes Las Herrerias." He says this like we should all know what he's talking about.

Only Meagan recognizes the name. She gets this exaggerated grimace. "Oh, boy," she says. "It begins."

"What begins, Meags?" Manny says. He scoots up beside Diego and gives him a little punch on the shoulder, and they exchange conspiratorial smiles.

"Uphill. The real climb begins. I remember this leg. It's hard. But I wish I could tell you it prepares us for what's to come tomorrow."

Bastien laughs, but otherwise there are groans all around.

"Man, girl, why are you doing this to us?" Manny says.

We come to a small wooden bridge and as we cross over the little creek beneath it, we can see the uphill path on the other side. Here we go.

CHAPTER 21

TROY SINCLAIR

IF TOMORROW IS WORSE THAN this, I don't wanna. We've been walking forever. I feel like we must be almost there. My calf muscles are screaming.

We're finally stopped for a rest. Faba Fountain. Everyone's just walking in circles guzzling water or sitting on the edge of the little stone wall. We just climbed a pretty big hill, but the next ones are even bigger.

"Soon, Galicia," Bastien says.

"Oh, I thought we were in Galicia this whole time?" Shania says.

"Me too," Diego says.

"So, so," Bastien says, after he takes a big swig from his collapsible water cup. "It blends."

"Can we stay here tonight?" Greg asks. I know I'll never get tired of looking at him, but I'm so over the guy. "My legs are on fire."

"Fat chance," Gil says. He laughs, but our fearless leader is actually on the ground doing leg stretches and rubbing his calves. He's in just as much pain as the rest of us. The old man is the only one who seems oblivious to the exhaustion that's on everyone else's face. "Have faith, Greg. Only about four more miles to O Cebreiro. You can do it."

"Yeah, and I can do the backstroke in a sewer, too, but I'm not about to."

"You're funny," Claire says to Greg.

A large group of peregrinos walk past us, sticks clicking, not even stopping for a break at the fountain. They must be insane.

"Buen Camino," a cute Japanese boy says to me. He smiles, and I watch him walk away. So cute. About my age, too, I'd say.

"Buen Camino," I say, returning his greeting. He turns back and offers another smile. He's walking with two girls who are lost in their own conversation, oblivious to our interaction. I give him a short wave, and he turns back to his friends.

Just before they round the next corner and disappear from view, he turns back one more time and returns my wave. And, just like that, he's gone. My cute new pilgrim friend.

"Okay, gang," Meagan says as she jumps down from the stone wall surrounding the fountain and does a few quick jumping jacks. "Time to hit the road. If I remember correctly, we'll hit some nice shade soon. It's gonna help combat the uphill battle we're in for."

"In for? Lady, we're in it. What did we just do? Wasn't no flatland."

"And now we can finally designate Greg as our resident comedian and cheerleader," Gil says. "Thank you, Greg, for showing us your true stripes."

"Don't mention it, Gilbert. Just put me in your backpack and we'll be even."

"Nice one," Claire says.

"Come on, let us go," Bastien says. He stores his collapsible cup, takes out an old-fashioned thermos, and fills it with water from the fountain. "Fill up before you go. Water, water, water. Oui."

We do as he says, all taking our turn at the tap, and then we set out for our final walk of the day.

*   *   *

AT THE TOP OF A long, drawn-out, uphill battle that has me considering abandoning some of the stuff in my backpack along the side of the road, we come to an almost flat section in the road, and just up ahead there's a café. Tables and chairs are set out on an oversized patio in front of the little shop.

I begin to pray to all the fairy godmothers in my head. *Please, please let us stop here. Please, God in heaven, let us have a little break.*

As if to answer my prayers, Bastien says, "Let us pee." He smiles as he arrives at one of the tables, shucks off his backpack, and lets it slip to the ground. He plops down in a chair and, for the first time, I can see a hint of exhaustion in his face. He slumps hard.

Thank God and baby Jesus.

By the time I reach him, his table is already full. I go to the one beside it. Claire, Shania, and Manny join me. Everyone else is already seated with Bastien.

We sit in silence—every one of us—as we catch our breath. That was a killer hill. It's getting really mountainous. Like, everything is changing. We're pretty much *on* a mountain. Even the plants and trees are different. It's mostly evergreens now. And wherever we walk, I feel like we can see for a hundred miles. It's all so vast.

"Hey, dude," Manny says, nudging my side. "That guy over there is looking at you. I think you have a fan."

My face explodes in heat as I look everywhere, trying to see who he's talking about. Eventually my eyes lock on the boy who said hi at the fountain. Ooh. My face burns a deeper level of heat.

"Nah," I say. Feeble, I know.

"Um, yeah." Shania actually winks at me. "If that boy doesn't have the hots for you, Troy, I'll eat this loser's hiking socks." She motions to Manny, and he laughs. We all know Manny has the smelliest feet of all of us. Combined.

I fake-gag, like I'm going to throw up all over her. We all laugh, and the boy across the patio smiles even more. Yeah, he's definitely looking at me. He's sipping a café con leche and completely staring at me as the girls with him continue to talk nonstop in their own little world.

I get up to go inside to use the washroom and maybe get a café con leche. But Manny misunderstands my intentions.

"Ooh," he says. "My boy Troy gonna make a move. Slick shit, dude."

I punch his shoulder and give him the evil eye. "Not quite. I'm going to the washroom."

He pretends the punch hurt while the others laugh. I walk away and try to see out of the corner of my eye if the boy watches my exit or not.

He does. I turn back when I step into the café, and he's so totally looking at me. Oh my God. He's getting up. He's coming toward the café.

Like the coward that I am, I run for the washrooms as soon as I scope out the signs for them. I say another prayer, this time to the owner of the café who chose individual washrooms over communal ones.

Oh my God, oh my God, oh my God. My go-to panic mantra.

I can do this. I'm a fierce warrior, a peregrino. I quickly do my thing, wash up, and stand holding the doorknob, ready to take on the world. Or, at least this tiny corner of it that contains a cute Japanese boy just outside the door I'm too afraid to open.

I take a deep breath and step into the hall leading to the rest of the café. Without looking at anyone, I make my way to the counter and attempt to casually order my café con leche.

After I thank the lady who serves me, I take my passport from my back pocket. I present it to her, open at the first page with empty squares. She positions her stamp inside a square, and with a little force she pushes the plunger. With a soft *kerflunk*, I have a new stamp.

She quickly grabs the pen from behind her ear and jots today's date under her stamp, which is a picture of her café logo along with a Camino cake.

"Buen Camino," she says. She smiles and turns away. I thank her, but she's already moved on to the next customer and the next café con leche.

Off to the side are a few shelves filled with peregrino souvenirs. I see the boy pretending to be fully fascinated with some scallop shell trinkets. It's a ruse. They're the same shells we see at every single stop. He's so cute: shorter than me, with perfectly coiffed jet-black hair. His eyes are so brown they look black. They were the first thing I noticed about him at the fountain.

This is the part I'm terrible at. I hope he's better at it than I am. He already said hi back at the fountain, so maybe.

I make my way over to the shelf and pick up a small leather purse with a yellow shell embroidered across the front. I'm opening it and looking at the pockets inside when he finally makes his move.

"It's so cute, right?" he says. Perfect English. I stare into his face and notice that he has a tiny diamond earring in his nose. Hot. "But what's inside is what really matters." He smiles again and he's so adorable.

"I know. Function over fashion, right?" I feel like a dweeb. I consider running out, until he agrees with me.

"Wouldn't have it any other way," he says.

My shoulders relax and I unclench my teeth. I hadn't even realized I was clenching them. I put the purse back on the shelf. Not enough compartments. Can't have everything loosey-goosey in the bottom. It's a cute purse I would never use.

"Kei. Kei Amano." He offers his hand, and I take it. It's small in mine, soft.

"Troy Sinclair. Toronto."

"New York state, here," he says. "Those two talkers out there are my older sisters. I'm on the Nonstop Talking Camino Tour. Looking to be rescued." He's so totally coming on to me he doesn't even try to hide it.

"Oh." I almost scream. Sudden realization excitement. Sue me. "Happy Fourth of July!"

"Ha. Yeah. Thanks. No fireworks for me, I guess."

"Maybe. There's probably a ton of Americans walking the Camino. Maybe somebody'll set them off?"

"Maybe." His smile is incredible. And I *love* the stud in his nose. It picked a perfect nose to be a part of, too. Am I pathetic? Who cares? He's a cutie.

"Let's go outside." After I say it, I pray for an empty table on the patio so we can sit alone. "We can go get your coffee and find somewhere to sit away from all the chatter."

He pretends to wipe sweat from his forehead. "Phew. Thanks, Troy. You're saving my life."

I laugh, because he's cute and because I know that's not really what is happening here. He made his pass, and I've accepted. This has nothing to do with him escaping his sisters.

Ten minutes later he knows my dog's name and I know Wagon Wheels are his favorite food. Raspberry Wagon Wheels. Not the originals, because they're just sad and pathetic raspberry wheel wannabes. He's seventeen, the same as me. His mom is from Japan and his father is from Montana, third-generation American, and my parents are from Toronto and so are their parents.

Basically, the more he talks, the more this dummy is falling for him. Like it could ever happen. In my head, I'm trying not to calculate the distance between New York state and Toronto while simultaneously imagining the flower patterns of our china.

Kei's sisters thought the Camino would be a great experience for him. They walked it with their mother during the summer before *their* last year in high school. Back when their mother was still healthy enough to make the trip.

His mother died last year, just before Christmas. Cancer. They couldn't convince their father to shut down his dental practice long enough to come with them, even though he hadn't had a holiday in years.

I know so much more about him than he knows about me.

The focus is just about to switch over to me when Meagan interrupts us. I see her shadow loom over us before I see her.

"Sorry, Troy," she says, "but it's time to go."

Her words pull me out of the security of the little world Kei and I have made for ourselves at this table.

"Oh, yeah," I say, sounding just as startled as I feel. "Sorry. This is Kei. Kei, Meagan."

I look where the others are sitting, and every single one of them is staring back at me with a great big stupid grin on their face. I feel the heat rise into my cheeks once again, but I don't care.

"Hi, Kei," Meagan says. "Sorry, but we have to steal Troy away. Time for us to make our way to O Cebreiro."

"Nice to meet you, Meagan." He stands and extends a hand. Meagan shakes it. "What refugio are you staying at, if you don't mind me asking?"

"Not at all," she says. Kei and I look at each other like Meagan's about to call the numbers of the million-dollar lottery and we're eagerly holding our tickets. But, seriously, what are the chances? "Albergue de O Cebreiro."

"Oh my God!" he says. And I can almost see him waving his winning ticket in the air. "That's where my sisters and I are staying. We'll see you there."

I do my best not to jump up and down when I get to my feet. The two of us just beam at each other.

"Awesome. See you there. Nice to meet you, Kei." Meagan walks away, turning to wave before she reaches the table where everyone is still ogling us like crazy people.

"I'll see you later then," I say to Kei. I can't keep the excitement out of my voice. But I don't want to.

"Sure, Troy. It was really nice to meet you." We do a little one-shoulder hug, and he speaks into my ear, "I can't wait."

"Me too. Later." I turn to walk away. As I do, they're all bowing to my awesomeness, and I seriously consider dropping dead of embarrassment. But if I did that, I wouldn't see Kei later tonight at the refugio.

CHAPTER 22

DIEGO NELSON

Now we're in the mountains. Walking on a mountainside. Green hills as far as the eye can see. I'm alone. I just need some time to myself. It's the open spaces. So much room to think about Moms and my abuelita. I miss her so much.

We just left this amazing little town with stone buildings and straw roofs. It looked like Hobbit land, or something. Right out of the Middle Ages. Everyone snapped selfies and Insta pics of the amazing houses. Everyone but me. I should have, to show them to Moms. But the more I walk today, the sadder I feel. I don't know why I'm doing this.

"Just up ahead, my friends. The border marker. We will finally be in your Galicia. For real."

"Want to carry me the rest of the way, Bastien?" Greg says from behind me. Suddenly he is my guardian angel, staying close. He's the only one behind me. I was lagging, so he keeps making sure to stay behind me.

"Ah, no," Bastien says. "This old man is weary of footsteps, son. This, my last Camino."

"Oops," I hear Greg mumble to himself.

"Tired, Bastien?" Meagan asks.

"This is a tough day, mademoiselle."

"Indeed," Gil agrees. "Almost to the top of this one, though. One hill at a time. We'll make it."

"Yes, yes." He stops for a second and takes a deep breath and smacks his stick on the hardened earth of the path. We've been walking a narrow dirt path filled with a scattering of uneven rocks. "At the top, we will find the Galicia marker."

"I'd rather find an A & W and a tall mug of ice-cold root beer at the top," Greg whispers so that only I can hear. I look back at him, and he smiles and closes the short gap between us. "Sorry. I think I'm dehydrated."

"You've been my shadow today, Greg," I say.

"Sorry, man." He offers me a guilty smile. "It's just what I do. At home, I look after my little brother. I know you're hurting, man. I'm just worried about you. I hover when I worry. Sorry. Didn't mean to stalk you."

"No, no. It's all good, bro. You can walk with me, though. You don't need to walk behind me."

"Thanks, bud. You hanging in okay?"

"Sure, yeah. Long day, though. I'd love that A &W root beer, now that you mention it."

"Sorry I brought it up, Diego." He laughs. "I just set you up for more disappointment."

I laugh. We continue in silence.

Sure enough, once we round another corner the monument Bastien told us about comes into view. No A & W anywhere in sight.

The monument looks like a bigger version of the mile markers, only, instead of coming up to our knees, it towers over our heads. It says Galicia in big red letters under a red Galician cross with crests beside it. And a scallop. And way too much graffiti.

"Wow," Greg says.

"Right?" I say. The others already have their phones out, taking pics and getting others to take pictures of them beside it.

I drop my pack and stretch. To my left, opposite the monument, I can see forever. I'm just taking in the view of rolling hills and valleys in the distance when Bastien puts an arm around my shoulder. I look at him, and he smiles. And for the hundredth time since my tumble yesterday, I'm happy we found him. I'm happy he found me.

"They say there is a place in these hills, Diego, where you can look back and see Ponferrada. That's where you began, yes?"

"Yes, Ponferrada. But that's impossible. No way we can see Ponferrada from here."

"No, no. It is true. The castle of the Knights Templar, no?"

"Yes," I say. "We stayed right across the road from it. It was incredible."

"Oh, yes. Magic. And the pizza in the plaza, Diego. I am an old man, but I would walk from Toulouse where I live for that pizza, my friend. But others on The Way, they have told me they have seen Ponferrada from the hills near O Cebreiro. Somewhere, somewhere."

"That's amazing."

"It is, it is. And how about you, my friend. How are you this day?"

We stand apart from the others, and I'm glad to be alone with him. I feel I can be more myself. It's easy to cry with Bastien and not feel stupid or bad about it. He still has an arm around my shoulder and he squeezes a bit tighter when he sees the tears come to my eyes.

"I'm okay," I lie. He ruffles my hair with his free hand.

"You will be. You carry your abuelita to the cathedral of Santiago. Here." He taps his heart. "She will be proud of nieto Diego. So proud. But, this you know."

He fills me and empties me all at once. I turn my head into his shoulder, and he allows me to have a little cry.

When I'm done, I see that the others have grouped together just beyond the monument and that they are patiently waiting for us. The looks on their faces make me less uncomfortable about crying. These guys are pretty cool.

I wrestle my backpack onto my shoulders, and then we rejoin them and prepare to set out on the day's final leg.

"One hundred and fifty miles or so to go," Gil says. "We're almost to Santiago."

"Not quite," Greg says. "But I dig your enthusiasm."

As I make my way over to Shania to maybe walk with her, Greg takes it as his sign to stop mothering me. He moves on ahead to catch up with Troy, of all people. Not sure they really dig each other.

"Hey, you," Shania says.

"Hey, yourself," I say. We smile at each other and it's nice to be back with her. It's been a while.

"You okay? I mean, I know you're not okay. But are you okay?"

"Sure, yeah." I shrug, and we begin to walk, falling in behind Claire and Manny. "I'm just really tired. Not sure what I'm doing this for anymore, Shan."

"I hear you." She reaches for my hand and takes it in hers. This girl who was a storm of chaos and anger when we met a lifetime ago. I've been wanting her hand in mine for a few days now. It feels nice. We walk in silence, just the two of us, and nobody interrupts us.

Even when our hands become slippery with sweat, we both keep holding on.

Pretty soon, we come to a mile marker that says *O Cebreiro, K.151*. It stands in front of a short stone wall that looks a thousand years old; every nook and cranny of it is filled with moss. Even the downward-facing scallop shell on the mile marker is filled with moss. Everything about the town looks old and damp. And beautiful.

"Made it," Shania says. She raises her free hand, and I high five her. Now we're facing each other and all hands are touching. I take this opportunity to hug her. When I do, she's rigid at first, like she didn't know I was going to do it. Like she didn't want it. I didn't even know I was going to do it. But she softens into it. I want to kiss her. Instead, we let go.

Everyone else kept walking. They stopped at an ancient church. It's not like the thousands of other churches we've seen that all look alike. Its shape is different. Surrounding it are more of those stone houses with hay-thatched roofs. Some of them are even round. Every road in the village is made up of cobbles and rocks. One of the oldest towns so far, for sure.

As we join the others, Bastien is front and center being the tour guide.

"Inside this Santa Maria, there was the blood and the flesh. The Madonna who blessed the sacrament, maybe," Bastien says.

"Hey, Diego," Manny says, waving me closer to the front. "My boy here is Catholic. Listen to this, Diego."

I come up beside Manny, but not because I believe anything Bastien is telling us. Just because. Because of my gran, I listen. Shania follows me.

"We go inside, yes?" Bastien says. He almost whispers this, like a prayer. "We go inside."

We all follow him as he makes his way inside.

"It happened that a snowstorm came in 1300 and the priest was no longer interested in the faith. When he thought no one would come because of how bad the storm, he got angry and... stomp stomp stomp."

We're all inside looking around the church. It's tiny and it's big, all at once. A man stands off to the side, in a little booth. He has an ink pad and a stamp and he waves us all over.

We form a little line, taking out our credencials. We take turns getting stamps as the man welcomes us to O Cebreiro and stamps our passports. He says *Buen Camino* to each and every one of us as the stamp comes down on the page. We thank him and then huddle around Bastien as he continues to speak.

"Madonna of the Sacred Miracle," Bastien whispers, pointing out the statue. "A farmer walked through the storm, yes, and it made the priest bitter. That someone showed up, that someone should have so much faith in the dying church that he grows to despise."

We move toward the altar. Greg stops and sits down and Meagan joins him. Everyone is quiet, following Bastien's lead.

"The bread, they say, became flesh. And the wine, it was blood. Not only for the priest who had also lost his way, but also for the farmer who had come through the impossible snow. Two men healed. One in faith and one in warmth."

He turns to us, smiling. He likes to be in the spotlight, but not because he likes the attention he receives. With Bastien, you can tell it's because he likes the attention he gives.

"And the Madonna," he whispers. We need to lean in to hear him. "The Madonna, she saw it all. Yes?"

CHAPTER 23

SHANIA REYNOLDS

THURSDAY, JULY 4TH – *Day 6 – O Cebreiro, Troy Finds Love, and Diego – Oh, and Another Day of Double Entries.*

I have to stop this or I'll get a bad reputation. I'm writing in my journal a second time. Again. It's not like we're going to get bonus points for this or something. I'm so pathetic.

This town is awesome. Later we're going to walk around a little. For now, we're just chilling in our rooms waiting for supper. Every single one of us is writing in their journal. I'm guessing some are playing catch-up. I'm not mentioning any names, Claire and Greg. I haven't seen either of them writing since day one, and their pens are going fast and furious. Court-mandated journaling. That's pretty awesome.

I'm in love with Troy. He's such a sweetie. The way he and that boy were back at the café. He can't even sit still, knowing the kid's coming here tonight. He might explode. He made all of us promise to be on our best behavior too. Or he would kill us. Twice, he said.

Bright side. I've been rushing to get to the bright side. I know it's tragic what's happened with Diego's grandmother. But today I somehow found the courage to hold his hand. Not just a little, either. All the way from our last stop to O Cebreiro. Holding Diego's hand is like holding onto fire. Only, it's a fire that doesn't burn your skin. It just makes it warm with a heat you never want to lose. That's my bright side. Diego Nelson.

"Come on, Manny," Greg says after he whips his journal across his bed. "Let's break outta here. If we're stealth-like, we might be able to get some wine downstairs before Gilbert and Meagan come back."

They went for a walk around town. They said they would do it now and leave us to do it on our own after our group meeting. Cool of them.

"Nah," Manny says, "Count me out. I'll come down, but not into wine here. Nope."

"Cool beans. More for me. You can be lookout."

It will not end well, if Greg gets into the wine. I don't want to be around when this one crashes.

"How about you, Diego?" Greg says as he and Manny head for the door. "Coming down?"

"No, I'm good. Just gonna rest for a bit. You go ahead."

"I'll come," Troy says. He slips his journal under his pillow and runs to catch-up. He'll most likely go to keep an eye out for his new *friend*.

"Wait for me," Claire says. She follows them downstairs, journal in hand. Yep, she's playing catch-up. Definitely.

And just like that, Diego and I are all alone in this big room.

It surprises me when he sets his own journal down and comes to join me on my bed. He sits at the foot, but looks out at the room instead of up at me.

"Hey, you," I say. I rest my foot on his lower back. He turns and offers me a small smile.

"Hey."

"You okay?"

"Yeah, sure. Just feel kind of funny. This afternoon was nice. Sorry my hand was so sweaty. It was really hot."

"No big deal, Diego. I'm sure some of it was mine. You don't have to apologize."

"I like you, Shania," he says. But the look on his face isn't what it should be. He's close to tears.

"Hey," I say. "What's wrong? I like you too, you big dummy. It was a little shaky at first, Diego, but I think that was more me than you."

I try to give him just the right smile, like I'm sorry but not sorry for being so testy. I *did* practically kick and scream my way into this trip. He just happened to be in the wrong place at the wrong time.

"I just, I don't know what I'm doing?" He looks into his lap. He's making an effort to keep it together. I'm not sure he's going to win. "I have nothing to go home to. My grandmother is gone."

"Diego, no. You have everything to go home to. Your mom. She sounds amazing. You have *her* to go home to. Every step you take out there, you're walking closer to seeing her again. And when you're with *her*, you'll be with your grandmother."

He smiles. "Thank you for that."

"Don't mention it. We should go downstairs. Or I won't be responsible for what I'll do to you." We both blush, and I can't even believe the words came out of my mouth. I meant them innocently, but they grew bigger once they left me. Oops.

He sits silent on the edge of my bed and allows time for my moronic words to dissipate away to nothing.

"My grandmother couldn't come to the airport. I said goodbye to her the day before I left. She had a doctor's appointment when we had to be at the airport. I thought it was okay back then, but now I wish I got to see her one last time before I got on the plane."

"Come on, Diego. Don't beat yourself up. She loved you. You got to say goodbye to each other. I know she was happy you were walking the Camino, because you told me. Just because she wasn't at the airport doesn't mean anything. Hell, my dad just went to work the day I left. And my mom, she doesn't even work. She just got up and went out to wherever she goes every day. A goodbye at the airport is not what it's cracked up to be."

"You never told me that." I realize I've said too much. I wasn't going to tell him about my parents. I guess I got lost in the moment. "Your parents didn't take you to the airport? Are you shitting me, Shania?"

He sounds angry. He slides up to the top of the bed and sits at my side.

"Yeah," I say. "Obviously not something I'm proud of. What do you think I jacked a car for? They just don't notice me. They don't see me. But it's okay. I have Flibber and Dillon. For now, I guess that's enough. Dillon's an ass, but he's *my* ass. I talked to him three times since we got here. And we text every day. Nothing from my parents."

"Are you kidding me? That sucks, Shan."

"Yeah, but I'm used to it. It's not as big a deal as it sounds. Not when you don't expect anything from them." I wonder if he can tell I'm lying through my teeth, that every single day of my life I expect something from them that doesn't come.

"Yes it is. It *is* a big deal. I would die if Moms did that to me. I can't even… yeah… it wouldn't happen."

"Rub it in," I say, pushing him from behind a little too hard. I was only joking, but I almost fling him off the bed. "Oops. Sorry. Didn't mean that."

He turns and he's smiling. We're on my bed together. That fact hits me just as he leans closer.

"Nobody deserves to be treated like your parents treat you," he says. "I don't care what you did or why you did it. It doesn't mean it's okay to shut out your own daughter. They're shits for doing that to you. You know that, right?"

"Yeah, sure I know that. I could write a book on that topic. Queen Shit and King and Emperor Shit. I guess that makes me a princess."

"I like you," he says.

"I like you too, Diego Nelson."

"Can I kiss you right now?"

"Can you do me a favor and not ask if you can kiss me and just ki—"

Diego cuts my words off with his lips. They swallow mine, and he leans closer, and we're kissing each other full tilt. I could get used to kissing him. His lips are so full, and he's got this soft growth of black hair over his upper one, not quite a moustache, and it feels so good.

Diego puts his hands on my cheeks, and I'm lost in his grip. We kiss until my mouth hurts and the light outside the big bedroom windows begins to change. When we part, my lips feel puffed out to twice their size, and Diego's look just as beat-up as mine feel.

And it's so good. I hope the others don't figure it out. Then again, who cares? I mean, we did hold hands today. They must know something's up between us.

"We better go downstairs." I laugh because we're both breathing heavily, and, if I'm as flushed as Diego is, our flimsy cover will be totally blown. "Supper will be ready soon."

"Okay," he says. "Maybe you should go first."

I look at him, perplexed. "It doesn't matter. We can go together."

"No, we can't. I can't go yet." He blushes and looks down at his crotch and brings my pillow over to cover his lap. "I'll be right down. I just need a few seconds."

"Huh? Oh." Brainiac Shania finally clues in. "Sorry. Yeah. Ha ha. I'll see you down there, then?"

"Yeah. I'm good. Save me a seat." I look at the pillow in his lap and I laugh. He covers his face with his hands. "Thanks. I'm glad you're not making me feel self-conscious about it or anything."

"See you down there." I get up and wriggle my way out from behind him. I get off the bed and give him one last kiss before I leave. I grab the pillow and run with it to the door. When I look back, he's covering himself with his hands. I wave and throw him the pillow.

"Funny, Shania. Real funny."

I take the stairs two at a time. My smile is going to crack my face in two. I could get used to this.

TROY SINCLAIR

FINALLY. I'VE BEEN SITTING ON this wall forever. Every peregrino who came walking into town must have thought I lived here. Every time I said *Buen Camino*, they just smiled and thanked me instead of returning the greeting.

I see Kei's sisters first. They're walking alone. It looks like they're both talking. I wonder who's listening.

I jump off the wall, move over to the mile marker, and lean against it. It's my attempt to look casual.

My heart skips a beat, because I expected Kei to be right behind them. When he isn't, I panic. But I'm an idiot. Where else would he be? They wouldn't be walking along like nothing's wrong if something happened to him. Unless, of course, they were too busy talking to notice him falling off the side of the mountain.

Troy. You're an ass. Still, I feel relief when he finally comes into view.

Now I realize I'm going to look desperate waiting for him. I'm about to run back to the albergue and sit in a corner with a look of indifference on my face. Too late. He sees me and waves his arms in the air. So much for making my escape. But his enthusiasm makes me feel awesome. And a little less foolish about my own enthusiasm.

I wave my arms back just as his sisters take a breather and look in my direction. They see my wave and look behind them and see Kei returning the wave. They look at each other, and one says something. The other one bursts out laughing. Nice. Now I feel like an even bigger dweeb.

I rest my arms at my sides and wait for Kei to finish the climb. His sisters arrive first.

"Hi, you must be Troy?" One of them asks, but I'm pretty sure she already knows the answer. "I'm Mia. This is Becky. We're Kei's sisters."

"Nice to meet you. Yeah, I'm Troy. Guilty as charged."

"He's a little excited," Becky says. "Straight ahead?"

"Yep. Just up that road. The big one with the chairs out front. And all the peregrinos," I add, smiling.

"Thanks," Mia says. "We'll leave you to him. See if you can't calm him down some. He's a bit too excited. I hope you're ready for the Kei energy."

We all laugh as they continue on to the albergue and I wait for Kei to finish his climb.

"Hi," he says. His forehead is covered in perspiration, and his hair is slightly less wild than it was earlier. It's tamed in the heat. But even wilted, he's no less hot.

"Hey," I say as I extend a hand. "Let me take your pack for you. I've had time to rest."

"That. Would be amazing." He peels it off and hands it over. I sling it over one shoulder and, instead of heading for the albergue, I sit on the stone wall behind the mile marker. I let his backpack drop to the ground at my feet.

"Have a seat. We still have time before supper."

"Sure. Mia will save me a bed. She's anal about stuff like that. All about the details. Especially now."

He sits down beside me and reaches for the water bottle in the side pocket of his backpack. "Want a drink?"

"Sure." He hands me the bottle, and I take a deep chug. "Thanks."

I hand it back, and he guzzles the last third of the bottle.

"Man, I needed that." He swipes a hand across his forehead, and his hair just naturally starts to go in the opposite direction like it was trained that way. "So?"

"What?"

"I think I may have told you my life back there. I know almost nothing about yours. You were saved by Meagan."

"Right. Guilty. Yeah. Age? Done. Dog's name? Done. I don't think I got to my brother. Avery? Did I mention him?"

"Nope."

"Well, I have a brother. Avery. We're twins."

"There's two of you?" He puts one hand to his heart and starts to exaggeratedly fan himself with the other one. "Look-alike? Or the other kind?"

"Identical."

Now he's falling into the grass at my feet. "Oh my God, that's hot," he says as he springs to his feet and makes a show of wiping off the grass and dirt.

"Funny."

"I try, Troy Sinclair. I try. But, seriously? Two of you? Swoon."

"Thank you, I think."

"I like you. I don't want you to save me from my sisters. I just want you to save me."

"That's sweet."

He offers a hand to help me off the wall, and even though I don't really need help getting off a two-and-a-half-foot wall, I take it. I hop down and scoop up his backpack with my free hand.

"To the albergue." I point the way because I'm such an expert on the town of O Cebreiro.

"Lead the way." He releases my hand, and I regret it already.

When we reach the courtyard in front of the albergue, I can already smell the amazing Galician soup.

"Oh, man," Kei says. "I could literally eat my own arm. It smells so good. I don't know what I want first, food or a shower."

"Better take a shower. You might just have time. Probably going to be busy after supper. I already had mine. I don't like to fight for shower space."

"I wouldn't fight you for mine. We could share," Kei says, and my face burns. "Gotcha. Man, do you blush easy. It's gonna be fun teasing you."

We step inside, and I give him directions to the washrooms upstairs and hand him his bag. He goes off in pursuit of his sisters, to check out his sleeping quarters before he takes a shower.

"Whoa, Troy. What is up with that?"

It's Greg. The hairs on the back of my neck stand up. There's something about his tone I don't like. I don't trust him after that night in Cacabelos.

"What do you mean?"

"Nothing. Just that you seem to be moving a little fast, is all. Getting your freak on with your new *friend*?"

"How is that any of your business? We're just talking. What's it to you?"

Claire glances up from her journal. When she sees us, she comes over.

"What's up, Greg?" she asks.

"Nothing. Just talking to Troy about his new boyfriend."

"Oh, really," she asks. "Did he tell you he has a new boyfriend?"

"No," Greg says. "But I have eyes. It's obvious they're hot for each other."

"*Really*?" I say. The pilgrims around us glance over to see what's happening. "You're seriously going to be like that?"

"What? I just asked about your little *boy*friend."

"No," Claire says. "You're teasing him."

"Settle down, Claire. Why is everyone taking everything the wrong way? Stop being so sensitive."

"Because you mean it the wrong way." She looks prepared to rip his face off. "We're used to people like you."

"People like me? I was just teasing him. I don't see what the problem—"

"Yeah, you do," Claire says.

She whips out her phone and starts scrolling through pictures. When she finds what she's looking for, she turns the screen to him.

"See that," Claire says. "That's my girlfriend. Her name's Zoe. Zoe and I recognize homophobic behavior. People don't always throw things or hurl slurs. Sometimes, it's just casual teasing disguised as banter. And when we get angry, they try to laugh it off by saying things like, *I was only joking*, or, *I was just teasing*. Or my favorite, *stop being so sensitive*."

"Are you calling me a homophobe? Because that's just *not* right. I didn't know you were gay, though, Claire. That's a shame. You're kind of cute."

Claire slaps Greg, and he stumbles backwards. I reach out to break his fall, just in time.

"I'm not here for you," Claire says. "You don't even know when you're insulting people, do you? You're so offensive."

"You didn't have to hit me." He turns to me, like I'm his friend or something because I broke his fall and saved him from splitting his head open on the stone floor. "She hit me."

Everyone's staring, but as I scan the room I don't see Meagan, Gil, or Bastien. They must still be out on their walk. Thank God. I'm pretty sure physical violence is on their *Don'ts* list.

"Don't look at me. You had that coming. You have a long way to go if you think you're not homophobic. The gays don't typically enjoy it when you tease them about their sexuality or make weak jokes about their relationships. And here's a tip, asshole. Don't insult a lesbian by suggesting she's missing out on something special with you. What is with straight guys, anyway? You're so gross."

He gives me this look that says, *what the hell?* When I don't respond, he turns and goes upstairs. I'm not buying his *what did I do?* crap. He knows.

"Sorry about that," I say to Claire.

"You have nothing to apologize for, Troy," she says. "We're good."

"But are we?"

"What do you mean?"

"I just want to know, Claire." I lean over to whisper because I don't know who might be listening and I wouldn't want anyone in our group to overhear my question. "Are you going to take off, or what? It's all I think about when we're out there walking. I don't want you to run away. You won't tell me what's wrong. There's no point in running. Don't you want to see your girlfriend when all this is over?"

"Yeah. I do. But on my terms. And that's not going to happen. Not ever. My parents wouldn't allow it. I'm just so tired of the shit in my life. Let's go outside."

I scrunch up my face, unsure leaving now would be a good idea.

"It's okay. We have a few minutes. Come on."

"Yeah. Okay." We leave the albergue, and there's an empty table against the wall of the building right by the entrance, so we sit down.

"What crap do you have, Claire? You have a girlfriend. You're out at school. That sounds pretty awesome to me."

"Because you only see a bit of the picture. You don't see everything. Sure those things are amazing. And Zoe is the best thing that ever happened to me. But, Troy, my life is more than that. We have to hide. We have to have these secret expressions for our love. The lime ones mean *I miss you*, the orange ones mean *kiss kiss*, and when we share them it's nowhere near the same as when our lips actually touch. It's what we have to settle with. So, there's that. Don't you ever feel like escaping?"

She pulls out her ever-present bag of Skittles and pops a few. This time, she offers the bag to me. I only take a few, though, trying to be respectful of her and her girlfriend.

"I'm sorry, but not really," I say. "Where would I escape to? If something's bugging you, you can't just leave it behind. I know ignorance too, Claire. I've experienced my fair share. I'm only here because I snapped when I heard one too many gay slurs last semester. I lost it and actually punched a couple of kids. Well, swung hands, anyway. Not exactly a fighter. They taunted me every day for the entire semester. I took it and took it and took it. Until I couldn't. After I hit them, I threw a chair through the plate glass window that led to the front office. And tore a banner off the wall beside the window."

With each of the deeds I list, Claire's mouth opens just a little wider. I continue.

"And I smashed the trophy case. I kicked it in with my Docs, actually. Felt good. But not good enough. Because then I took the team-autographed baseball bat out of the trophy case and proceeded to smash trophies and stuff in the cabinet."

"Holy crap," she says. There's laughter in her eyes. She totally looks impressed.

"I don't think you have to tell me about people messing with the gays. Greg, in there? He's not the first and he's not the worst. And he won't be the last. I'm trying really hard not to react the way I used to. The problem is theirs, not mine."

"Oh," I continue, "And I also threw a garbage can at the principal when he tried to stop me. And then I ran out of the school and kicked the first car door I came to. Poor Mrs. Powers, the school secretary, who had just lost her husband. The woman's like, a hundred and eighty-seven."

I finish and take a deep breath. Claire's laughing. "You made half that shit up, didn't you?"

"Nope. Sorry, but it's all true. The therapist called it blind rage. The cops called it a whole list of offenses and didn't care a stink about the therapist's findings."

"All new level of respect, Troy. Whoa. Don't mess with the angry gay. And, you're a funny guy."

"Don't think I haven't noticed you didn't completely fill me in on what's bugging you, Claire," I say. "You don't have to, but just so you know. I'm here if you ever want to talk about it. Can you please just *not* run away, though? At least while you're on the Camino."

"I can't promise that. But I can almost promise. I want to fly the coop, Troy. I saw this as a perfect opportunity. Far away enough that maybe they wouldn't look for me. Or at least they wouldn't find me. Europe's a big place."

"And you're just talking crazy."

"Let's go inside. They must be feeding us soon. I'm starved. It's going to be dark soon. You got my back with Greg? If he tries to stir shit with Gil and Meagan?"

"Sure," I say. "That was the first thing I thought of, actually. The lecture. But I don't think he will. People like him. He won't want to broadcast his failure."

I stand up, reach for the door, and hold it open for her. She steps inside, and I follow her. We arrive just in time for Kei to appear, refreshed from his shower. He's wearing tan shorts and a red tank top and he's everything I want right now.

"Hey, you."

"Hi, Kei. Let's go find a seat." I can't take my eyes off of him so I let him find the seat and I follow him to it like a puppy. The aromas that were near crippling to my hungry belly are even more overpowering now. Soon all the peregrinos milling about also take their seats.

The trays of food come from the kitchen one after the other. Soup, salad, chicken, bread. And lots of wine, but not for us. Claire joins us, sitting across the table from Kei.

Diego comes barrelling down the stairs, and he and Shania come and sit beside Claire. The looks on their faces tell me everything I need to know.

Manny is at the very end of the table, talking to some older lady who's bundled up like it's the middle of winter. She wears a coat and has a scarf wrapped around her head. They're having a lively conversation. She pours a glass of wine for Manny from her bottle. He glances over and sees me. He raises a shhh finger to his lips and raises his glass to the woman, and they cheer. And he was the one who said he wasn't into drinking.

Is it stupid that I feel like these are now my people, my family? I didn't even realize what I was doing. I'm taking inventory of my group, making sure they're all present and accounted for.

As we all start reaching for food, I introduce Kei to everyone. The front door opens and Bastien barrels in with Gilbert and Meagan at his heels.

"We eat," Bastien bellows as he sets his walking stick against the wall and takes a seat at the long makeshift table.

As I look about the room, there's only one person noticeably missing. Greg. As much as he was an ass, I feel bad he's not here. I try to concentrate on Kei and the food in front of me, but I need to fix this. I excuse myself from the table.

*   *   *

I FIND GREG SITTING ON his bed, punching the hell out of his pillow. He's in a blind rage. *That* I can relate to.

"Oh. Hey, Troy," he says when he notices me. He actually attempts to sound casual, which is ridiculous. Then he looks away, embarrassed.

"You okay?" I ask.

"Honestly? No. This has been a shit year for me. Getting away from my life was the best part of this so-called punishment. But also the worst."

"Sounds bad," I say. I want to say more, be more sympathetic. But I'm still angry. Besides, he should be the one coming to me. He looks at his pillow, like he has just noticed it's there. He chucks it aside. "My parents, man. They use me as some sort of pawn, me and my little bro. We're just two more of the possessions they're constantly fighting over."

"I didn't know you had a little brother."

"You didn't ask. We haven't exactly been bonding, Troy. I know you think I'm starting off badly. I mean, I get it. I am. I try to joke around a lot and sometimes I go overboard. I'm pissed off. But it's not your fault. I don't know why I keep taking potshots at you. I'm such an asshole."

"Welllll? That's pretty much true. I can't argue with you there."

"I'm sorry."

I contemplate his apology. He gets up from his bed and starts to walk toward the door. He signals for me to follow him.

"Really, Troy. I'm sorry. None of my shit is your fault. I'm not usually such a jerk. I'm sorry."

I follow him to the door. By the sounds coming from downstairs, I can tell supper is now in full swing. Time to get down there.

"You should probably apologize to Claire. You went way too far."

He covers his face with his hand and shakes his head. "Man, I am unstoppable. Monumental."

"Assholes are sometimes like that," I say. He looks hurt for a split second, but then sees the half-smirk on my face. We stop in the hallway before heading downstairs.

"This has been the year of the divorce in my world," Greg says. "My parents spent the entire year dividing their empire. My brother? He has special needs. And he's adopted and already had a messed-up start. So he's not taking the chaos so well. The only thing that kid ever wanted was stability. A place to belong. My parents gave him that. And they used to be pretty passionate about it, about making sure Robbie felt safe and wanted and a part of *us*. Until they didn't. When they fell apart, it's almost like they forgot how to be parents. Forgot how much Robbie needed saving."

"That sucks so much, Greg," I say. "I'm really sorry. But I gotta say, as bad as it is, I don't see why you think it gives you an excuse to pick on the two queer kids. I can't figure out if you're homophobic, an asshole, a bully… or all three."

"Yeah," he says. "I get it. I promise you, though, I'm not homophobic. I don't expect you to believe me. I'd think the same thing. I didn't mean to hurt you. Or Claire."

"You saw us as the weakest links and you struck. That seriously sucks. Do you see that, at least?"

"Yeah. No excuse. I don't know what to say."

I'm getting angry all over again. "Don't say anything, Greg. Just be better." The noise downstairs pulls me in. I'm still so hungry. "We need to get down there before there's no food left. Truce? For now?"

"Thanks, Troy. I'll try not to be such a jerk."

"Don't try, man." I'm not going to be a pushover. "I will call you on your crap every time. Stop thinking it's okay to tease queer kids. We've had enough. Oh, and you owe Claire a huge apology."

"I know." He looks downstairs. "It's the first thing on my list."

"Let's go eat. I'm starving. And it smells so good."

"I hear that," Greg says. We finally make our way downstairs.

CHAPTER 25

DIEGO NELSON

WE HAD TO PROMISE WE wouldn't get "into mischief" tonight before Gil and Meagan would let us go out. Easy. I just want to be out here holding Shania's hand, stealing a few kisses, and thinking about home and my grandmother. Not interested in anything else.

"Where to?" Manny asks. We're all standing around waiting for someone to make a suggestion. I can't believe we all want to spend our free time walking around in the dark, when we already spent the entire day walking.

"How about this way?" Troy says. Not like it matters which way we go. He leads the way as we set off to explore the little village. I'm pretty sure we'll cover the entire place in about two minutes.

Troy brought his new friend Kei with him. He seems nice enough.

"I know the plan was to escape the adults, but I kind of miss not spending time with Bastien tonight," Shania says. I couldn't agree more. I don't know what I would have done without him last night. "I mean, it's kind of lame walking around. Didn't we already do this? Like, *all day*?"

"Get out of my head. That's exactly what I was thinking."

"Sure you were, Diego. Right."

"No, really." We're holding hands, and it wasn't even like it was a decision or anything. We just stepped outside, and I took her hand and that was it.

"So, you two an item now?" Manny tries to butt in between us. He's skipping around like he's on fire. Then he leans against my back like he's trying to get a piggyback. Troy said Manny drank wine at dinner. I wouldn't be surprised if he's a little lit. He's sure acting like it.

"I don't know. Mind getting off my back, dude? Don't want you to take us with you when you fall flat on your face and break your neck."

"No. I'm good," he says. "Just a little shine." He laughs this maniacal laugh, but he lets go. Shania shushes him, because this town is dead. It looks like everyone who lives here goes to bed at eight. Manny makes his way to Troy and Kei. New victims.

Claire and Greg walk together, staying far behind everyone else. This surprises me after what Shania told me about their fight, which I would have seen with my own two eyes had I not been upstairs waiting for things to calm down. Let them work things out themselves. Last thing we need is more drama on this trip.

"So, are we?" Shania says.

"Huh?"

"An item? Are we an item?" She looks down at our interlocked fingers and then gives me an overexaggerated inquisitive look and giggles.

I'm so bad with girls. Really. We all know how the Sabrina Vincent fiasco went down. I couldn't even get that girl by lighting a celebratory fire in her honor. To be fair, though, that was probably not the best way to go about it.

Now here's this girl who's looking at me like I matter, and I didn't do a single boneheaded thing to get her. Unless, of course, it was the tumble down the muddy hill that cinched it for her? Just so we're clear, I did *not* do that on purpose to get the girl.

"Earth to Diego? I didn't know it was going to be such a difficult question."

"Nah, nah," I say. "It isn't."

Kei and Troy have stopped in front of a house and they're talking amongst themselves.

"Well, then. Are we?"

"I just. I'm having a hard time believing you'd want to. For me? The answer would be yes. I'd like that."

"Who hurt you?" she says. I can't read the look on her face, but there's laughter in her eyes. Not sure if she's asking a serious question or not. "I just mean, Diego, you're gorgeous. And the way you talk about your mother and how nice you are. And, man. I was so angry when we met. Like, *hostile*. Just being around you makes me feel better about all the crap in my life. It's insane you think you couldn't be enough to get any girl you'd want."

"My track record speaks for itself." I smile, try to wave it off. I don't like talking about myself like this. And I'm not fishing for compliments. She squeezes my hand.

"Well. I want to. So, I guess that settles it. We are." We stop beside Troy and Kei, who are staring at the house in front of them.

"You are what?" Troy asks.

"An item?" I say, but it comes out as a question. When I speak it out loud it begins to feel real in my head. Shania Reynolds and *me*. This girl who wanted to kill me and everyone else, just six days ago, chose me. I'm not even going to tell them she's my first. Maybe before all this is over, I'll even call her my girlfriend.

"That's amazing, Diego," Troy says. He side-hugs me and it surprises me. But it's also cute. The guy's okay. Then he looks at Kei.

"Yeah," Kei says. "You can tell them."

"Awesome." He kisses Kei's cheek. "So we were thinking about kind of being an item, too. *Only*." He raises his hand quickly to stop Shania and me from saying anything. "Proviso. We've decided to spend our time out here together, *for now*. I mean, obviously we know how this is going to play out, right."

"Dude." I'm about to congratulate them, but then I remember Kei is American and I do the math. The possibility of anything long-term vanishes pretty much instantly. I don't know whether to be happy or sad. Still, I grab his shoulder and give it a little shake. "I'm happy for you."

Shania hugs him. "I knew you had it in you, Troyboy. You picked a cutie, too." She pats Kei's shoulder. "Nice."

I notice none of us use the words boyfriend or girlfriend. Not yet. At this point, it would probably just jinx us.

"When we get back to the albergue, we're going to ask his sisters if we can walk the rest of the way together. At least we'll have a few days."

"That'd be nice," Claire says as she and Greg finally catch up. "You guys look cute together." She holds her hands out and frames them, making a box with her fingers like she's going to take a picture. Kei laughs.

"It's all him," Troy says. He looks at Kei like Kei is everything. And I know the feeling.

"What's wrong?" Troy says. He lets go of Kei's hand and steps over to Claire. He puts a hand up to her face and wipes away tears. I hadn't even noticed. Then he looks to Greg and his face turns quickly to anger. "What happened, *Greg*?"

"Dude, no," Greg says as he takes a step back.

"It's okay, Troy," Claire says. "It's cool. I was using Greg as a sounding board, talking about my shit. He apologized and then he just listened. Turns out, he's really good at listening."

Troy looks at both of them like they're insane.

"After what happened earlier, I wasn't sure," Troy says to Greg.

Troy disappeared right before supper and came back downstairs with Greg. I missed everything before that.

"I'm an asshole," Greg replies. "We've already established that. No way around it. But I apologized. I swear, bro, we were only talking this time."

"Okay. But like I said, I'm gonna call you on your crap," Troy says. Boy is hard-core. "Bygones be bygones, Greg. Especially if Claire was willing to forgive you. Think before you speak in the future. Easy as that."

"True. You're right."

"Oh, I know I'm right. That's why I'm telling you."

I look at Shania and raise my eyebrows exaggeratedly. She gives me the look that says *not now*. I know she's thinking the same thing, though. Troy's playing tough. He's like David to Greg's Goliath.

"Are you okay, Claire? Really?" Troy says.

"Yes, Troy," Claire says. "I swear. Greg apologized, I accepted. Then we talked about some of my stuff. I talked, he listened. All's good."

Greg looks at Troy and smiles. He's got one of those *see, I told you so* looks on his face. Troy backs down a bit, appears to accept Claire's explanation.

"I have an idea," Kei says. "How about we go back to the refugio. I think I walked about a thousand steps too many today."

This relieves any leftover tension. We all agree with Kei.

"Wait, wait," Shania says, jumping away from me and taking center stage in front of us. "Guys. We totally need a group selfie in front of this amazing house. I mean, look at it."

It's incredible: thatched roof that looks like it goes on forever and stone walls. If this were Hollywood, we'd be on the set of some crazy medieval movie with dragons and shit. It wouldn't even surprise me if a dragon came swooping out of the sky right now, blocking out the moon, and landing in the road beside us. It's *that* cool.

"You're right. Instagrammable," Kei says.

Shania turns her back on us and holds her phone out at arm's reach. "Get behind me, everyone."

"Wait." Kei again. He grabs a selfie stick and a clicker thing out of the little shoulder bag he's carrying and hands them to her. "Here."

"Kei to the rescue," I say.

Shania Bluetooths the clicker and snaps her phone onto the selfie stick. We all stand behind her as she aims the shot.

"Okay, can everyone see themselves on the screen? Ready? Smile!"

She takes the shot and then keeps moving the stick around at different angles and taking shots. We all make ridiculous faces and hold fingers up behind each other and stick out our tongues and stuff. Then we take turns snapping pics with couples and different groups and Shania promises to share them with everyone.

Time for bed. Tomorrow is the real horror day. We're all feeling pretty good right now, being out alone. Free. But it's all going to change tomorrow, I'm guessing.

We run back to the albergue and, despite the silence of the sleeping town, we let out a few hoots. And there are definitely some outbursts of laughter.

Only one window opens before we get back to the albergue. We laugh even louder when a woman's voice makes a big *Shhhhhhh* sound as we fly past another incredible medieval house. Oops. We definitely *are* delinquents.

CHAPTER 26

SHANIA REYNOLDS

Friday, July 5th – Day 7 – Is that even possible? 7 Days? & Diego!

Last night was a blast, but we're all feeling it this morning. Still, I'm not bitter about it or anything.

When we got back to the albergue, all the peregrinos were in the common room gathered around the big fireplace. Guess who was sitting on the ginormous hearth playing some beaten up acoustic guitar and singing some folksong? Yeah. Bastien. The man who can do everything.

Of course we joined them. That old man sang for over an hour. Felt like we were at a concert. All the other peregrinos clapped like mad and shouted their praises at him. And when he sang "American Pie" for Kei and his sisters… I could cry just thinking about it now. All the Americans in the room, they got wild excited. Some lady cried and sang along. She couldn't sing, but she did anyway. And, yeah, it was beautiful.

I love Bastien. I think every single peregrino in this whole refugio loves the man. They're all swarming him right now as he tries to finish the last of his breakfast. They're thanking him, and taking pictures with him, and laughing and shaking his hand. And he's taking it all in. The old man is drinking in every drop of this affection. I love him. And he's all ours. He's walking with our group again today. He told us he would make sure we all got to Fonfría in one piece. And when he said that, he winked at Diego… who tapped the bandage on his forehead and laughed.

So we're all hungover, but not from booze. Just… just… from what? Life. We're life hungover.

And we're about to head out to the worst climbing day of our Camino. Mountain day. My legs don't feel like mine. They're harder. I hope I don't get all Hulk muscles down there.

Oh. Yeah. Bright side. As if the whole entry wasn't all bright sides already. Diego. It's official. We're an item. Not entirely sure what that means, but I love the sound of it. Man, I hated the guy on day one. Who would've thunk it? Total boyfriend material, though. All mama's boys are.

I finish with my journal and tuck it into my backpack. I'm ready, really I am.

"*Buen Camino,*" a woman says to me as she places her passport into a breast pocket in her shirt and closes the snap over the pocket. That reminds me. I still need to get my passport stamped. I smile and return her Buen Camino before she slips out the door with a group of pilgrims.

I get my passport stamped by the hostess and thank her for everything. It's been amazing.

Everyone's here, ready to go. Even Claire. She may have given up on making us wait every day. I'm guessing we're all a little softer than we were on day one. Maybe Gilbert knows what he's doing with this program. Maybe it's not all a bunch of granola crunch bullshit after all.

"Okay, we go," Bastien says as he clicks his walking stick on the floor to get our attention. He doesn't just get ours. Everyone left in the albergue turns toward the sound of his voice. "Goodbye, my fellow peregrinos. May the god you choose go with you this day. Fonfría, Fonfría."

He turns and heads out the door to a dozen or so goodbye *Buen Camino*s from those we'll leave behind. He waves, and we follow him outside.

"This is a day in your lives," Bastien says as we assemble around him on the narrow cobbled roadway. He points the way. "This is the way."

And we're off.

"Boy's coming with me for a bit," Manny says, hauling Diego away from me. Diego makes a show of struggling to stay with me, but we're both good with it. I nudge myself over to Bastien and decide to walk with him.

"Salut, ma chère," he says. As we walk, I'm somehow comforted by the clicking of his stick. "Today is to be beautiful beyond measure."

"That's good to hear. Everyone's been building it up so much, it's getting pretty scary in my head."

"No, no. We have conditioned for the climb, no?"

"Actually, I was kind of thinking that. My legs feel stronger."

"We will walk beside highways today, and in woods, and on cliff-sides, and through small towns. A little bit of everything. All uphill."

He had me right up to the end. Oh, well.

"Hey, can we walk with you guys?" Troy asks. I'm glad Kei's sister let him go on ahead with us. Before we came along, he was pretty much walking by himself anyway.

"Sure," I say. "Bastien's just giving me the highlights for today."

"My sister told me to drink lots of water," Kei says. Troy rolls his eyes. "She said she didn't want to come upon my body in the woods later."

"Ha ha. Yes. The last woods before Fonfría, they will be the worst. They are, how do you say, never-ending."

We start an incline as we head out of O Cebreiro. It opens up to highway soon after we leave the town and it's all winding road. We walk beside a guardrail, and the view is incredible. I can see for miles.

We walk for a mile or so in silence. Everyone's trying to find their pace with the incline, which seems to increase with every step. There's a constant grshh, grshh, grshh sound of crunching gravel as we make our way, punctuated by the fump, fump, fump of Bastien's stick on the shifting surface.

"Look at that," Troy says, breaking the silence we've fallen into. "Wow! What is that?"

"That is where we come from, Troy. The town. O Cebreiro." Bastien points with his stick. "See. The church of the Madonna miracle. There."

"Oh. I didn't realize. Yeah. I can see all the roofs. Weird."

"We travel in a wobble today. Very confusing."

"Yeah, I thought it would be over there." Troy points in the other direction.

"Yes," Bastien says. "Wobble, wobble. Here, there."

We continue in silence, like we all know talking is too much of an energy drain. It's a constant climb. We need to conserve our energy. The only one talking nonstop is Manny. He's up ahead talking Diego's ear off, like the climb is nothing for him.

I don't hear Diego saying much in return. Seems like a one-way conversation.

We soon arrive at another small town. Diego and Manny get there first, but we're not far behind them. And Meagan and Gilbert are right behind us. *Liñares*, the sign at the entrance says.

We stop and allow Claire and Greg to catch up with us. Everyone is breathing heavily. I feel like, we made it! But I know we're not even close. The sun hasn't climbed much in the sky since we set out. Still morning.

"Phew," Meagan says. "That was hard work."

"Seriously," Greg says. He sounds like he's going to die. Or cry. Or both. Since we're all standing still, he starts to tear off his backpack.

"No, no, wise guy," Gilbert says. "We're not stopping. No breaks yet. We were just waiting for everyone to catch up."

"Oh my God, you're killing me. This is child abuse." Greg moans, but readjusts his backpack. "I'm reporting you to Children's Aid."

"Good luck with that," Meagan says. We all laugh, but not too much. Because, you know, we're all dying.

"We walk into town together," Bastien says. "Soon, we come to a break, Greg. After we leave town, there is something to see. We stop then, oui?"

"Oh, yes. I know where you mean," Meagan says. She takes out her pretty-much-destroyed guidebook and checks it. "Yes. We'll definitely stop there, Bastien. The kids will want to take pictures."

"Yes." He takes a drink of water. He's been taking sips regularly since we first set out. I wonder how old he really is. He must be at least seventy. Today, it's showing.

Troy and Kei share a bottle, while everyone else goes for their own bottles. It's like we all took the cue from Bastien. We keep walking into the town. It's still uphill, but there are flat parts here as well.

Halfway through the town, Gilbert points to a church. We all slow down, but nobody stops. He walks as he reads from his guidebook.

"La Igrexa de Santo Ex—"

"Estevo," Bastien corrects. "This simply means the Church of Santo Estevo. This church, it is from the twelfth century."

I take a quick sidelong shot, stopping just long enough for it to not be blurry. I'm pretty sure I've taken more pics than anyone else in our group. Maybe when I get home, I'll start a blog.

This makes me think of home, and I push the thought away because it's depressing. Diego can't wait to get to Santiago so he can go home and see his mom. I want to see the cathedral, and get there and all, but I don't want this trip to end. The last thing I want to do is go home. I feel so alone there. I think I'd die without Dillon. Dweeb that he is.

Soon, we are outside the town. After we pass the mile marker, we hit a rough pathway that runs alongside the road. I glance behind me for Greg's reaction to the path ahead of us, and he rolls his eyes. It is literally straight up.

"Greg's not a happy camper," I say to Bastien.

"Soon we stop," Bastien says.

"I'm not too happy myself," Troy says. But his face is beaming. He and Kei have been holding hands since we left the albergue.

"Only a mile up this hill, kiddos," Meagan calls back to us. I sigh with relief, but the moan from behind me tells me either Greg's not buying it or he thinks a mile is too much.

"Too little, too late, lady," he says to Meagan. "You're still being reported."

"Sure thing, bucko. Just keep walking. You're the only one complaining."

"I'm the only one brave enough."

He could be right.

We walk on. The guys ahead of us pick up their pace a bit, but we stay back with Bastien.

As we come toward the top of this hill, everything opens up around us. A statue comes into view. At first I can only see the top, and then more and more of it. A man holding his hat on his head, fighting against a heavy wind as he walks into it.

And it's true. Even today, on this impossibly hot day when we're all sweating buckets under this hot sun, there's a wind here. It's only hot air, but still. Definitely a wind.

"Alto de San Roque," Bastien says. Meagan and Manny and Diego and Gil have already made it to the statue. They stand waiting for us. "That peregrino, he fights the winds of the top of the world, yes?"

We can see all the way across to the mountains in the distance. It looks like we're even with them. We're so high. The wind is strongest by the statue.

We all remove our bags. Greg collapses beside the statue and spreads himself flat out in the grass. Claire sits cross-legged beside him. Troy and Kei climb the stairs at the back of the statue and go right up to it to take a bunch of selfies together. They're building their Camino memories in pictures.

I think of doing the same thing with Diego, but hopefully we will have a life together after the Camino. At least *we* both live in the same city. Troy and Kei won't have that option. I lie down in the grass beside Greg while Bastien sits down on the short stone wall beneath the statue and lets out a deep sigh. He's done. And we're not even there yet. Poor Bastien.

Diego finally makes his way over to me.

"Hey, you," he says. He sits between me and Claire and leans down to give me a peck on the cheek. "You okay?"

"Sure. It's hard, but not so bad. Look at these views."

"Amazing, right. It's so dope the way the guy is bent into the wind like that," he says, pointing up to the statue. "It's like you can see him fighting against it. Like he's a real person. Perfect."

"Yeah," I say. "The actual wind is part of the statue. Hey, wanna walk together after this?"

"I'd like that, Shan." He takes his eyes away from the statue and smiles like his face will break, like this is exactly what he wanted.

"Sure, leave poor Manny out of it. I can take a hint."

"Walk with us, bro," Greg says. It's the first sign of life he's given since flopping on the ground. He doesn't even open his eyes.

"Thanks, bud. A true friend."

"Whatever," Diego says. "Pffffft."

"Hehe." Manny laughs and gives Diego a peace sign. "Just kidding."

"When are we leaving?" Troy says, coming down from the statue. Kei follows close behind him. "We're ready to go."

Everyone just looks at Troy. He's way too perky. I'd hit him but I'm not about to get up off the ground to do it. Too wiped.

CHAPTER 27

TROY SINCLAIR

AFTER THE SHORT BREAK AT Alto de San Roque, I can't help but feel sad. It seems stupid to get so emotionally involved with someone. Kei and I took so many selfies at the statue. But looking at them hurts. It only makes me realize how short this relationship is destined to be.

No matter how many likes my new *us* profile pic gets, he's going to disappear once we get to Santiago de Compostela. He'll be this dream that may or may not have happened. This pretty boy who may have been.

It's depressing as hell.

"Hey. Penny for your thoughts?"

"I was just thinking about us, actually." I'm walking blindly, holding his hand and flicking through pictures one-handed. I'm putting my faith entirely in him to guide me past any danger zones I don't see.

"Cute pics, right?" he says. "I changed my profile pic too."

"I know. You tagged me," I say. Facebook friends already. It must be love. "My dad's probably gonna friend you so he can grill you on the importance of safe sex on the Camino."

"Shut up," he screams.

"How do you think I feel? I have to live with the man."

"My dad doesn't know I'm gay. I don't think he'd care. He's pretty liberal, but my sisters don't want me to tell him. They panic about everything. They feel responsible for him since my mom died. They mother both of us."

"It sounds nice though. I mean that they try so hard."

"Yeah. They're pretty amazing. They just don't ever turn it off. I can't believe they allowed me to walk ahead of them. It's unreal. Even if they did change their itinerary to stay in the same albergue. They don't usually let me out of their sight."

I put my phone in my pocket. I stopped looking at pictures a while ago.

"You seem lucky to me," I say. "My brother and I? We don't have much in common. I mean, he's okay. But we're not as close as we should be. Dad tries, but it doesn't work if it's forced. You wouldn't find us on the Camino together."

"Whatcha talking about up here?" Claire asks, coming up alongside us. "Ooh, look. Another town."

"Another break, I hope," Greg says from behind us. He catches up with Claire just as we arrive at the mile marker.

Straight ahead is a sign. *Hospital da Condesa K.145.*

"One forty-five," Greg moans, almost crying. "How is that even possible? All that climbing. All that walking. That's all we did so far today? We're in *The Twilight Zone* on some kind of treadmill that keeps changing the scenery while we stay in place. I'm gonna die."

"You sound like me when we started out." Shania is quite a bit ahead of us, but anyone within a five-mile radius would have been able to hear Greg's lament.

When we walk into the town proper, the road is cobbled, and there are short stone walls on either side. The others have stopped just up ahead at the building to the right. They head toward its doors while Gil stands in front of it, waving us inside like an air traffic controller.

"This way, folks," he says, waving his arms dramatically. "This way. Lunchtime."

"Thank God and sweet baby Jesus," Greg says, ripping his backpack off his shoulders. It falls to the ground, and he makes a big show of bending down to pick it up.

Claire gives me this look, and it's like we're spiritually connected or something. I laugh.

"No," she says. "Thank—"

And in unison we both say, "Sweet Creepy Jesus of Cacabelos."

We laugh hysterically, like pee-our-pants level laughter. Gilbert looks at us suspiciously, but everyone else just looks at us like we're crazy. We complete the transaction with a high five.

"In you get, all of you. Let's go, let's go." Gilbert finishes his arm-waving and follows us inside.

The others are already sitting at a table.

"What was that Jesus thing all about?" Kei asks me. I pull out my phone to find my Creepy Jesus pics and show him. "Ah. Okay. Yeah, I did *not* see that. *That*, I would remember."

"Washroom?" I say to no one in particular. I'm about to burst. Shania points to the far corner of the café, and I make a run for it.

"I'll get you a café con leche and a piece of Camino cake," Kei says.

"Sounds good," I say, waving as I leave.

Gilbert corrects Kei before the washroom door closes behind me. "Tarta de Santiago, Kei."

When I come back out, everyone's staring at Claire's phone screen and laughing. She's no doubt showing them Creepy Jesus.

"And how many other times have you guys snuck off on these middle-of-the-night outings without our knowledge," Gil asks. His voice is stern, like we're about to head for a month of after-school detention. But his face belies him. His eyes are filled with laughter.

"Just that one time, boss," Claire says. She unconsciously pulls some Skittles out of her pocket and pops a few. "Unless you count that time we snuck out and went to the rave in Ponferrada on day one. At the castle. So many drugs. Manny even hooked up with a puta."

"Okay," Gil says. "You totally had me until the Manny part. Can't picture that. But bonus points for knowing how to say hooker in Spanish. I'm impressed, Claire. You guys really *are* learning something on the Camino."

We all laugh. Bastien shakes his head and *tsk tsk*s us but he's also laughing. I'm going to miss these people. And not just Kei. All of them. Even Greg.

"What's wrong?" Kei asks in the silence that follows the laughter.

"Nothing," I tell him. "Absolutely nothing."

"You just looked sad there for a sec."

"Nostalgic. For *this*. For this moment. Does that makes sense?"

"Totally," he says. "Yeah, I get it. I keep missing things as they're happening out here. Like everything that's making me happy is also making me sad."

"Exactly." I almost shout. I hold a hand over my heart. Bastien smiles. He's been listening to our conversation. He slowly nods his understanding and puts a hand over his own heart.

"Saudade," Bastien says. The other conversations at the table die away as the others hear him speak. "It is Portuguese."

"Seriously, Bastien," Shania says. "Is there any language you don't know?"

He smiles but he has something to say. And I for one want to hear it.

"It means nostalgia. Deep, deep in the heart nostalgia. A, how you say, melancholy. For something missing, something absent. Something you want but may never again have. Saudade."

"That's it, Bastien. Yeah," Kei says. "I get sad thinking how much I'll miss everything that's happening. The moment."

"Much like saudade, yes?" Bastien says. "Maybe not so much in the English. But close. Missingness? My wife, she say... give me a moment."

He looks into the distance as he recalls his wife's words. In all this time, I never once heard him mention a wife. Actually, I'm not sure he's said anything personal about himself.

"Ah, oui," he says. "My Simone, she say, *the love that remains*. When the person is gone. Or, maybe, for us now, when the place is gone. When the Camino family is gone. Saudade. The love that remains."

Everyone is completely silent when Bastien finishes speaking. And not just everyone at our table. Those close by have also been listening. Bastien wipes an errant tear from his eye. He laughs, but it's a laugh with a deep sense of... of saudade.

"Wow." It's Diego who breaks the silence. Tears well in his eyes. "Saudade. Yes."

"You, my friend. You know, yes?" Bastien says. "Your abuelita, no?"

"Yes," Diego says. He nods deeply, and Bastien nods with him. When I turn to look at Kei to see if he's taking in this emotional moment, he's also nodding. We can all understand the feeling we were reaching to define.

Leave it to Bastien to define it.

"My wife," he says, mostly to Diego. "She pass. In March. Four months ago. Her heart, it was tired. I am loss without her. Lost. We were together for fifty-three years. Long time, yes? Saudade."

I want to jump up and hug this sweet man. My heart hurts for him. I look to Kei again, and he puts a hand on my knee under the table and makes this face like his heart just melted away to nothing. Another follower of the Church of Bastien.

"I'm so sorry, Bastien," Meagan says. And we all offer our belated condolences while Bastien attempts to make light of the moment, even though he has just described in perfect detail how overwhelming what he's feeling is.

"We go," he finally says, incapable of receiving any more of our affection.

We gather our mugs and plates and phones and journals and stuff and head to the front of the café.

"Passports, guys," Meagan says. But she doesn't have to tell us. It's automatic now. We already have them out. "Well-trained, children. Well-trained."

Greg gives her a dirty look. "Who you calling children?"

"Just you children, Greg."

"Well played, Meags," he says. He presents his passport to the man behind the counter. The man stamps it and gives it back to Greg with a *Buen Camino*. One after the other, we all get stamped.

Once we're finished, we head for the exit and search through the dozens of backpacks for our own, haul them up, and leave the café behind.

CHAPTER 28

DIEGO NELSON

Well, that was more emotional than I thought it would be. That word. It almost killed me. It's how I've been feeling for days. Like something is missing. Like I left my heart somewhere, but I can't remember where.

Saudade. Yep. Thank the universe for Bastien.

I kind of wish I didn't cry, though. Now it feels like Shania is mothering me again. She's holding my hand but like she has to. Not like she wants to. Sometimes I feel like a bird with a broken wing. I just want to see Moms.

"The church here is exactly like the one back in O Cebreiro. Look," she says.

"Yeah. Sort of. Same roof." The Galician cross rises out of the top of it. The same one that was on the cake back at the café. I don't really have anything else to say, though. We keep walking in silence, and I know Shania feels pretty useless. I don't want her to. It's just… I'm not sure there's anything anyone could say or do that will reach me. Maybe they're not supposed to. Maybe I'm supposed to be sad.

"Where are we even going tonight?" Manny asks, coming out of nowhere from behind us. "Does anyone remember?"

"*Um*, Fonfría," Shania says. She's such a smartass. Queen of Sarcasm. "Literally everyone but you remembers, loser."

"Oh, yeah," he replies. "Thanks for breaking it to me gently."

"Manny, you kill me," she says. Manny starts talking to her about the music he's listening to, and I let go of her hand.

"You guys walk. Go ahead, Shan. I'm good."

"No, no."

"Really," I kiss her. She turns back to Manny, and they keep talking as they move on at a quicker pace than my dragging, sorry ass is willing to go. I'm probably better off by myself for a bit. No need to pull Shania down with me.

"Wait," Greg says from somewhere behind me. "Are we actually going downhill? Praise God."

Dude has lost his juice.

"Not for long," Meagan says. She is walking ahead with Gil, Bastien, and Claire. Now I get why Greg is behind me. I think he's doing it again. Shadowing me because I'm alone. Because I'm sad.

After a few more minutes of walking alone, someone comes alongside me, and I assume it's Greg. But when I look out the corner of my eye, I realize it isn't. The man has a beard and is wearing what seems to be a Tilley hat. He's also using two walking sticks, which I can't believe I didn't hear.

"Buen Camino," he says in an Australian accent. He's wearing a jacket in this heat. He must be nuts. I give him a look, and he says, "Yeah. I know. Getting a lot of those looks. I'm actually hot. I put this on this morning and haven't stopped to take it off."

"Buen Camino," I say. "It's gotta be almost eighty-five degrees out here. You should be dying in that thing."

"Yeah," he says. "Where I come from it's thirty, but I hear you. I really should put it away. Don't know why I even brought it. I just started back in Cacabelos. You must be American, then?"

He talks a lot. Dude doesn't even stop to breathe.

"No, Canada. I was translating the temperature. I thought Australia did Fahrenheit like the States. Oops. Sorry."

"Yeah, we're part of the Evil Empire, just like you." He smiles, transfers one of his walking sticks to the other hand and offers his hand for me to shake. When he takes his hand back, he says, "Bill. From Darwin, Australia."

"Diego. Toronto. So you just started out? Who you with?"

"All alone. I was on my way to Paris and made a side trip. Always wanted to experience the Camino de Santiago. Better a little bit of it than none. Paris next week and England the following week. Abbey Road. The Beatles. A little trip to relive the glory days. That'll be my *real* pilgrimage."

"You don't look old enough." There's gray in his hair, but not a lot. Beatles are more my grandmother's era than Moms's.

"There is no *old enough*, Diego. And no young enough. The Beatles are for everyone."

"Huh," I say. "Maybe."

"Ain't no maybe about it. I'm forty-eight. They're my band just as much as my father's."

"I kind of dig 'Yesterday.' Not trying to be funny, but 'The Long and Winding Road' too."

"Nice one," Bill says. "I've seen enough of that in the past couple of days to last me the rest of my days."

"My abuelita—my grandmother—played those songs for me. I love them because I loved her."

Greg comes up alongside us. He gives me a look that says *I'm here for you, dude*, looking all sympathetic.

"That's sweet, Diego," Bill says. "It was nice talking to you. I'm off. Trying to do this thing in less time than it takes. Time to motor on. Onward and upward, right?"

"Buen Camino, Bill," I say.

"Maybe we'll see you in Santiago. Who knows? Buen Camino, Diego." He nods hello to Greg and says "Buen Camino" again.

"Buen Camino," Greg says. And the stranger from Australia is off. I watch as he passes by Manny and Shania, and then Claire, Bastien, Gil, and Meagan, exchanging *Buen Caminos* with all.

I look at Greg and he still has that sympathetic look on his face. I pat his shoulder. "I'm okay, dude. Really. I'll be fine."

"Just checking, Diego. Good deal. Glad to hear it. I'm here if you need me."

"Thanks, bud. Appreciate it."

We're walking on a sort of laneway now. Rocks and pebbles. My calves are burning, so we must be starting another uphill climb. Here goes.

Sure enough, we're soon all huffing and puffing. Those ahead have slowed down, so we're all walking together. We're all struggling together. Manny and Shania have come back to join me and Greg. I take Shania's hand, but soon it becomes too hard to hold hands and climb.

"Holy hell," Troy says. He and Kei are leading the pack up the hill, but he's losing ground. "I can't do this."

"Up, up, up," Bastien says. "I'm seventy-four years old, Troy. You can do this."

"Don't make me feel bad about complaining, Bastien. It helps me climb this ridiculous hill."

Bastien laughs, but cuts it short to catch his breath. "Merde," he mumbles.

"Bastien," Meagan says, exaggerating her disgust. "You wash your mouth out."

"Oui, oui," he says. But he brushes her comment away with his hand and laughs again.

"What's it mean? What's it mean?" Manny says. He's the only one not struggling on this endless hill.

"It means shit," Kei says. Troy's mouth opens in a big O of shock.

"Some genius you are, Manny," Claire says. "And you call yourself Canadian? Even an American knows more French than you."

"Kei!" Troy says. He punches Kei's shoulder, but he laughs.

"What? It's only shit," Kei says. A burst of laughter goes through the whole group.

"Troy wouldn't say shit if his mouth was full of it," Claire says.

And we all lose it again. Bastien has to stop walking as he coughs out the last of his laughter. We all fall back into silence and struggle the rest of the way up the path.

After another half hour of endless, relentless climbing, Meagan chirps, "Finally. Thank goodness."

"What? What?" Greg asks. "Please tell me."

"Alto do Poio. Now, we are highest." Bastien says this like he's saying a prayer. He looks as though he could pass out any minute. And I don't think his age has anything to do with it, because I definitely feel the same way. "We are at the top of the world, now, my fellow peregrinos."

There's a general sigh of relief among the group, but just when relief is setting in, it's disrupted by Greg.

"That's what you said at the last Alto place, Bastien. And I was stupid enough to believe you then. You're going to get reported, too, if you're not careful."

He winks at Bastien when it's clear Bastien's not quite sure he's kidding. Bastien winks back and smiles.

"This is the *other* top of the world," Bastien says. We all laugh. "Almost there, my friends. Maybe four kilometers." He holds his thumb and forefinger together in a pinch. "Not quite. Little bit less, maybe?"

"I'm holding you to it," Greg says.

We walk on until we come to a sign that says *Alto do Poio – altitud 1.335m.*

"That sign's high," Greg says.

Shania says, "Oh, you're good."

He bows and almost loses his balance. Note to self, don't try to bow while walking uphill.

Soon we come to a large white building at the side of the road with a green awning that says Bar *Puerto O Poio.*

"Those are magic words," Greg says.

"Yeah," Gil says. "We're stopping here, Greg. But you can just ignore the first word. If you're lucky you can watch Bastien and me drink a beer."

"You're mean," Greg replies.

"Yep." Gil turns into the dirt driveway and we head toward the front door, passing a small group of peregrinos milling around outside at the tables scattered about. The red chairs all have the Coca-Cola logo across their backs, and I think that's the best idea of the day. I'd kill for a Coke about now.

"Gang, if Bastien and Kei will excuse us," Gil says, looking at the two of them with an apologetic smile, "It's time we had some alone time. Talk a few things over."

"Now? Can't we stop and catch our breath first?" Greg says. He's full-on whine now. "Can I at least get a Coke before our meeting starts?"

"Of course, Greg," Meagan says. "Don't be foolish. Bastien and Kei? After we all have a bio break and grab snacks and drinks, the eight of us are going to meet back here at this table." She sits down to claim the table in question. "You two will wait for us, right?"

"Sure," Kei says. He heads into the café.

"I'll sit with Kei. You go, you go. You have your little meeting of the criminals. Go, go." Bastien winks and sets his eye on a table across the patio.

"Thanks, Bastien," Meagan says as he makes his way over to the table, drops his backpack, and slumps into a chair. He's obviously exhausted.

"Well," Gil says. "Back here in five, gang. See you then."

There's a Coke in there with my name on it.

CHAPTER 29

SHANIA REYNOLDS

Friday, July 5th – Day 7 – Oh My God! Fonfría Forever! Long Live Fonfría!

We're here. I'm not leaving, ever. This place is incredible. It was pretty cool up in the common house. I was already happy there. With the games room and the couches and the everything else. But then we came down here, to the dining hall. I'm speechless. This is going to be a short entry. I can't stop looking around. It's this little stone building, just down the hill from the albergue. Completely round, with this high, high roof that looks like straw. It's all one room.

What's weird is… it's SO much bigger on the inside than it appeared to be on the outside. And we're all sitting at this gigantic table that curves and follows the round shape of the room. Diego snagged us chairs on the inside, against the wall. He's the best.

Greg sits down on my other side and his presence gives me a reason to chuck my journal aside. I stick my pen in my back pocket and take a drink of water.

"Hey," he says. "How's the journaling going for you? I can't seem to keep up."

"I guess okay. I keep writing in it, anyway. Where's yours?"

"In my backpack. In my room." I give him a strange look. I don't even have to say anything. "Yeah. I hear ya. Loud and clear. I can't write in it if I don't take it out."

"Glad we're on the same frequency. Exactly what I was thinking."

"Hey, can I have your bun?" Diego asks. He can never get enough to eat. I didn't notice this when we weren't so close. I guess he's only comfortable asking me for all my food now, after we've exchanged saliva. I roll my eyes but I also hand over my bun. "Thanks, Shan."

"You never share your buns with me," Greg says.

"Ha ha." Funny guy.

We're interrupted by this boom, followed by a loud clacking sound that makes me jump a little. At the end of the table, the hostess, Rosa, stands with a pot in one hand and an incredibly large wooden spoon in the other. It's the decorative kind old people have on their kitchen walls, more like a paddle than a spoon. You could definitely steer a canoe across Lake Ontario with it.

There's a murmur from all the peregrinos, ourselves included.

"Tonight, we dance," she says. Her husband Paulo comes through the front door. He wheels this enormous pot in front of him. It looks like a witch's cauldron. As he comes to a stop beside his wife, she sets the pot down on the end of the table and sticks the spoon into the cauldron.

Paulo shrieks like a banshee, and there are more murmurs and gasps among the peregrinos. And laughter. The anticipation in the room is electric.

Beside me, I hear Greg mumble, "Whoa." Out of the corner of my eye, I can see him sitting there with his mouth wide open, waiting.

Something amazing is about to happen. I can feel it. I take my eyes off the cauldron just long enough to glance at Diego. His face is filled with laughter, and it makes me happy. I reach for his hand under the table, and he finds mine and squeezes. We turn our attention back to the couple, afraid we'll miss something.

Everyone across the table from us are now either turned sideways in their seats or have turned their chairs to face the couple; their mostly eaten suppers are forgotten.

"But first, we make magic," Rosa says. "And then we drink!" She begins to stir the contents of the cauldron with the oversized spoon. When she stops, she picks up an orange and a knife and holds them above her head.

Then, as she begins to remove the orange peel with the knife, she starts to tell us a story about the concoction she's making. The room is a din, but I swear she says something like, "Owls, barn owls, toads, and witches." Like a real-life incantation. This is Harry Potter stuff.

The peel just keeps spiralling and spiralling above the cauldron, in one continuous piece. This lady doesn't stop until the orange is completely bald. Now, that's impressive. The peel falls away from the orange and disappears into the liquid brewing in the cauldron below. Then she stabs the orange with her knife a bunch of times and drops it in after the peel.

Rosa says, "Demons, devils, goblins." Then she asks Paulo for something that sounds like *orujo*. Paulo comes back to the cauldron with two large bottles of alcohol, holds them higher than his head, and pours. The streams fall right into the cauldron as he whoops out loud.

I hear something about worms, vermin, witchcraft, and the tears of Mother Earth. She says something about water and goes on to tell us more about the ritual. She calls it something, but with everybody oohing and awing it's hard to hear her. It sounds like *Queimada*. I think she's saying a spell *and* explaining things as she goes, so it's hard to tell which is spell and which is explanation.

My phone is dying or I would film this entire thing. Dillon would so devour this stuff. I can't believe I wish my brother was here, but I kind of do.

I don't know where Paulo puts the bottles of booze, but he dances back to the cauldron, spins around it, and drops something inside. Raisins?

"Coffee beans," Rosa says, smiling at her husband as he steps over to the table to grab something else. He picks up a little burlap satchel tied with twine.

"Now you're speaking my language," Troy says from his seat across the table from us. He's a coffee hound. He and Kei exchange a look and burst into laughter.

"That man is gor*geous*," Kei says, a bit louder than I think he meant to. If I can hear it, so can everyone else around us. Kei's hand springs to his mouth, which forms a surprised *oh*. He and Troy laugh some more and lean toward each other to whisper. Pathetically cute.

He's so right, though. Everyone in the room knows Paulo is gorgeous. He's Black, with a goatee, and gray peppers his hair and beard. He wears a tight white V-neck T-shirt that shows off his iron-man body. Kei is *not* wrong.

Rosa does the peeling thing all over again with a lemon. Then another. She talks nonstop about the ritual warding-off of evil spirits. When she says something about the clay pot and how it represents Mother Earth, it's the first time I notice the cauldron isn't cast iron.

Rosa says something about Satan and Beelzebub's inferno, burning corpses, mutilated bodies. When I hear, "farts of the asses of doom," I turn and look at Diego. He's already looking at me. He squeezes my hand and smirks. For a split second, we're frozen in time. Then we burst out laughing before turning back to the show. That's what it is, really. A show for the peregrinos.

Paulo opens the little pouch and dumps the contents into the cauldron with a fanning of his hand, like he's performing magic, while Rosa tells us what they are.

"Sugar, yes. And spices we will not say. Secret spices for the evil spirits." She winks. It's all so over the top. I can't stop smiling, though. It's so awesome.

Rosa continues with the spell, mentioning unmarried women, cats, goats, brooms, and sand. She pulls out a big-ass ladle and begins to madly stir the concoction with it.

Paulo lights this thing that looks like one of the torches the villagers used in *Beauty and the Beast* when they stormed the castle. It's all straw and crap, twined tightly on the end of a wooden stick. As quickly as it appears, he's touched a lighter to it and it explodes into flames.

Peregrinos gasp, hoot, and clap. I can't believe the things that keep happening to us on this trip. Amazing. After the first peregrino leaves his chair, we all follow his lead. It's a swarm to the front as we race for the best views of the couple and their cauldron.

As Rosa reaches into the mixture with the ladle and hauls out a full scoop, Paulo touches his torch to it almost quicker than the eye can see. The liquid in the ladle comes to life with fire. But not just any fire, it's all blue and rainbow-tinged and dancing up the handle of the ladle, threatening to consume Rosa.

With just a little blow, Paulo extinguishes the torch, drops it to the floor, and kicks it to the corner of the room behind them. He doesn't even look back to make sure it's fully out. I bet he's done this a million times, perfected the act.

Everyone claps as Rosa lifts the ladle high to allow the blue-flamed potion to pour back into the cauldron. We giggle as the liquid's surface in the cauldron bursts into flame. She scoops and pours, scoops and pours, scoops and pours over and over again.

"Hear roars of those burning in firewater." Her face is deathly serious, except for the laughter in her eyes that gives it all away.

"And when we drink this beverage," she promises in her incantation, "we're free of the evil in our souls and of any charms against us."

After a couple minutes, she ends her spell with an invitation to friends to join them in their *Queimada*. She nods in Troy's direction, motions for him to join her. She couldn't have picked a better assistant. He's bouncing up and down and practically crying with excitement. He makes his way over to her like he's the next contestant on *The Price is Right*. She hands him the ladle and mimes the movements she made with it.

Troy lifts a full ladle of the fiery potion as high as he can before tilting it and allowing it to pour back down into the cauldron. Greg has his phone out and is taking pic after pic of Troy as he ladles again and again.

Rosa makes a motion for the return of the ladle, and Troy reluctantly gives it back to her. She invites the next person and the next. Anyone who wants to goes up and copies her ritual, and soon almost everyone in the room has taken part.

"The fire drink that banishes evil, yes?" Rosa says once the noise has died. Then she slams the lid onto the cauldron and lifts it off almost immediately. All the flames are gone. Tendrils of smoke rise from the cauldron.

"And now we drink," Rosa says. From nowhere, Paulo wheels over a cart filled with clear glass mugs. Rosa begins to sloppily ladle the punch over the mugs, back and forth. She gets nearly as much on the tray as in the mugs. Soon, they're all full. "Together," she says.

Greg looks around for Gilbert or Meagan and finally spots them. With one look I know he's asking them if we can have some, because of the alcohol.

"Just this one time," Gil says. He tries to put on a stern expression, but it doesn't quite work. He hasn't broken a single blood vessel since I decided to stop swearing around him a couple days back. He's lightweight. "Don't think about making a habit of it."

"Yes, sir," Greg says. He salutes Gil and turns back to us, all smiles. "Shall we?"

We do. And it's so good. The fire's gone, but I can feel the heat of the drink all the way down to my toes. So good. What a bizarre taste. I hope I don't forget how to describe it when I try to relive this moment for Dill. Wow. Fonfría!

CHAPTER 30

TROY SINCLAIR

It's gonna be a hard day for everyone. Not just me and Kei because we stayed up all night talking. And not just because everyone's exhausted from yesterday's walk.

Every peregrino back at that albergue was pumped after the potion show last night. Even Bastien, who scoffed and called it silly hocus pocus.

Can we pause for a moment to appreciate the fact an old man like Paulo can look so fine and dance even finer? *Paulo. Insta*-crush. For both Kei and me. We heard someone say they thought he's Cuban. However he got to Fonfría, we're just happy he got there. Paulo's pic got more likes on my Instagram than any other pic from the trip so far. And, he's like fifty. That's gotta say something.

He taught us how to samba. After that potion, Paulo taught everyone how to move. Not just Kei and me because we wouldn't leave him alone. We were like a couple of schoolgirls. At one point there were thirty-plus peregrinos dancing around that big room in a conga line. *That* just does not happen anywhere.

Kei's sisters missed the punch, but they got there in time for the dancing. Mia is an amazing dancer. So is Becky, actually. Kei? Not so much. I was so embarrassed for him. It was painful watching him and even more painful knowing he *thought* he was amazing.

Anyway, we're all tired and dragging our feet today. We stayed up too late. Diego's worried because Bastien stayed at the albergue to get another hour of rest. He said he would find us later tonight, but I don't think Diego believed him. It's like Diego's lost his faith in humanity.

It's also just the four of us. So much for walking as a group. It was nice while it lasted. Even Greg. I wouldn't have any pics of me playing with that fiery punch if not for him. He's really trying.

Diego didn't want to leave when everyone else was ready, so Shania asked if we could wait around with her.

Claire, Greg, and Manny went with Meagan and Gil. They're supposed to meet us here in Triacastela, but we've been dragging our asses all day. Diego's clearly attempting to stall us as a ploy to give Bastien an opportunity to catch up. I'm okay with it, really. But he should just say so already.

"Well, what should we do?" I ask. We've peeked inside a couple cafés. One of them, long enough to get coffee and a stamp. "You're the boss, Shan."

"I don't know. At least we made it this far," Shania says. "If we don't find them in the next five minutes, I say we keep going. We'll find them in Samos. I'm sure they kept walking. You know Gil. After the first couple days with Claire, it drives him bonkers to wait. We're probably pissing him off big time. I say we just keep moving until we get to Samos. If we see them, we see them. If we don't, we don't."

I have to agree with her. I want to ask her to get Diego out of his funk so we can walk a little faster, but I can tell he's fragile today. I don't really feel like rocking the boat.

"I'm sorry, guys," Diego says. "It's my fault we're lagging behind." It's pretty much the first thing he said since we left Fonfría, unless of course you count the times he tried to defend his pace.

"It's no biggie, Diego," I say. He's practically dragging his feet. "We all meet up at the end of the day anyway."

"Yeah, but—"

"No. Don't do that, Diego. Come on," Shania says as she grabs his hand. "It's okay. Come on, let's go."

I feel so bad for him. I'm usually so good at talking to people, but I'm not sure how to handle this one. Poor Diego. It's like he's lost a second person. He hangs so much on Bastien for helping him deal with his grandmother.

I take Kei's hand, and we make our way out of town. Maybe Bastien will walk with Kei's sisters. Maybe, just maybe, he will somehow stay with us the rest of the way to Santiago.

*   *   *

IT'S STILL EARLY AFTERNOON WHEN we decide to part ways. Actually, it's Kei who makes the decision. We've travelled through a number of small towns, mostly in silence. The terrain has been a mix of everything from the side of a highway to a forest to fields, pretty much the way it was before the O Cebreiro to Fonfría mountain climb. It's downhill as well as uphill, so nothing too hard.

With three or four miles left to go, Kei finally can't take the pace any longer. He turns to me and says, "Let's just go already."

We're both tired of dragging our feet to keep back with Shania and Diego.

"Just wait," I say. I stop and, thankfully, he stops with me. "Hey, guys. We're gonna carry on ahead if that's okay with you. We're almost there anyway. Do you mind?"

I look first to Diego, but he doesn't make eye contact. When I look to Shania, she shrugs. She's defeated. She's not having a good day.

"Go ahead, guys. Don't worry about us. We'll be right behind you."

"Thanks." I wave and turn back to Kei. "Let's go, then. Before I change my mind."

I can't help but feel guilty. Like I'm abandoning them.

"Bye, guys. We'll see you there." Kei waves. "You okay, Diego?"

"Sure, Kei," he says. "See you when we get there."

I hope to God Bastien finds his way to our albergue tonight. Diego was keeping it together so well. Looks like he's going to crash without his savior. I don't mean that in a mean way at all. Bastien is everything.

Kei perks up almost immediately as we pick up the pace and leave the two of them behind. Soon, they're nowhere in sight.

In no time, we come upon a little creek running alongside the path. Kei consults his guidebook map to see if he can figure out what it is.

"I think it's Rio Sarria," He says, pointing to a river on the map with a long skinny finger.

"Really? That doesn't sound right. We're not going to Sarria until tomorrow."

"Well, look." We stop dead in the path. The sound of the gently flowing water makes me realize just how hot I feel. And sweaty. Kei's finger traces the river on the map and, sure enough, it passes through Samos. It looks like it follows the path all the way into town.

"Huh," I say. "Who knew?"

"Well, for starters, probably the cartographers who made this map."

"You're very funny." I smack his hand and make him drop his guidebook. Before he has a chance to pick it up, I grab his shirt and pull him close. "And cute. Very, very cute. Anybody ever tell you that?"

He laughs, forgets the map. "Sure. All the time."

"They better not." I feel brave, so I pull him even closer and kiss him. "Wanna stop for a few minutes?"

"Sure," he says. He pushes me away and picks up his book. After he slips it back into the side of his backpack, he turns from the path and says, "Let's go down by the river."

"But someone may see us."

"Live a little, Troy. Besides, what were you planning on doing?"

The blood rushes to my cheeks, and I die. Then I shrug. So embarrassed.

"Ha," Kei says. "You're way too easily embarrassed. It's really cute." He takes the short grassy embankment down to the river, and I follow close behind. We're both already taking off our backpacks.

We land in a heap at the bottom and drop our packs beside us. Before I know what's happening I'm flat on my back feeling the weight of his body on top of me. He gives me a few deep kisses that leave me breathless.

Kei rolls off to my side, and I look up into the cover of trees above us and the cloudless blue sky beyond. It's a perfect day. I don't care if we're tired from last night and I don't care that we just walked for hours in misery. We're together.

The closer we get to Compostela, the more I panic about what comes after. Lying here in the grass next to Kei, I don't have to think about things like that. I can just be beside him.

I put one arm behind my head and slip the other under Kei's neck. He shimmies closer and snuggles against my chest. We sit in silence and listen to the trickle and roar of the flowing river as it makes its way into Samos.

"I could live here," Kei says. And I know he doesn't mean here, just outside Samos in the Spanish countryside. I know he means with me, just the two of us, in this moment.

"Yeah," I say as I close my eyes against the sparkle of the sun filtering between the gently shifting leaves. "Me too, Kei."

With my eyes still closed, I turn my head, lift his mess of jet-black hair, and kiss his forehead. And we fall asleep to the sound of water, the perfection of a gentle breeze, and the smells of the most perfect summer day of my life. A smell I'm sure I'll remember forever.

CHAPTER 31

DIEGO NELSON

AS WE ROUND THE CORNER onto the side street where our albergue is, Gilbert and Meagan step outside its door onto the cobbled sidewalk out front.

"Wow," Gil says, "Took you two long enough."

I smile apologetically, because I know today is totally my fault. I'm acting like a spoiled little kid. Might as well stamp my feet or kick and scream. Total temper tantrum. I did not see this funk coming. I hadn't realized how much I had come to lean on Bastien since my grandmother died.

"Sorry," I say. "My fault."

"He's just kidding, Diego. You're the first to arrive," Meagan says, beaming. "Did you see the gorgeous monastery on your way in? I say we go back and check it out while we're waiting for all the slowpokes to get here. It was one of the highlights of my first Camino. You guys'll love it."

"What? Seriously?" Shania says. She ignores Meagan's comments about the monastery. "I thought Claire, Greg, and Manny walked here with you guys?"

"Oh, yeah," Meagan says. "I meant besides Manny. He's with us. He's upstairs having a shower. Claire and Greg stopped for a rest back in… where was that, Gil?"

"Lusío," Gil says. "Yeah, they were having a rather heavy conversation, wanted to stop at a café. Manny almost stayed back with them, but changed his mind last minute. So here we are. Waiting for everyone else."

Gil glances at his wrist, pretends to look at a nonexistent watch, and shakes his head. I offer him a weak smile.

"How long have you guys been here?" Shania asks.

"Oh, almost an hour now. We had a beer at the little pub on the corner." He points behind us, and we turn and look back. There's a bar patio with tables, chairs, and umbrellas set up at the bottom of the street across from the corner we just passed.

"We're just going to go dump off our stuff and go see Manny. We'll be right back." Shania slips out of her backpack and carries it to the albergue door.

"Front desk is just inside," Meagan tells her. "Let them know you're with us. They'll give you a key. Have showers too. No hurry. We'll wait here. Tell Manny to come with you. We'll walk to the monastery together."

"Sure thing," I reply. I follow Shania inside.

I'm not worried about Kei and Troy. Doesn't take a rocket scientist to figure out what they're doing. They're probably making out somewhere.

It's Claire I'm worried about. Troy told me all about her plan to take off. Even if she *did* say she changed her mind, it doesn't mean she really did. I hope he did the right thing, trusting her enough to not tell Gil.

Shania gets the key, and we climb the narrow stairway to the top of the albergue, two flights up. Another dorm room with eight beds. We'll all be sleeping together again tonight. I hope there's a single here for Bastien. He said he would call ahead. I hope he did.

Manny's sprawled on his bed with just a towel wrapped around his waist. He's holding his phone an inch from his face and talking into it.

"Yeah, dork. You can use it. It's not a problem. Just don't go snooping around in any of my drawers or stuff. Don't make me hit you."

I hear this ridiculous giggling on the other end. Manny waves to us as we enter the room and raises a finger to let us know he'll just be a minute.

Shania heads straight for the bathroom at the back of the room. En suite. Bonus.

"Tav. You being good for Mama, right?"

"*Yessssss*, Man," a little kid voice responds, all exaggerated, with a drawn-out moan on the end.

"Can you get her for me, little dude?"

"Okay, okay. Coming up." I can hear a bunch of movement on the other end, like the kid is running with the phone. "Mama. Mama. Manny's on the phone for you."

"Tav. Tav? Hey, Tavish?" Manny says. He looks at me and shakes his head as if to say *little brothers are such a pain in the ass.* "Tavish!"

There's clatter on the other end and then silence. Manny turns the phone screen toward me as I plunk my pack on the bed right next to his and sit on the mattress. The screen is filled with the cutest little face I've ever seen. It's a miniature version of Manny's, only with a much bigger afro. And the kid's wearing a pair of black-rimmed glasses.

He turns the screen back to himself and says, "I love you, Tav. Okay. You watch our room. I'll be back in a few days, bro. Put Mama on now, 'kay."

"Sure thing, man. I'm on it. Love you, too. Bring me sumpin', 'kay?"

"You bet, little man." Manny jumps off the bed, cinches his towel tighter and heads for the door. Just as he steps outside into the hall and begins to close the door, I hear him say, "Hey, Momma."

As I hear the shower start, I lie down and try not to think about the fact that Bastien didn't walk with us today. And I try not to think about the fact Claire might be out there causing Greg a world of pain. I hope she didn't bolt. Those two were just starting to get along. I believed it when Troy told me she changed her mind about taking off. I hope he was right.

*   *   *

SHANIA TOSSES A PILLOW AT my face and it wakes me from a deep sleep where I dreamed my gran had come to meet us back in Fonfría. It was so real. I could see her sitting at that long banana-shaped table last night and watching everyone dance. Her face was full of laughter, but as I tried to make my way over to her, the conga line kept getting in my way. I was clawing my way through it, getting angry at everyone, when the pillow hit my face.

I jump up and toss the pillow to the floor with an angry, "Awwww."

"Whoa, maniac," Shania says. She's in a towel, fresh out of the shower. "Chill. It's just a pillow."

"Sorry." I let out a sigh of relief. "Dream."

"I left the room for five minutes tops. How could you possibly be dreaming?"

I smile apologetically.

"Freak. Get ready. You can jump in the shower when I get back. They're waiting for us downstairs," Shania says. She grabs her backpack and returns to the bathroom.

Manny steps back into the room. He tosses his phone onto his bed and lets his towel drop to the floor as he reaches for a change of clothes.

"Dude," I say. "I don't want to see your junk. Put it away."

"Yeah. Sure you don't. Then stop looking, my man." He pulls his boxers on, but it's too late.

"Dude."

Manny just laughs and finishes getting dressed.

*   *   *

WHEN I STEP INTO THE street, it's just the four of them waiting for me. I had hoped to at least see Troy and Kei. I knew it was too much to hope for Bastien.

I feel so much better after my shower. Like a person.

"Ready to see the Mosteiro de Samos?" Meagan asks. "It's one of my favorite places on the whole Camino."

She's excited. I can tell by the way she's practically on the balls of her feet.

"Show me the way." I can feel myself clawing up out of today's funk. Shania takes my hand, and we head down the street.

The monastery is just around the corner. It's humongous, the first thing we saw as we approached the town. It's a great big sprawling fortress, a compound of buildings with a garden right in the middle of it. Pretty much looks like a little village all by itself.

Along the way, Meagan fills us in on what we're about to see, and how we can walk the balcony all the way around the circumference of the inner courtyard. She gets even more excited as she tries to describe the paintings on the balcony.

We head directly for the courtyard and spend a little time walking around the gardens before climbing the stairs to the balcony.

Meagan was right, the paintings are phenomenal. What I didn't realize was that she meant murals. The *actual* outside walls are covered with angels, monks, nuns, demons, horses, battles, mountains, and stuff. I snap a million pictures because I know this is something Moms would love to see. It makes me sad because my abuelita would have gone mad for this. It's like a Catholic Mecca or something.

"Holy shitballs, Diego," Shania says, breaking the silence we've all fallen into. She yanks at my hand until I come to a stop just past the next doorway. "Look."

She points to the next mural, where a guy is sitting on a cement ledge. A demon sits in the background. The guy's all muscle, in shorts and a ripped top. His hair is windblown, and he's pointing off to the side. He looks terrified. The old lady behind him looks to where he points. She's just as scared. Same with the whole crowd behind her. Even the creepy little dog-like thing wrapped around the guy's foot is looking off in fear.

"Holy shit. That's you."

"Shania," Gill says. "Words. Please. Really?"

"Oops. Sorry. But look."

"Wow," Gill says, first inspecting the guy in the painting and then turning back to look at me. "Your doppelgänger, Diego."

"His what, now?" Manny says as he runs over to see what the fuss is about.

"Twin stranger," Gil says. "It's German. Your lookalike is your doppelgänger."

"Dude, I know what a doppelgänger is. I'm a freaking genius. And maybe if Diego was buff like me, he'd look like this dude. Scrawny D just doesn't measure up to that guy."

"Very funny," I reply. He's right, the guy's got muscles I'll never have. But his face? Whoa.

We all gather around the painting. It's bizarre how much it looks like me. I follow the guy's pointing finger and it leads to another ripped dude. But this one's not only terrified. Clearly, he's in pain.

Like he's dying. Some angel is either yanking him away to his death or trying to save him. Can't tell which.

Shania makes me stand in front of my doppelgänger as she takes a bunch of pics. She wants one where the guy's pointing finger is pointing at me, so it looks like I'm the one he's terrified of, so I humor her and everyone laughs.

"Your mother's gonna shit herself when she sees this one."

"Shania. Words."

"Sorry, Gil." She walks away, leaving Gil to shake his head with the regret of a disappointed parent. He looks at me as if to ask, *where did I go wrong?* I shrug and smile. He'll just have to learn to live with her or go crazy trying to change her.

I run to catch up with Shania, who's already checking out other murals farther along the balcony.

When we've done the loop, we walk down the big stone staircase and assemble at the bottom.

"Well," Meagan says. She pulls out her phone and looks at the screen. "It's almost supper time. We should start to head back to the albergue. Hopefully the others will be there by now."

She glances at Gilbert, and you'd have to be slow not to see the uneasy expression on her face.

"Okay, gang," Gil says. "You heard the lady. Let's go. We'll do the rest of the tour when we're all back together. Let's move out, shall we."

CHAPTER 32

SHANIA REYNOLDS

SATURDAY, JULY 6TH – *Day 8 – Bastien Comes Home & Troy & Claire & Greg*

I swear, my journal is becoming more about everybody else than it is about me.

I think time is different out here on the Camino. That's the only explanation I can come up with. When Bastien finally made it to our albergue just before supper, it was almost dark. I thought Diego was going to explode. It was like his long-lost father had come home from the war.

The weird thing is, we all felt the same way. We all missed him. It really does feel like he's a part of our lives. You know someone for a few days here, and it's the same as a lifetime on the outside.

Diego almost cried. And I almost cried seeing how happy he was to see Bastien. I swear, I was gonna go out there and drag Bastien here myself if he didn't show up. Even Kei's sisters arrived before him.

Kei and Troy were walking past when we came out of the monastery. Troy went bright red when he tried to explain how it was we were able to get to Samos before him. In the end, we just shamed and humiliated him like the good friends we are. We knew he and Kei had found somewhere to hang out alone. Together. And their guilty expressions told us everything. That, and they both actually looked dishevelled, like they'd been messing around.

The three of us—Bastien, Diego, and I—are going out for a walk around town in about two minutes. I'm in the lobby waiting for them.

Gil and Meagan are here, too, blowing their gaskets. Greg and Claire still haven't shown up. It's dark out, everyone's already eaten, and they're still no-shows. Gil is pacing like a wild animal in a cage. He keeps going out in the street and coming back in to say, "No, not yet," to Meagan. Each time he does it, she looks more pissed off.

I would not want to be Greg or Claire right now.

"Where in the name of hell have you been? What happened? Did you get lost?" Gil practically shrieks when Claire comes slinking into the albergue with Greg at her back.

I put my journal away in my small bag and prepare to make a quick exit. I don't want to get caught in the crossfire.

When I look up at Claire, her face is a mess, like she's been crying for hours. "It's my fault." She stands in the middle of the lobby, shoulders slumped, as though she's prepared to accept whatever punishment Gil decides to give her.

"Can I go upstairs and get out of these clothes now? My job here is done," Greg says. He says it like he's had enough of everything.

Gil looks too angry to move. Or speak. Like he's afraid of what he might say. He stands in the center of the lobby shaking his head.

"I think you better stay put, young man," Meagan says. She bolts from the chair she's been attempting to sit in while obsessively tapping her feet and compulsively checking the time on her phone. "I think the two of you owe us an explanation for your lateness."

"It has nothing to do with me. Can I be excused, please? I really need a shower, Meags."

"Greg. I said no. You're not going anywhere until you guys tell me where you were. Sit." Meagan points to the chair she just abandoned.

"I didn't let anything bad happen to her. I brought her here, didn't I? I'm so sick of this. It's just like back home with Robbie. I save the day, and no one appreciates it. I don't know why I even bother."

"Sit," Meagan repeats.

Greg growls, makes his way over to the chair, tosses his backpack to the floor, and plunks himself down. He folds his arms and gives Meagan a dirty look. "Happy?"

Meagan says, "No, Greg. Not really."

Gil doesn't open his mouth. I think his head might explode if he does. He was never this mad when he was freaking out about my constant swearing.

Bastien and Diego come clomping downstairs, unaware they're entering a battle zone. Everyone's frozen in this diorama of a family on the verge of destruction.

I smile at them, and the three of us make our way to the door before anyone else moves or says another word. We somehow cut through the tension in the room and escape into the cool night air.

"That was intense," I say once we're free. "What took you guys so long?"

"Sorry, ma petite. I was telling to Diego the story of the scared souls on the monastère mural."

"Did he tell you his face is on that wall?"

"Ha ha. Yes. Oui. The murals, they are the stories of the life of St. Benedict. It might be his death in the picture of Diego. I am old, Shania. I cannot remember like before, but the boy in the mural? Maybe he points to the dying saint?"

"Cool," I say. I'm not surprised Bastien knows. "So. Where are we going?"

"Just through the town and then over by the river. Where we saw that fence with the scallop shells," Diego says.

"Sounds good."

"Aye. We walk and we walk all the day long. And then we come out at night and we walk some more."

"It seems strange not hearing your walking stick, Bastien. You left it in your room?"

"It is on another journey." He smiles and winks at me as we make our way across the road and walk past the massive monastery.

"Huh?" Diego says. "Did you lose it?"

"I gave it to a woman. She needs the click-click-click more than me, yes? In Lusío, with the path that went down, down." He holds his hand out with his fingers pointing to the ground, like he's signing downhill. "Diego falls down the up, and Maria, she falls down the down."

"Are you kidding me," I say. "You made another rescue today? Are you some kind of Camino superhero, Bastien?"

"Ha ha. We all rescue each other on the Camino, Shania."

"What are you walking for, Bastien?" Diego asks after a moment of silence passes between us. The emotion in his voice is so strong, it's obvious this is something he's been pondering. His desperation is palpable in his clenched jaw.

We reach the scallop shell fencing and stop. The river is below us, and the soft rushing sound of the current is soothing to the ear.

"Well. The last Camino, maybe it was to take the soul of my daughter with me to Santiago. To Finisterre, the end of the world. And, later? Muxia."

I rest a hand on Bastien's shoulder. This man who is so good to everyone. He's had so much damn death. "Your daughter?"

"She die. Very sick. She had cancer. Before my wife became ill."

"I'm so sorry, Bastien." Diego pats Bastien's hand, which rests on the top of the iron fencing.

"It was several years ago. Four." He looks off into the darkness of the water below, as though he could conjure a past where his daughter was still alive. "I took her only in my heart on that walk to Compostela."

"That's so sweet." I have no other words.

"As my wife's heart is dying, and I sit by her bed and I watch her fade, fade, fade—she becomes a ghost in her body—I dream only of the Camino. Of taking her in the same way together we take our Chloe. I dream only of the people, and the trees, and the mountains, and the yellow arrows to point the way to the cathedral and St. James. Of the click, click, click of the sticks, yes?"

He smiles but it's a smile that holds the deepest sadness ever. I think back to the day I was dragged here kicking and screaming and I imagine him yearning for the same thing I would have sold my soul to get out of.

"I only want to complete this way to Compostela. I am very tired. If I can help only a boy who falls at my feet in the mud or a woman who struggles to reach the bottom of the hill, that is enough for now. I take my wife with me. I carry her here."

Bastien pats his chest, but not where his heart is… more in the center. We fall into silence while we ponder his words. I feel guilty for almost missing out on this because I hated the idea so much I tried to take the punishment instead. Thank God my father wouldn't allow it.

"I didn't know why I walked," Diego says. "Because I was bad? But then I thought, no, that's only why I got here. Not why I walk. I think we're all walking away from something or toward something. Maybe, some of us, even both."

Diego surprises us by putting a hand on the fence and springing himself up and over it. His legs swing in the air, and he lands effortlessly on the grassy incline on the other side.

"Now I know. I have my abuelita with me." He turns to us and he looks slightly mad, with this crazy smile and tears welling up in his eyes. He pounds the middle of his own chest.

Then he turns toward the river, steps down to the bank, and jumps in. Clothes and all.

"Diego," I stage-whisper scream. He's lost it.

"Ha ha ha. Leave him be. Leave him be. It is safe. The river won't take him here, Shania. It is little, little."

Then Bastien looks me in the eye and winks before he struggles impossibly to get himself over the same short fence Diego hurdled with ease.

"We go?" he whispers when he finally manages to get himself down on the other side. He is completely spent, but he still turns and makes his way down to the water. I must be crazy, because I follow them.

CHAPTER 33

TROY SINCLAIR

IF THE OTHER NIGHT WAS any indication, things are beginning to get real on this Camino de Santiago.

Our not-so-little group walked past the one-hundred-mile marker yesterday, on our way to Morgade. After Claire and Greg's little stunt the night before, it's amazing we all made it to that marker alive. It felt like we were prisoners all the way there. Gil was even strict with Kei until he realized he should probably tone it down a bit.

Try taking a selfie with nine of your closest friends, especially when half of them aren't speaking because they're pissed off at one another. We had to kneel and lean in all together against the stumpy little mile marker. It wasn't easy. Thank God for my Kei and his lifesaving selfie stick. There was a line of peregrinos waiting to get that shot too. It's probably the most popular mile marker on the whole Camino.

Anyway, we finally arrived in Morgade yesterday as the sun was about to set. It was our longest day. Almost twenty-five kilometers. And, though we were herded together under the watchful eye of our angry shepherd, Gil, and his faithful sidekick, Meagan, I talked to no one but Kei. Which was okay by me.

When Claire attempted to butt in and bribe us with a fresh bag of Skittles, I shut her down.

The albergue was gorgeous, and Kei and I fell in love with it. We imagined ourselves living there and growing old together. It was all stone and wood and precious, with butter yellow walls and quilts. We kept to ourselves to avoid the drama.

I keep thinking about the disappointment I'm going to feel once we reach Compostela. The more excited the others get, the more desperate I feel. It's ridiculous. I can't imagine not having Kei's face in my life.

We've walked all morning, and the sun is beginning to scorch. I swear, it's getting hotter every day. Kei and I set out early, but we were the only ones allowed to break from the group. I think Gil trusts me the most of our group of hooligans. After yesterday, I'm just glad to be rid of them all for a bit. A guy needs to breathe.

"The guidebook says they took the church apart brick by brick, numbered each and every brick, carried them up the big hill, and put it all back together again," Kei says while I'm busy watching my feet walking down this ridiculously steep hill. "Do you think that's true? It says they literally moved the town up the hill."

"You should watch where you're going. You're going to kill yourself."

"Nah," he says, lifting our interlocked hands. "I have complete faith that you'll steer me away from danger."

"You probably shouldn't," I say. But he's done the same thing for me several times. "I don't know about the church, but you're totally missing this."

I point off to the right where this huge bridge has come into view. A small town stretches up and away from the water on the other side. We're far above it, looking down upon it. It's a postcard.

"Wow," Kei says. He stuffs his guidebook back into his backpack. We keep walking, taking in the amazing views of the approaching town as we go.

The closer we get to the river, the more the steep road down to it swerves and curves. We lose sight of the town several times as it disappears through the trees.

We pass several peregrinos who zigzag from one side of the road to the other to cut down the angle of the incline and save their feet.

"Wanna try that?" Kei suggests after it's obvious we're the only ones not zigzagging.

"Nah," I say. "Let's just run. More time to ourselves once we get there."

"If we fall on the way down, I'm suing you for malfeasance."

"Big word. Such an American concept." We laugh and continue on our self-destructive path to the bridge in the distance.

*   *   *

THE PLAN TODAY IS FOR all ten of us to have a picnic just beyond Portomarin, the town on the other side of the bridge.

Kei and I stop at a grocery and pick up some crackers, Twizzlers, and beef jerky. And a can of sardines. Our contribution to the picnic. The Twizzlers are Kei's idea. He's not allowed to have junk food back home. His dentist father.

We're sitting on some steps beside the Church of San Xoán—the church that was moved brick by brick up the hill before they flooded the valley—when everyone comes walking up from the bottom of town. Claire, Shania, and Greg are first to appear, followed by Meagan and Bastien. A few minutes later, Manny, Diego, and Gil arrive. They all wave.

I point to the store with one hand and lift my bag of picnic food with the other. "We're all ready."

"Awesome," Meagan says. "We'll be right out."

After they all have their purchases and have taken the necessary cathedral shots, we start out of town.

"Anything happen we should know about?" Gil asks as he comes up alongside me and Kei.

"Nope. Smooth sailing. Thanks for letting us take off early."

"Not a problem, my man. I trust you." He smiles but raises a finger. "Unless and until you give me a reason not to, that is."

"Thanks. Good ole reliable Troy. That's what they call me back home."

"Nothing wrong with being reliable," he says, before dropping back to fall into step with Meagan.

Soon we cross a small footbridge over another part of the river. The road winds uphill right away. It's almost nostalgic when I hear Greg moan and complain from somewhere behind us. I look at Kei, and we laugh. So much for our earlier peace and quiet.

CHAPTER 34

DIEGO NELSON

"And at the top of this world, we give thanks for Portomarin," Bastien says. He waves an arm in the direction we came from. "To Troy's sardines, to this big sky above, and to the large hawk who circles us. Our spirit guide on this day of our journey, maybe."

Bastien holds his plastic cup up to the bird, and we all copy him.

"Amen," he says. We join him. It is one of the rare occasions Gil and Meagan have allowed us all to have a taste of wine. After the toast, we dig into the pile of food spread out between us.

We sit in the long grass beside the path, directly at the top of the enormous hill we just climbed. The sand of the path is almost orange. The sides of my hiking boots have taken on the color. Almost all of us are in our stocking feet, and our shoes are piled on the path. Claire is barefoot, and her feet are almost as orange as the sand.

"This is the best food I ever tasted," Shania says. Pretty much everyone agrees.

In the quiet that follows, we devour the bizarre mix of food. Everyone just grabbed stuff at the grocery, so we have so many random things to pick from.

When Gil and Meagan clear everything away, sorting piles of trash and leftovers, Claire stands up. She gulps down her cup of wine and clears her throat.

"I have something I want to say to everyone. I have an apology to make. Can we have today's group meeting now? But can Kei and Bastien stay for this one?" She looks to Troy and keeps his gaze while she continues to speak.

Gil nods for her to continue.

"I've been a little… messed up lately. Back at Samos I ruined Greg's day by dragging him into my drama. And I sort of dragged everyone else into it too."

"You don't need to apologize, Claire," Troy says. Dude sounds almost angry, though. "We all have our own crap to deal with."

"I'm serious. I need to talk about this. It's why I'm here. It's why I feel this ache that just won't go away." She pounds her chest and breaks down a little. She's tryna keep it together, but I don't know.

"Sweetie," Troy says. He stands up, goes to her side, and guides her down to the ground. They sit cross-legged, and Troy says, "Okay. I got you. Say what you need to say." He keeps one hand on her shoulder.

"Thanks, Troy."

He nods and pats her shoulder. My Troyboy is in his element now, mothering Claire through it.

"Back home I feel like I'm disappearing. I'm not allowed to be who I am, and it's wearing me down. It *has* worn me down. I'm afraid if I go back, I'll vanish completely. And I know I've been so miserable here and bringing everyone down, but it's because I love it here. I know that doesn't make any sense, but I keep missing it as it happens. What's that word Bastien said a thousand years ago? Saudade?

"I'm dying of saudade. For this place. For being able to feel like myself. For casting a shadow here. My heart races when I think about going home. That's why I keep thinking of just leaving this path and disappearing into Spain, into Europe. Into the world. You guys are the only thing keeping me from doing it.

"I feel crazy. Like I'm being pulled in two directions." Claire stops to take a breath, and Bastien hands her a handkerchief from his pocket. She blows her nose and wipes tears from her eyes. "Thank you."

"What's wrong, Claire?" Shania asks. "If your parents are anything like mine, I get how you'd feel invisible."

"It's not that, Shania. It's not invisible. I think I could deal with that."

"What is it, then?"

"Guys. I'm not sure we should be talking about this," Gil says. "Maybe we can just graciously accept Claire's apology, finish picking up, and be on our way."

"No, Gil. I want to say it out loud. I want to get it out."

Gil has this look on his face. He's worried for Claire, but there's more to it. I don't know if he's comfortable with how personal things are getting. He gets up and reaches for the bag of garbage.

"Gil," Meagan says softly, almost imperceptibly. She raises a hand and nods at the ground beside her. Gil takes the hint and sits back down.

"My parents are strict conservatives and extremely religious," Claire says. "Like, they live for their church; they're nuts. I'm pretty sure you all know I'm gay. I talk about my girlfriend, Zoe, whenever I can because I miss her so much." She pulls a bag of Skittles from her pocket. "I eat these things like crack just to feel closer to Zoe because back home we use them to communicate. We devised a secret language between us where Skittles are our vocabulary. Because we need to be a secret. I need to get out of that oppression, out of that house, or else…"

Claire allows her words to trail off.

"Or else, what?" Shania says. I reach over and squeeze her hand because she's pushing and pushing. She should just let Claire speak and get it out. "Ow," she says. I give her a look and hope she can read my mind right now and shut it.

"A few months back, they sent me away to this *weekend retreat.*" She air-quotes. "Like three weekends in a row. You know, to get me to give this up."

Claire holds up her bag of candy, and I can read Shania's mind even before she asks the question. I squeeze her hand again to stop her. She looks at me like I'm the one with the problem.

"Give up being gay," Claire says, answering Shania's unasked question.

"Oh, man, girl," Manny says. He has the same stunned look on his face as everyone else. "That's just so wrong."

"Conversion therapy?" Troy says. "You didn't tell me this. Why didn't you tell me this? Are you fucking kidding me? Oh my God, they're nuts. You poor girl." He hugs her. She accepts it, but only for a second. She wants to keep it together.

Gil says exactly nothing about Troy's use of the F-bomb. And my boy *never* swears.

"It's not what they call it. But, yeah. Pretty much conversion therapy. I'm going to get out as soon as I can figure out a way. Until then, I just can't be who I am. I already know that. Mostly, it's okay. I deal and deal and deal… until I can't do it any longer. It gets too exhausting. I just put on this face like everything's fine and I'm not this monster they can't stand or relate to or accept."

"I'm really sorry, Claire," I say. I don't know what else to say because I can't imagine Moms ever going against me for any reason.

"That's just not right," Shania says. "That's messed up."

"We've been talking to Claire, guys. We had a discussion with her back in Samos," Gil says. "We're going to see if we can't get her some help when we get back home. She's promised not to make a run for it before we get to Santiago. And I believe she's telling us the truth. Right, Claire."

Gil winks at Claire and smiles. The two of them share this look with Meagan. I sometimes forget why we're here, that these two are our guardians, that counseling is happening out here. This is pretty much as heavy as it gets.

"I already told you, Claire," Greg says. "I got your back no matter what. I don't give a flying shit. If anything like that shit happens again, they'll want to run as far away as possible. If I find them, they won't like what I'll do to them."

"My little assassin," Claire says. She laughs, wipes away more tears with the handkerchief. "To think a few days ago I slapped his face so hard for being an asshole, it left a handprint. Anything can happen on the Camino, folks."

This is the tension breaker we all needed. We laugh, but not much because, man. I don't think I ever heard of anything as heavy as this.

"Maybe we should hit the road, gang," Meagan says. "Like Troy said, Claire. There really isn't anything to apologize over. I think the rest of the kids have your back. Considering the impossible pressure you've been under, it's no wonder you're struggling."

"Thanks, Meagan."

"Don't mention it. Now look what you've done. You've made this old man cry, even. Imagine that." Meagan climbs off the sweater she's been sitting on and reaches across to pat Bastien's knee. "You okay?"

"I'm fine, I'm fine, oui." But he doesn't look fine. I want to bash Claire's parents in the face for hurting him. He points to the sky above us. "You see, Claire. The hawk. He stays for you. To allow you to tell your story. He can take some burden, maybe, yes? Fly away with it."

"I hope so, Bastien," she says.

We're all on our feet now, and the picnic is pretty much put away. Time for the last half of the day's walk. To Gonzar.

I can tell Shania has something to say, but I don't want her to say it. I know Shania. She'll have all these questions for Claire and start freaking out about things. But arguing with her is hopeless, so I try another strategy to distract her. As everyone else struggles into their backpacks, I attempt to deflect the impending Shania tirade with my lips. With kisses.

As I get her into a lip-lock, everybody is quick to tease, but the tactic works. Soon everyone's walking away, rejoining the path, and I'm left standing in an open field kissing my girl.

CHAPTER 35

SHANIA REYNOLDS

Tuesday, July 9th – Day 11 – *How Can I Hate My Life When Claire…?*

I didn't want to journal last night when we finally got to the albergue in Gonzar. Yesterday put me in a real funk. First with the whole thing Claire's dealing with, and then, to top it off, I had to listen to a lecture from Diego about leaving her alone and giving her some space.

I thought I had it bad. I mean, yeah, my parents constantly ignore me. But I'm such a princess. They give me everything. They make sure there's nothing I want… even if they're not emotionally there for me. They're busy. It's not like they hate me. It's not like they try to change me. I mean, not the way Claire's parents are trying to kill her.

I need to talk to her. We never really got along all that great. Maybe I can fix it. I fixed it with Diego, after all. If I can fix that situation, I can probably do anything.

We're in a small café in a place called Palas de Rei, on our way to Ponte Campaña Mato. We're almost done walking for the day. It seriously feels like everything's wrapping up. I'm going to miss this place and these people like I've never missed anything before. Except maybe how I miss Flibber right now. I'd give anything to kiss his silly face.

"No, no," Bastien says. "*Hórreos.*" This is about the third time I heard him pronounce the word for Greg, who is adamant in his insistence that the "little houses" he keeps seeing in the small towns we've been walking through are coffins for the dead. Greg's arguing that people store bodies in these little houses over the winter because the ground freezes. Because some guy named Louis from Seattle told him this. Everyone is laughing but Greg. He's just annoyed.

I put my journal away to listen. I've seen the long miniature houses on stilts all over the place. No clue what they are. I could see how someone would mistake them for that. They're almost the size of coffins, taller with fancy little roofs on them. But I also didn't think that's what they were.

"Greg, my friend. No," Bastien says, sounding a bit frustrated himself. He speaks as much with his hands as with his words. "I tell you this promise, these are not houses of the dead, little coffins in the sky. Merde. They are granaries for the farmers and villagers. To keep their stock dry and away from the riffraff of rodents. I promise you, this is so. Not these houses of the dead corpses you speak of."

Greg does not want to give up.

"But Louis knows. He said—"

"*He said, he said, he said.* Nonsense. The man does not know. Someone is a joker. Someone told him this to make him the fool, the ass's ass. They are granaries."

"Dweeb," Manny says. "Come on, bro. You don't think Bastien knows of what he speaks?"

Greg's face turns beet red, and his frustration shows in the way he shakes his head. He's not going to win this one. When he accepts his defeat, he gets up and makes his way to the washroom.

"His Louis, he is a fool or a trickster," Bastien says. He grumbles under his breath and there is more laughter.

"On that note," Gilbert says, rising to his feet. "How about we head out of this one-horse town and get moving? Onward to Ponte Campaña Mato, my little lovelies."

Every one of us groans. This is the second time he's made the horse joke. As we walked into town, there was a solitary horse standing in a field by itself, and he mentioned it then. In his own head, Gil is the funniest person he knows.

*   *   *

BY THE TIME DIEGO AND I arrive at the albergue, we're both spent. This does not stop us from walking around the large property or finding a quiet place alone to make out. I keep worrying I'm going to wake up at the end of this trip and realize it was all a dream and I didn't really get the boy. I can't even believe I used to have to keep reminding myself to be nice to this guy. He's like Flibber. The only thing in the world Diego wants is my happiness. Even if he does sometimes try to keep me in check. That. Will. Never. Happen.

We're sitting on this homemade wooden bench under an apple tree, at the very end of the property, when I see Claire come out the back door of the albergue. She takes something over to the outdoor sink, turns on the tap and starts scrubbing the thing in her hands under the running water. She must be cleaning her underwear, something we've all been doing every night. Pack light, wash, and rewash.

"It looks like she's trying to murder her poor gotchies," Diego says. The words sound like he's attempting to be funny, but his face is all seriousness. He's rigid and stern. His cheeks are tight, like he's clenching his teeth.

Diego seems to be taking this thing with Claire hard. I also think he doesn't want to discuss it with me because he thinks I may snap. Which I may.

"Can I talk to her yet, Diego?"

He takes his eyes away from Claire, and his facial muscles relax.

"I would do anything for Moms, Shania," he says. "And I would have done anything in the world for my grandmother. Anything. How could her parents love her and do that to her, Shan?" He stops talking and kisses me. It's gentle at first and then a little rougher.

"I would never in a million years ask someone I loved—or anyone—to change who they are." He's angry. It's like he's been holding it in since the picnic. "I don't want that kid to go home after this. They're breaking that little girl's soul, Shan. It ain't right. Nobody deserves that. There's some things you just don't come back from. People die when they break."

There's something inside Diego, I swear, that's the same color and brightness as the thing that burns in Bastien and makes him so magical. They both have it. No wonder they found each other.

He takes my face in his hands and plants another rough kiss on my mouth. Then he gets up, turns, and walks toward the albergue. At first, I assume he is going to talk to Claire. Instead, he walks past her, opens the back door, and steps inside.

I guess he was giving me his blessing.

Claire finishes up at the sink, turns the water off, and brings her underwear over to a clothesline between the albergue and myself. There's some old-fashioned covered-wagon lawn ornament between us. It blocks my view at first, but she steps around it. I smile, and she takes it as an invitation to join me.

"Hey," she says.

"Long day, eh?"

"Not the longest. That was yesterday." She makes this face like she's exhausted, for emphasis. I know yesterday wasn't the longest day of walking, so it's obvious she's talking about dealing with her shit at the picnic. "Compared to yesterday, today's been a walk in the park."

"Yeah. I guess you're right," I say.

"I just had some face time with Zoe. She's my rock. I can't look at her face and not feel better. She *gets* me."

"That's an awesome feeling."

"The best." She sits on the bench beside me.

"I'm sorry we haven't been the best of friends out here," I say.

She shrugs, smiles. "Nah. Don't worry about it, Shania. We all landed here pissed off. Well, except for Troy, maybe. And your Diego. But we all have baggage. They probably *expected* us not to get along anyway. You know what they say about girls."

"True. Bitchy, don't get along, kill our own. I hear you. But then, other times they say we got each other's backs, protect each other, and gang up. Can't have it both ways. I should have tried to make friendly, though."

"Three more days of walking," Claire says. "Still lots of time to bond, right?"

I smile. There's only one thing on my mind, though. What she's gone through. I can't find a way to bring it up. Every sentence I try to string together comes out wrong according to my internal editor. At least Diego would be proud that I'm consulting my editor. I usually speak first and think later. Maybe the Camino is slowing me down that way.

"I sometimes feel like a ghost in my own life. If it weren't for my brother, Dillon, and my dog, Flibber, I'd be hopeless. My parents, they each have these lives where every second of every day is mapped out. They actually get nervous if they find themselves at home, accidentally short on scheduled chaos. So I sometimes feel like nobody cares. Like, if I disappeared they wouldn't even notice. I know it's bad when I start talking out loud to the dog."

"Ha, ha. I've been there. They know our greatest secrets. Shit, my dog… she should probably have an honorary degree in psychology by now. She's gotten me through so many rough patches. I think—"

"What did they do to you, Claire?" I interrupt, because I can't take it anymore. I've been biting my tongue for over twenty-four hours.

"It's okay, Shania," she says, like she's the one who has to placate me. "I'm fine. Zoe is the most amazing girlfriend. I'd be a wreck without her support. Ha, like I'm not one already. It's just, those people had this way of getting in my head. They blamed my parents, my upbringing, my babysitter, my teachers, everyone, for me being gay. They had me believing at one point that I wasn't born this way. That's the scariest part.

"The thing is, I'm not even sure my parents knew some of the shady stuff they pulled on me at that *little program* they signed me up for. Mom and Dad just needed *the gay* to be taken out of their daughter by any means possible. My mother goes faint when she hears the word lesbian. She can't even deal with that.

"I came home that first weekend kicking and screaming, but I soon realized it wasn't gonna stop until I got some kind of *clean bill of health*. So eventually I started to lie, to tell them how I was *feeling better*." She air-quotes these last two words. "It worked for a bit, or at least I thought it did. Then my parents were convinced I needed to *complete the program* before they could be guaranteed it would fully take in the long term."

"Whoa," I say. "That's insane." The light in the sky has changed and the noise from the albergue grows as resting peregrinos come to life. People make their way from the sleeping quarters to the dining hall.

"How do you think I made my way to the Camino? I couldn't take the bullshit. I snapped on the program. I snapped on my parents. Nobody within a hundred miles of my life was safe. The camp—as they liked to call the place—had me on break and enter, mischief, and destruction of property. I only destroyed property because the assholes weren't there at the time. It probably would have been murder charges if they had been."

I stand and offer her a hand up. Claire takes it and stands up. I hug her and she allows me to do so.

"I'm sorry this happened to you. It's so messed up; I don't even know what to say. I didn't know they still tried shit like this, Claire. For real."

"Yeah, well." She shrugs, and we make our way back up to the albergue. "If they can disguise it as some kind of religious camp and get away with it, they do."

We're practically the last ones to enter the dining hall, but naturally my knight in shining armor has saved seats for both of us.

As we sit down, Claire says, "I could eat a horse."

"Too bad we left that one-horse town behind us, Claire bear," Gil says. "Otherwise, I could have hooked you up."

"Ha ha," she says, totally deadpan. But then she laughs. Not because it's particularly funny, but because it's kind of what you do with friends. "You're pretty funny, Gil. Not."

"Eat your soup."

"Yes, sir."

I can't believe I'm going to be saying goodbye to these people in just a few more days. It doesn't seem possible. Time means nothing on the Camino, because I swear I've known all of them forever.

CHAPTER 36

TROY SINCLAIR

TODAY WE ARRIVED IN CASTENADA. One of the best moments possibly in the history of the Camino happened today. We stopped in Melide for lunch. The town is famous for their *pulpo*, or octopus. We'd been hearing about it since our journey began. Yours truly, I should add, did not partake of the delicacy. Ew.

Anyway, Greg—smartass that he is—thought it would be a good idea to scare the hell out of Shania with some octopus tentacles. When he stood behind her and dangled them in her face, though, it wasn't Shania who lost her mind.

Unfortunately for Greg, Manny was sitting beside Shania. And the second those tentacles fell into his field of vision, he went ballistic. He snapped and jumped out of his chair. The chair went flying back and hit Greg right in his junk. He went down like a bag of bones, tentacles and all, clutching himself.

Manny runs screaming like he's still not far enough away from the tentacles to be safe. His arms flail like he's walking through cobwebs. Meanwhile, Greg's on the floor shouting about his nuts, and Shania's still sitting there eating her French fries like nothing happened. Completely deadpan. That girl.

The best part is, Diego was sitting across from Shania pretending to take her picture, just waiting for Greg to strike. So Diego has a bunch of pictures of the chaos. Brilliant.

The best pic was caught the moment Manny went crazy. The look on his face. I mean, obviously I think he's one of the most gorgeous boys on the Camino. It's no secret. But his face in that pic? Priceless. But *not* pretty.

The albergue tonight is small. There are only three other peregrinos besides our group of twelve. We're all sitting in this huge common room overstuffed with couches, chairs, coffee tables, and bookshelves filled with books, puzzles, and board games. There's also a large floor model TV that may not have been used in years, if it even works at all.

Kei's sisters are sitting on one of the couches with Bastien, trying to convince him to pick up the guitar beside the fireplace and serenade them. I'm guessing he'll eventually give in. He's got this cute little smirk on his face, like he's holding out for more adoration. Cheeky.

There's a pile of old-fashioned photo albums on one of the coffee tables. The albergue owner used to get people to mail back photos and she's collected them for decades. Shania and Diego are cuddled into an armchair that's too small for them; they're poring over all the old photos and making up stories about the lives of the people in them.

Manny and Greg are playing a fierce game of chess at the dining table, and Claire is doing her best to churn their competitive natures into a frenzy.

It's comfortable. Everyone is chilling. Something about the hushed busyness makes me feel nostalgic. Sad. And so filled with stupid happiness.

I'm looking at Kei, who's sitting across the room by himself. He's playing with one of those Rubik's Cubes and failing miserably. I'm waiting impatiently for him to look up from his cube and make eye contact with me, but I don't think it's going to happen.

For what I'm thinking, it's now or never. Gil and Meagan went outside, the other peregrinos are talking amongst themselves, and the three albergue people are cleaning up after supper. I did the math carefully, accounting for every single person in the house. All present. And Kei won't look up from that stupid toy.

I get up from the 1970s spinning egg chair I fought so hard to score and I make my way over to Kei. I pray nobody's paying attention, because my motives are not pure.

I'm right in front of him before he finally looks up from his frustrations. When we make eye contact, I nod in the direction of the bedrooms.

Kei follows me down the long hallway and, thankfully, nobody seems to notice. Mission accomplished.

It's four to a room here. We're sharing with Gil and Manny, both presently occupied. I wait for Kei to come in behind me before I shut the door. Kei leans against the wall with a smile on his cute little face and says, "What's up?"

But he knows.

I take his hand and lead him to his bed. His sleeping bag is already spread out on top of the sheets, protection against bedbugs and anything else the sheets may be harboring, according to Gilbert.

Kei spreads out on the bed, and I lie beside him. As scared as I feel, as much as my heart beats out of my chest, I know this might be our last opportunity. When I roll onto Kei, he groans, but not as much as the bed. We both laugh nervously.

"Is there a lock on the door?" Kei asks. I see that there is. Reluctantly, I leave him to push in the lock in the doorknob. As I make my way back, I slip my T-shirt off. "Are we doing this?"

"Shhh," I say. "Can we just let whatever happens happen? We probably don't have much time."

I ease myself on top of him, and we start to kiss, taking it slow. I kiss the stud in his nose and Kei giggles. "Sorry. Tickles."

"I like you, Kei," I say. "A lot. I'm crazy about your beautiful face, your heart. I love the way you think. I'm going to miss you when this is over."

"I want us to find a way, Troy—"

"Me too. I do. With all my heart." I roll over and wedge myself between him and the wall and drape a leg over him. I snuggle my head into his shoulder and sigh. "I mean, think about where you live and where I live. And how we're only teenagers. It's so depressing."

"But," he says, "if we both want it, it shouldn't matter what we have to do to make it happen. Long distance." He runs a hand through his hair, attempts to tame it away from his face.

"I want it." I lift my head, lean up on my elbow, and kiss his open mouth. Even as I do it, I fear this will be our last time. But I can believe in the possibility of anything. Especially in this moment.

"We still have the next couple of days," Kei whispers at the end of our kiss. "We have now."

"Yeah. We do have now, Kei Amano."

"Yes we do, Troy Sinclair."

This time, Kei's the one who makes a move. He rolls onto his side toward me until I'm pinned against the wall. He snuggles against me and kisses me again.

"Just a sec." I strain to get free of the wedge I've gotten myself into. He lets me go, and I jump up over him and off the bed. I dart across the room to the light switch and flick it off.

After I stumble my way back to the bed in the dark, I'm careful not to smack my shins on its metal frame.

"It's so dark in here," Kei whispers, his voice silky and filled with nervous energy. It's the last thing I hear him say before I let myself fall on top of him. I try not to think about the way Dad insisted I come to Spain prepared. I try not to think about Dad at all.

CHAPTER 37

DIEGO NELSON

THIS IS A SAD DAY. It's the last one when we will walk toward an albergue. Because tomorrow afternoon, we'll make our way into Santiago de Compostela. The end of the road for us.

"We walk, you and I?" Bastien says, as I step off the doorstep of the albergue and walk down the long driveway to where he stands waiting. He's more eager today than he has been the past couple of days. The closer we get to Compostela, the more he seems to slow down.

I sling my backpack into place on my shoulders. "Ready. Let's do this."

Shania is still in the albergue with the rest of the kids and Meagan. Gil is just up ahead, across the road. He walks with Kei's sisters on either side of him. Everyone has made plans to meet in a place called A Calzada for lunch on our last day before Santiago.

I can sense everything rushing to an end, winding down. Every step is closer to Moms. And to a world where my abuelita is no longer here.

"You must be getting ready to see your mother at home, no?" Bastien asks, reading my mind. We head out on the shoulder of the road and kick the shifting gravel as we go. "She will be very happy to see her little boy."

"I hate that I left her when she needed me most. She's kicking around in the apartment alone. Everywhere she looks, she'll see my grandmother. And I did this all for some stupid girl who doesn't even know I'm alive."

"This does not sound like Diego of the Camino," he says. "That Diego walks for different reasons, not because of what he did."

He holds everyone to their truth, always. I forgot about Sabrina Vincent long ago. You set idiotic bonehead fires for girls like Sabrina Vincent. You live inside fires like Shania Reynolds.

"Yeah. I guess you're right."

"It is not often, I guess," he says, smirking. "We go this way." Bastien points to a dirt path that goes down the embankment, moving away from the road. As we take it, I can see that it leads to a tunnel under the road.

The concrete walls of the tunnel are covered with graffiti and paintings of peregrinos in various poses. They range from cartoonish to Michelangelo-esque.

"Wow," I whisper as we walk past a painting of St. James walking with his pilgrim's staff. I swear he's going to walk off the wall and join us.

"St. James. He's happy here. Almost home to his bones in the cathedral, no?"

"I guess so."

The last message on the wall before we leave the tunnel is *Life Is Too Short*, in a fancy graffiti script. I think of my grandmother and wonder if Bastien sees the message and contemplates his daughter's cancer or his wife's heart attack four short years later. I wonder if he has anyone else.

We walk downhill through a roughly paved lane with old stone houses close on both sides. The wall of one house displays a hastily painted yellow arrow, in case we're unsure which direction to take. I rush to keep up with Bastien. He's focused this morning. The new stick he picked up clicks a steady rhythm as we make our way deeper into the little sleeping town.

Up ahead, I see Gil, Becky, and Mia stop to let an old man with three cows cross their path in the narrow laneway. The man tap, tap, taps a long thin stick on the cows' butts to keep them moving.

By the time the cows pass, we have caught up to the others.

"After you," Gil says as he ushers us through with his hand.

"Onward to Arzúa," Bastien says, pointing the way ahead. "We stop there for café con leche, Mr. Gil?"

"I would kill for a coffee," Mia says. She fixes her long black hair into a scrunchie as we all start to walk. She looks like an older version of her brother, with girl hair.

"We see you there, then." Bastien strikes off at a quick pace.

"Late for the marathon?" Gil says to me as I walk away. I turn back and offer him a weak smile before I rush to keep up with Bastien.

We hit the outskirts of Arzúa and it opens up to a large boulevard with four lanes of traffic heading into and out of the heart of the town. Both sides of the road are filled with restaurants and coffee shops. We walk past a restaurant with an impossibly giant pan of paella in front of it, right on the sidewalk. My mouth waters as I catch the spicy aromas of seasoned rice, chorizo, and shrimp. Café after café beckons us inside, but Bastien shows no sign of slowing down, even though his breathing is heavy and he has this look like he's really struggling to keep going. After we pass a number of perfectly reasonable cafés, I become suspicious.

"Aren't we stopping for coffee, Bastien?" I ask. "Like we told Gil and the girls we would?"

"No, no," he says, pointing ahead with his stick. "We walk. We will stop at the church here for a stamp and then continue to Casa Calzada, no?" He pats his breast pocket where the top of his passport peeks out.

It's not like I have a choice if I want to continue walking with him.

We turn off the main strip, and the town opens further. We see a church with a large courtyard filled with trees.

"The church." He stops for a second, taps his stick on the road a couple times, takes a deep breath, and continues onward toward the church. "Merde."

Two nuns at the door greet our arrival. They are both ancient and they wear the scapular and cowl, so only their faces show. No hair. My abuelita would be happy. She liked the old ways of the Catholic Church, *when nuns were nuns.*

"Bonjour," Bastien says as he offers a great big Bastien smile. They light up at it, mesmerized by the kindness in his face. Just like everyone else.

"Ola," one of the ladies says as she hands him a pamphlet on the church. "Veña, entra."

The other nun opens the door to a cool rush of air-conditioned air.

"Ah, yes," Bastien says. "Lovely."

We step inside, and the relief is instant. I hadn't realized just how hot the day had become. The coolness on my arms and face as my sweat begins to evaporate is heaven.

As there are no other peregrinos nearby, the nuns follow us inside.

"Veña," the speaking nun repeats. The other woman has yet to speak, but her face is pure kindness.

They lead the way up the main aisle. I follow at their heels with Bastien behind me. The pews on either side of us are solid pine and polished to a blinding shine. The smell of lemons is thick. The scent fills the church. As I look about in every direction, I touch the back of a pew. It's buttery soft and chill to the touch.

Near the front, the sanctuary opens up, and there is a prie-dieu on one side and a pulpit on the other.

"Mon Dieu," Bastien says from somewhere behind me, a little more than a whisper. Both nuns look over their shoulders; their smiles fade momentarily. Perhaps at his choice of words? I'm pretty sure *My God* is a swear in here.

"Apologies, sisters," he says. I turn to him, and he smiles meekly, but there is something else in his face. In his eyes. Almost panic. And, even though my own sweat has dried up in the coolness of the church, Bastien looks as though his has gotten worse. He pulls a handkerchief from his pocket and dabs at his face.

As I turn back toward the sanctuary and the nuns, I hear a quiet thud. I turn in time to see Bastien hit the side of a pew on his way down, but not quickly enough to catch his fall before he lands on the stone floor of the aisle.

I scramble to his side, and already he's waving me away with his arms. "I'm fine, I'm fine, Diego." He sits and props himself up with one arm. "Just a little light in the head. The heat. I need no help."

I kneel to help him the rest of the way up anyway. By the time I get him seated in a pew, the sisters are at my side tsking and fussing.

"Vous n'êtes pas bien, monsieur," the talking nun says. I try to translate, with my terrible high school not-really-paying-attention French vocabulary. *You are not well, sir?* Spanish, I would have understood.

"Sit, sit. Sentarse. Asseoir," She continues, moving from one language to another almost effortlessly. "Por favor," she says to the other nun, who looks like she may cry. "Vai buscar auga." Though she's speaking Galician, it's close enough to Spanish. Water.

"I'm fine; I'm fine," Bastien repeats, pleading for the attention to stop. I sit beside him and rest a hand on his shoulder while the woman disappears to find some water.

"Monsieur, if you will excuse me," the nun who stayed behind says. "You are not fine." She puts a hand to his forehead. "You are too hot."

I follow her lead after she removes her hand, and she's right. He's burning up.

"Bastien," I say, a little shocked. "You didn't say you weren't feeling good this morning."

"Ha ha. Maybe I was trying to outwalk the cold, no? The Compostela waits for no one, Diego. Just one more day. It is a simple cold."

"You're sick."

"And I will be sick in Santiago. Not now. Now, we must walk. I rest tonight. I'm fine."

I know he keeps saying this to convince himself, as much as us, that he is okay.

"You're really pale, Bastien. You don't look fine." As I say this, I realize just how sick he looks. I try to remember this morning. I'm sure he didn't look like this when we set out. Even if I hadn't noticed, somebody else would have, for sure.

He leans back into the pew and sighs. The silent nun comes running up the aisle with a bottle of water in her outstretched hand. "Beber, beber," she says, breaking her silent streak as she encourages Bastien to drink.

While the nuns fuss over him, I go toward the back of the church. I pull out my phone and send a text to Shania to tell her we're in Arzúa and that Bastien is unwell.

She replies almost immediately, first with an *Oh no,* and then follows it with an *I knew it.* I wish I had realized, or she had mentioned it to me if she suspected it.

I'm afraid to be alone with him.

*　　*　　*

AT BASTIEN'S FRUSTRATED INSISTENCE, WE left the panicked nuns of Arzúa behind. Even though A Calzada is well over an hour away, he says one should never stray from the plan on the Camino. I don't remember that Bastien wisdom being brought up before today.

We walked deep into a valley, across a stream, and then had to climb again. A terrible day to have to hit everything but flatland. Bastien keeps telling me he's fine, but I can see how he struggles. The road is leaving him breathless.

We have made it to As Quintas. We veer off into a wooded area, following a mile marker. The trees get thicker as we go deeper into the forest path.

"We are close now, Diego. As Quintas. Soon we stop for lunch. Ten minutes, yes? Maybe fifteen. We look for A Calzada." He leans harder on his walking stick, but trudges on. "Then we rest. We eat and feel better."

I don't fully believe his sense of timing or his promise of feeling better after he's eaten something. These are his attempts to calm my panic and worry. I continue in silence, wishing more than anything that we had not set out alone.

Everything begins to hit me. Even as I attempt to keep it together, I know there's nothing I can do. A ball of tension forms a knot in my throat, and I can feel it every time I swallow. The tears begin to fall, and I have no choice but to give in to them.

"I don't want you to be sick, Bastien," I say.

"I'm okay, Dieg—" he begins, before he looks my way and realizes the state I'm in. "No, no, no. Don't cry, Diego." He takes out his handkerchief and hands it to me. Even though it's still damp from the last time he used it, I don't care. I wipe the tears.

"You're sick. The lady back there. She said you're not well. I don't think she meant you were having a bad day."

"Come," he says. "Sit."

We've reached an open area in the forest. There's a vast assortment of rocks spread out beside the path. Some are painted with little symbols or words. There are also sticks and twigs arranged in the shapes of arrows on the ground by pilgrims who came before us.

Off to the side, three boulders are large enough for us to sit on. Bastien leads the way.

"I do this for my wife," he says, once we're sitting down. I'm looking at my feet. I won't look at him while he speaks. I feel pouty. Before he continues, a small group of peregrinos walk past and *Buen Caminos* are exchanged. Bastien waves as they wander deeper into the thickening forest.

"I carry her in my heart as we both carried our daughter on our second Camino. To Finisterre and Muxia. Not her ashes, no. That is just, that is nothing. Ashes are not the person. The soul, it is gone from them. The soul is everything."

Bastien waves his arms about to encompass the air and the forest. I kick at the ground and I feel like a spoiled brat. I swipe at my eyes with the handkerchief. "I don't know what you're saying."

"This is my last time on the Camino de Santiago. It has carried me, and I have carried it… for all of my life.

"When I finish this walk, when I go to Muxia, I will say goodbye to this beautiful land. To this beautiful life."

"But you can do the Camino again. Someone else doesn't have to die for you to walk it again, Bastien. You can walk it on your own. For yourself."

"My friend. My boy." But he stops talking. We sit, and I listen to the sounds of the forest. I wait for him to continue.

A lone pilgrim passes and mumbles, "Buen Camino." He tips his hat as I look up and nod my hello. He turns back to the path and soon disappears.

"Mon petit criminel boueux," Bastien says. He ruffles my hair and laughs. "I picked you up from the mud, my little criminal. Was that not a life ago? Look at all the steps. To this, my goodbye Camino."

"But it doesn't need to be. You're not listening."

"No, my friend," he says with a newly stern voice. "It is you who does not listen."

"We should have walked with the others today. Gil would know what to do."

"There is nothing to do, Diego. I am fine. We will make it to A Calzada for lunch. To Santa Irene to sleep our last sleep. And to Santiago de Compostela tomorrow. We will make it."

I stand and face him. "Can we just go? We're close. Let's just get there and wait for the others. Okay?" I don't like the feeling in my chest, like something is chasing around in there, swarming... threatening to escape. If I can walk, I can get away from it.

Bastien sighs, defeated. "Yes, yes. We go."

"Thank you." I turn my back on him and walk to the path and take my first few footsteps. I don't know if I'm angry, sad, lost, or drowning. I just need to move. *Must keep walking.*

The soft thunk of Bastien's walking stick in the packed earth of the path tells me he's begun to follow me.

"I cannot, my friend," he says. He stays back, not matching my new pace.

"You cannot what?"

"I cannot walk this Camino again. I cannot do it."

The lump in my throat is back, but I march forward. I try to escape the words I'm doing my best not to comprehend, not to let into my life.

"Diego." The word comes with two firm stamps of his walking stick. "I have this thing that has also taken the life of my daughter.

I have cancer." I stop dead in my tracks but I do not turn around. I look at my feet as the panic rises within me.

"My last Camino," Bastien says. It's almost a whisper, but it's loud enough to rip a hole through my heart.

My feet begin to move of their own volition, even before I can fully process his words. The trees begin to fly by as I pick up speed, running over rocks and branches and the dusty pulp of last autumn's leaves ground into the earth.

I don't stop. I can't stop. Every time I hear my name called from behind me, louder with each utterance, I run faster. I refuse to stop running. And I won't look back.

CHAPTER 38

SHANIA REYNOLDS

THURSDAY, JULY 11TH – Day 13 – I Can't Fix This. And Tomorrow is the End of Our Camino

I thought I was doing this journaling thing right. Turns out I'm failing. I'm going to have to catch up on missed days. I bet Troy's is perfect... annotated, diagrams, tricolored ink.

Diego is destroyed, and I can't fix it. I hate when I can't fix things. I feel so useless. Bastien has the big C word. It's part of the reason he's out here on the Camino. It's like he's saying goodbye to his life.

By the time we met up with the rest of the group in A Calzada for lunch, the damage was already done. Diego was inconsolable. This didn't stop Gil and Kei's sisters from trying. They fussed over him on the patio while Bastien laid low inside the café, looking guilty.

I know he feels terrible for coming into Diego's life and causing him pain when he's already destroyed over losing his grandmother.

I think Bastien is like a sick dog with his death. He just wants to go away somewhere by himself, quietly lie down, pull the covers of the world up over his head, and disappear.

I hate my life. Sometimes. Even on the Camino. It gives and it takes, I guess. And tomorrow is the end of the walk. How did that even happen!

Bright side? It's kind of a riddle today. I can't describe what's happening, but it seriously feels more like the beginning of something than an ending... to be continued.

"You almost ready? We're gonna get going," Diego says, as his finger swoops in and flips my journal closed. He smirks, but there's no humor in his eyes.

I put my journal away and look up, expecting to see the others sitting on the barstools along the counter beside me. But Greg and Manny are standing at the front door pretending to look impatient. The other two must have already stepped outside.

"Oops," I say. "Sorry." I grab my backpack, and we make our way outside. Then, in a panic, I pull out my passport and run back inside for my stamp.

We're in A Brea. Almost at Santa Irene, our final albergue stop ever. And it's probably the first time it's just the six of us. The Banditos. *The Camino Club.* I think it was Manny who came up with that one.

When Diego and I got up to leave the café back in A Calzada, we planned to walk alone for the rest of the day. But Greg got up and said he was coming with us. He wouldn't take no for an answer.

Then Manny said he wasn't about to be left behind. His exact words were, "Yo, not without me, D. I got your back, bro."

Gil's face practically cracked, he smiled so big. Proof his diversion program was working or something. He loves when bonding shit happens between us.

Claire got up, threw on her backpack, and said, "Wait for me." Then she turned to Troy and said, "Well, are you coming or what? Let's go."

Nobody thought he would. He and Kei have been an inseparable unit. But Troy looked to Kei as if to ask for permission, and Kei just said, "Yeah, yeah. Go. I'll be fine. I'll walk with these guys to the albergue. I've hardly spent any time with my sisters anyway."

"Cool, thanks," Troy said. He kissed Kei goodbye and that was it. Gil and Meagan beamed like proud parents as we abandoned them on the café patio and set out. We walked nonstop from A Calzada to A Brea, almost two hours. It probably should have been less, but the guys goofed off the whole way here. Operation *Cheer Up Diego*. It may even be working.

Troy gives me this look when I rejoin them at the side of the highway just beyond the café parking lot. I hold up my passport. "Sorry. Forgot to get my stamp."

"Only about three kilometers away," he says, as he glances back to his guidebook. "Why did we even stop here?"

"Because Claire was going to piss herself and you *required coffee*," Manny says, groaning over his last words.

"Oh, Right. I was wilting and needed refueling. So sue me," Troy says as he returns his guidebook to his pack. "Straight ahead along the highway, people. We shall arrive at our destination in about half an hour."

"*Shall*, loser?" Claire says. "Really?"

"Watch it. I'm still undecided about you. Those who worship Creepy Jesus should not ridicule others."

Manny laughs. "You two are weird. Let's go already." And with that announcement, we're off.

We break up into twos to walk alongside the highway. I walk with Diego. Maybe sensing he doesn't have a lot of time to talk before we get there, Diego starts right away.

"Do you think I'm being too hard on Bastien?" he says. The look on his face suggests my answer could make or break him.

"Diego, you met him, what?" I try to do the math, but everything bleeds together here. "Three or four days ago. I know how you feel, like you've known him forever. Shit, I'm not even as close to him, and he feels like family. But when you think about it, he's just a guy who's along for a walk with a bunch of other people. Yes, I love him. And it's obvious you do. But I don't think he owes us anything."

"Whoa," Diego says. "So is that what *we* are, too? Just two people taking a long walk together?"

And I break him. Way to go, Shania. Your major fail streak continues.

"That's not what I meant." But I don't really know *what* I meant. Feelings are too intense out here. "I just mean, it's terrible he has cancer. He's a good person. We've fallen in love with this amazing man. He's given us so much. But we're going to get on a plane in Santiago and then another one in Madrid, get off in Toronto, and never see him again."

"Damn, Shania. I was hoping for a pep talk. You're not very good at this."

We kind of smirk at each other. We *sort* of chuckle.

"I've never done something like this. That man, Diego..."

"I know."

"You just needed space to take it in. He'll understand. With your grandmother and stuff."

"I left him alone in the woods when he was feeling like a pile of shit. He pretty much passed out in that church. He saved me, and I couldn't do shit for him so I ran."

I know he's wrong, but I can't put my finger on why. Truth is, I think all of us have been saving Bastien this entire time. We just didn't know it.

"And then when he finally dragged his ass into A Calzada, I wouldn't even speak to him at lunch. Like it's his fault he has cancer."

"Yeah," I say. "That *was* kind of shitty. I'm not gonna lie."

"Pep Talk Shania. That's what we should call you." He kicks at the gravel like he's pouting. "Damn, girl."

"Come on, Diego. The guy adores you. Who doesn't?" I laugh and grab his hand. "Not like you can't talk to him when they catch up in Santa Irene."

"Speaking of Santa Irene." Troy pushes between us, forcing our hands apart. "We're almost in Cerceda. We have to cross the highway just up there."

Troy points a few hundred feet ahead to a big sign between the highway and our skinny walking trail. It shows a stick-figure pilgrim crossing the highway.

"Yikes," I say as I look behind us for cars. None. But I do see Manny, Claire, and Greg attempting to do some of those eye-high, big-kick, Rockettes dance moves with their arms interlocked. While walking.

"Ten bucks somebody bleeds before this is over," Diego says after turning to see what all the commotion is about.

When they catch us watching them, they crack up even harder than they already were. Everything starts to crumble, and they break apart and stumble exaggeratedly, howling.

"Losers," I say, but I'm laughing just as hard. "We need to cross, guys."

"Aye aye, Captain," Greg says. The three of them run to catch up. "We could have used a fourth, Troy. Thanks for keeping us off balance, dude. We know where your loyalties lie."

"Um, yeah." Troy assumes the role of a crossing guard and herds us as we near the pilgrim crossing. "My loyalties will *always* be with the ones not making fools of themselves."

Troy's arms spread wide to hold us back, even though there's literally not a single car in sight in either direction. He walks backward to the edge of the highway and waits for all of us to stop walking.

"Look both ways," he says.

"Get out my way, Troyboy," Manny says. He kicks at the dirt like he's a bull who's going to plough through Troy. "Before I lose it on you for being too clueless to live."

This gets a rise of laughter out of Greg and an awkward little snort out of Claire.

"Fair enough," Troy says. He steps aside, and we all cross unscathed. "I was only trying to save your lives, you ungrateful beasts."

The others keep walking. After Troy finally crosses, Diego asks, "Can I see that stupid guidebook of yours? Mine's in the bottom of my backpack, and I don't feel like digging for it."

"We're almost there," Troy says. He attempts to brush Diego off. He doesn't like sharing his book. "Just down the road a bit."

Diego stares him down until Troy looks slightly shamed. He hands the book to Diego. Unlike Troy, Diego stops walking to read the guidebook. He doesn't have a death wish.

"We're stopping here," Diego says, pointing to a line on the page that lists a bar just up ahead before Santa Irene.

"Why would we stop?" I say. "We literally just stopped." We can practically see Santa Irene in the distance. I'm hot and sticky, and my feet are sore.

"Because we are."

"O Ceadoiro?" Troy says.

"Yep. That one." He closes the guide, passes it back to Troy, and starts walking. Troy looks at me like I should do something about Diego before it's too late.

"He's *yours*," he says. We're left standing by the side of the highway looking at each other. I shrug and start to walk. Troy follows.

"Why are we stopping?" I ask Diego again. He's now far ahead of us. He's on a mission to get to the bar. I can tell by the rigid way he's walking, we're going to be following his plan.

"Because."

"That's helpful." At Diego's new pace, we catch up to the others. I turn to Claire. "We're stopping before Santa Irene."

"Why?" she asks.

Manny moans. Like the rest of us, he probably wants to get to the albergue, kick off his hiking boots, and fall onto his bed.

"Because I say so," Diego says. "We walk into Santa Irene together."

"We don't have to stop to do th—"

"*All* of us."

"Ah. Bastien," I say. He gives me a tight-lipped smile and pulls forward. Troy starts to say something, but Manny glares him down, and his mouth closes before the first word gets out.

The five of us allow Diego to lead the march the rest of the way to the bar.

Once inside, we ditch our backpacks and take a table for four in the corner. Greg drags two chairs over from an empty table, and we all plunk down. No one speaks.

Manny, who can't sit still ever, drums his fingers on the table. When no one responds, he jumps up.

"Well," he says. "I'm getting a Coke. Anyone else wants anything, you'll have to get it yourself."

He hauls his wallet out and heads for the counter.

"Guys, I'm fine. I just wanna wait for Bastien and the others. That's all. Okay? I don't want to kill the mood on the last full day or anything. Can we chill a bit? I didn't mean to bring everyone down."

"We could have just as easily done the waiting at the albergue," Troy says. The look Greg gives him pretty much kills him. He slumps farther in his chair. Diego reaches across the table and pats Troy's shoulder.

"I'm sorry, Troy," Diego says. "It's been a shitty day. I don't know what I'm doing. I just got this feeling, like we should all walk into this town together. I want to do it with Bastien."

"Nah, I'm sorry, Diego. I'm just being bitchy. We can wait. Doesn't matter."

"If you guys wanna go on ahead, feel free. Really. I'm being an ass. I'll just wait here."

"Nobody moves," Greg orders. He slaps the table and stands up. "I got you, D. Diego's right," he continues. "This is our last albergue. We arrive together. I'm getting a Coke. Might as well get yourself one of those fancy coffee things, Troy, 'cause you're not going anywhere."

"Get me one too," Claire says.

"One Coke coming up," Greg says as he turns to leave.

Troy joins him. "I could do a café con leche any time. You don't have to twist my arm."

As they head to the counter, Manny comes back to the table.

"So," he says as he sits beside Diego and pulls his chair up close to him. "Isn't this the part, D, where we have that conversation about what happens after? You know, like in *Breakfast Club*. We gonna be friends after detention, my man? What about Troy? Claire? What's gonna happen when we see each other in the hall?"

This seems to immediately haul Diego out of his current slump. He's laughing before Manny gets halfway through his diatribe.

"Ooh, which one am I?" Claire says. Clearly, she's seen the movie too. Maybe I'm the only one who hasn't? "I'm already a Claire, so I could be Claire. I can eat sushi and—"

"Ha, ha," Manny says. "You kidding me, girl? I mean, *are you kidding me*?" He's loud. Loud enough to have Troy and Greg look over to see what's going on. They hurry back and sit down. Greg slides a Coke to Diego, even though he hadn't asked for one. Diego nods his thanks.

"What?" Claire says. "What's wrong with that?"

"Girl, you Allison. Ally Sheedy's character. Allison with a bullet. You'd be the dark mystery girl with the backstory and attitude. That Allison girl, she'd be the one on the Camino searching out your Creepy Jesus guy. Am I right, Diego?"

"*Welllllll*," Diego says. He's full-on smiling now, and I feel my whole body sigh as the tension in my shoulders slips away. "He's not wrong, Allison… um, I mean, Claire."

"Funny," she says. Greg hands her a Coke, and she thanks him, pops the tab, and takes a drink. Then he slides one over to me too. Sweet.

"Shania here would be Claire, of course," Greg says as I open my pop. Another movie fan. I *am* the only one. "Pretty little rich girl. Steals cars for kicks, even though she probably drives a—what, Shania? BMW? Maybe a Porsche? Mercedes?"

"Not even close." I wish I knew what they were talking about. "I share a car with my brother. If you want to call it that. He's in it all the time. And it's not a Porsche. It's just a Honda Civic."

"*Just* a Honda Civic?" Manny practically screams. "Girl, you're Claire. Bang on. Get it on. You don't even recognize your privilege."

Everyone laughs. I laugh along even though I don't know why and I'm pretty sure I've just been insulted.

"Anyway, can we get back to the question?" Manny says.

"Wait," Troy says. "Can we just make sure everyone knows I'm the Brian guy? Before we go any further. The Brainiac with a future brighter than all the rest of you losers. Thank you."

"This did not need to be discussed, brother," Manny says, even though I think that if there's a brain in our group, it's him. Manny's a definite candidate for this Brian guy. "We all knew this. My question… since we are at that point in our little Camino movie… we gonna be friends when this is done?"

"Of course. We're really nothing like those guys in the movie," Greg says. "They spent, what, six hours together in that library? We're here for almost two weeks, walking our feet off and smelling each other's stink every night. Come on, dude. Not even a question. We're solid."

"Greg's right," Diego says, dead serious. "I got my girl." He leans close to me, and I rest a head on his shoulder. "And my boys." He smiles at Manny and Greg. "And these two misfits."

"How do *we* get to be the misfits?" Claire asks. "Troy and I have more going for us than all the rest of you put together."

"Yeah," Diego says. "And you also have Creepy Jesus. *Soooo*, my little misfits."

Even I laugh this time.

"The comparison falls apart when you try to peg us into those guys," Greg says, coming back to the characters. "I mean, obviously I'm Judd Nelson's character. The bad guy with a good heart. But so is Diego. And so is Manny. But Manny's as much a Brian as Troy. Don't forget what brought Manny here, children."

"The gun in his locker? I mean, damn. That is exactly why Brian was in detention. Manny's Brian. But he's also Emilio Estevez's jock character. Manny's a total athlete, no? The whole point of the movie was that all the characters had a bit of each of them in them. Remember the essay they finally conned Brian into writing?"

"Oh yeah," Manny says. "At the end. True, bro. About each of them being a brainiac, a psycho, an athlete, a hood, and a princess."

"Yeah," Diego says. "Wow. So true."

I look around the table, and everyone's nodding and agreeing.

After a long pause, Diego says, "We're friends."

He takes turns looking all of us in the eye. After he makes his way around the entire table, he says, "Forever. Peregrinos."

We grow quiet and look around at one another. Claire sighs and smiles.

"Yeah," Troy says in something just above a whisper. "Friends in the afterlife."

Manny raises his Coke in the air. "To the Camino Club."

"Amen," Diego and Greg say at the same time. We all raise our drinks together and seal his words with a toast.

In the silence that follows, Troy clears his throat. "Ahem," he says. "I'm so glad we've had this little kiki, kiddies. Because I plan on leaning heavily on all of you for about a month or so after we get home. I'm about to be brokenhearted and I'm going to need, oh, I don't know, about five shoulders to cry on."

"Kei?" I say. Damn. New York is far away. And he chose to walk with us this afternoon instead of with Kei. Wow.

"Yep. Kei. I never expected to find a Kei on this walk."

"We got you, Troyboy," Greg says. And I know he means it.

CHAPTER 39

TROY SINCLAIR

Last day. I thought I would be the first one downstairs for breakfast. But when I step into the dining room balancing my tray of scrambled eggs and my café con leche, I find Bastien and Diego sitting together at the long wooden table.

I make my way over to them, but as I go to sit down I hear bits and pieces of their conversation and realize I've walked into something a little too serious to interrupt.

"Oops, sorry," I swerve to avoid sitting beside Diego. "Good morning, gentlemen."

"Hey, Troyboy," Diego says. He smiles and pops a forkful of egg into his mouth.

"Troy," Bastien says. "Happy last day of the Camino, son. Today, we walk to the cathedral. The jewel at the end of the journey, no?"

"Yeah," I say. "I can't wait." And despite the fact that my heart is being torn out of my chest knowing it'll soon be over, I'm honestly excited to begin it. I'm dying to see the cathedral and the swinging of the Botafumeiro in the church. I've read about the ceremony over and over in the guidebook. And I also watched a dozen videos of it on YouTube. I'm looking forward to smelling the burning incense as it swings through the air.

"Your life, it begins after Compostela, yes? You shall see." He smiles and takes a sip of his coffee.

"Listen, guys. I'm gonna take my tray outside and sit on the patio. Looks nice out."

"You can sit with us, bro," Diego says.

"Nah, I'm good. Thanks, though. You guys go ahead and have some time alone together."

I leave them to their thing and step outside. What a gorgeous day to walk to Santiago. The sun is shining, and it's not stinky hot like it was yesterday.

I sit at one of the two park benches that rest against the outside wall of the albergue. As I start to shovel the eggs down, Greg joins me on the other bench.

"Hey, dude," he says as he tucks his hair behind his ears. I swear, it got three times blonder since we arrived in Spain. He's full-on surf dude now. "Ready for this?"

"Ready as I'll ever be, I guess."

"What about Kei? What's going on there?"

"Yeah. Trying not to think about it."

"Sorry. Didn't mean to poke. That must suck, dude."

"That's okay. It's gonna be one of those days. I'm going to be an emotional wreck for so many reasons today."

We sit in silence as we finish eating. When I see that Greg has nothing left on his plate, I ask him, "So what's waiting for you back home, Greg? You're very private. Share."

"Well," he begins. "Pfffft. That's a hard one, Troy. Where do I even begin?"

"Well, that sounds intriguing."

"Remember how I told you about my parents' divorce and how my brother is getting lost in the fallout?"

"Yep," I say. "That seriously sucks. I couldn't imagine my parents splitting."

"The splitting wasn't the worst part," he says. "It's the way they both became so self-centered. Like their drama is the only thing in the world. I'm so stressed about Robbie. I'm gonna be looking at schools soon. Last year I was excited about college, you know. I was going to pick somewhere far away and stay on campus. I was so pumped. Their marriage spins apart, and all my prospects go out the window with it. There's no way I can leave Robbie now. This, being here? This is bad enough. Who knows what he's gone through since I abandoned him?"

"Come on, dude," I say. "You did *not* abandon him."

"Nice of you to say, but I knew the score. I never should have messed up the way I did. He's the one it hurt the most. Robbie needs stability more than anything. He can't deal with change. I mean, not at all. It destroys him. Anyway, now I'm looking at schools close enough for me to get home before supper every day. Just so he can have some kind of normalcy. Because my parents have become incapable of giving him that. I feel like raising him has become my main responsibility. I'm so stressed."

"I'm sorry, Greg," I say. I don't know what else to say. It sounds like he's doing the right thing, and there's nothing else he can do without abandoning his brother. "Sounds like you have a lot of crap to deal with."

"Yeah," he says. He shrugs, though, like he's blowing it all off. "But, seriously. We're talking U of T, Ryerson, York. They're all amazing. I just had this image of going away for school, you know. Guess you can't always get what you want."

"Yeah, but you got us," I say. I laugh, but I'm also serious. This has been cool. Nothing makes a friendship like living twenty-four seven with people. "One good thing came out of your life of crimes and misdemeanors."

"Ha," he says. "Yeah. Guess you're right. I'm sorry I was such an ass at first, Troy. I'm just really mad at my parents. I made you a target. That was shitty."

"Nope. It's okay. We already did this. You don't need to apologize again."

"Buen Camino."

We look up to see an older woman walking past the house. She has wild gray hair with a bright blue streak in her bangs and wears rainbow leggings and a lime-green T-shirt that reads: *Free Your Mind Instead*. I love her already.

"Buen Camino," Greg and I reply simultaneously.

"Enjoy your day, gentlemen. Santiago awaits!" She holds a victory fist in the air. "It's happening!"

We're all smiles. Greg laughs. "You go, girl," he says.

"Where are you from?" she says, slowing down. "I'm Betty. Taos, New Mexico."

Greg points to himself and then to me. "Greg and Troy. Toronto."

"Go, Canada! Enjoy, boys. See you at the cathedral."

"Buen Camino," we repeat. She smiles and walks on.

"Where was I?" Greg says. He stands up and puts out a hand and I give him my plate. He sets it on top of his own.

"We all have our own little clouds, Troy. Otherwise we wouldn't be here. Happy people don't fuck up."

"That sounded just a bit like Bastien wisdom, in a weird unedited-for-potty-mouth way."

"Yeah, well," he says, as I open the door for him. "Maybe he's rubbing off."

"Wouldn't be such a bad thing."

We go inside to prepare for the rest of the day. Our last day. Wow. I can't even believe it.

*   *   *

"Okay, gang. Our last group discussion before Compostela." Gil says, once we're all packed and ready to go. He and Meagan sit on one of the beds and the six of us surround them. "Time to think about what we've learned out here, eh?"

"Can we just cut to the chase," Claire says. "We've all fessed up about what brought us here. Manny, with his *accidental* weapons charge, Shania with her grand theft auto, Troy with his roid rage Captain Destructo 'incident.' Diego, the arsonist Casanova. And me, the B & E expert who likes to break things just as much as Troy does."

She stops there and makes a show of counting to five on her fingers. She slowly raises a sixth finger while she glares at Greg. "According to my calculations, that leaves one delinquent without a story. My, my. How *ever* did that happen?"

"Rules," Meagan says. "Nobody on the program is required to divulge their crime to the rest of the group. Gil and I? We both know everyone's story. The rest of you? You only get to know what each of you wants to share. Greg doesn't have to say a word."

"Blah, blah, blah," I say. "Come on, Greg. Give it up."

The other guys start up a *Yeah, Greg, Yeah, Greg* chant.

"Now, guys." Gil wriggles on the bed. "Let's not pile on. He has every right to—"

"No, no," Greg says. "They're right, Gil. If I want to be part of this club that nobody on the outside would ever want to be a part of, I should at least share my story."

"Okay, kiddo. But you don't have to. Don't feel forced into it. That's not what we're about."

"Nah. It's all good, Gil. I was talking with Troy at breakfast about stuff and, yeah. I'm ready."

"Cool," I say. "Let's have it. Speak."

Claire laughs.

"Can I just start off by saying I don't think I really belong with you losers. Yeah, I did something bad. And, although the thing I did is the same thing one of you did, I did *my* bad something with the very best of intentions. So, not a criminal."

"Yeah, and the anti-gay camp didn't deserve to be taken down by yours truly," Claire says.

"Okay, okay. Maybe you're the possible exception, Claire. I give you points for socially conscious criminality. Sincerely."

"You're stalling," I say. I sit down on the bed opposite Gil and Meagan. Shania and Diego join me.

"Okay, okay. So it was a perfectly sunny spring day. Robbie, my little bro, was freaking out about some LEGO dilemma. He sometimes snaps over stuff. One of his many issues. He's a seven-year-old on the autism spectrum. He'd been inside for a few days, and I could tell he was suffering from cabin fever. His schedule was completely messed up, and you can't do that to these kids.

"But Mom was out of town on some business trip, and my father lives across town now. I didn't want to deal with his passive-aggressive crap. He'd bitch about Mom leaving us alone instead of sending us to his house. He'd be pissed at her instead of coming and getting us. And pissed at me for not calling him sooner.

"There I was with this kid who's having a breakdown because his LEGO weren't doing what he wanted them to do. The sun was shining. I knew the Boardwalk would be a perfect distraction.

"Robbie loves the beaches. Especially Woodbine Beach near the end of the Boardwalk, where they have all those volleyball nets. When they're out and there's games going on? Man, he's a one-kid cheering section.

"I packed Robbie's favorite beach toys. He has all these sandcastle molds. I packed a lunch, a couple beach towels, and sunscreen. I did everything right."

He stops. The look on his face is fierce.

"Then we walked to the town center, and I made my way around the parking lot until I found an unlocked car. I got Robbie inside and jacked it. That kid needed a break. I had to do what I did to give him the day of magic he needed. His meltdown was epic. My parents put us through a year of hell, and Robbie was pretty much destroyed by everything. I was taking that kid to the beach, no matter what. I no longer cared."

"What the shit?" Shania says. "How many times did you joke about me being a car thief?"

"Shania," Gil begins.

"I know, words. Last day, Gil. Come on."

"Nope. Rules are rules."

"They suck," she says. But she's smiling. "Who doesn't say shit? Besides, he gets to joke about my—"

"Words."

"Shhhh," I say.

"We drove down to the Boardwalk, and I took Robbie to the beaches. We would have been fine, too. The parking's pretty far away from where we actually walked to. When the cops found the car, we could have just walked away and found another way home.

"But with all the crap I packed for Robbie, I had so much to carry from the car. And he was freaking out, half meltdown and half excited to get to the lake. I left the most important thing behind on the passenger seat. My wallet."

"Whoa, dude," Manny says. "That's mad crazy."

"Wow, Greg," Diego says. "That's, you know… stupid."

"Gee, thanks," Greg says. "Sorry, D. I guess I just don't have a criminal mind. Not like you. It takes real skills to start a fire when all you really need to do is pull the alarm. I mean, same result without the arson charge. Yeah. I'm stupid."

"Well played," Diego says. Everyone's laughing and I think it's the beginning of a lighthearted day. And also an emotional one. This is going to be so strange.

"Just one more thing," Greg says. "As much as this will probably make Gil cringe and Meagan cry, I'd do it all over again. I'd do anything for Robbie. Anything."

It starts to make sense to me now, the reason Greg has been so overprotective of Diego since his grandmother died. He's a champion of the underdog. He doesn't like to see the people in his life suffering. He's a good guy.

"Okay, guys. Okay. Can we get back on track now? We only have a few minutes left before we need to set off. Anyone want to start off on the topic of what we've learned so far on the journey. Tell me how things are going to change when you go home?"

We're all quiet as we look around the room at each other. Shania is the first to raise her hand. Her eyes well up with tears before she even begins to speak.

"I hated all of you people before I stepped out my front door back home in Toronto. I wanted to die. And I was angry at each and every one of you. Especially you, Gil." She points to him, and he shrugs *who me?* "With your face-cracking smile and your optimism. I did *not* want to come here. And I hated this stupid-ass diversion program shit most of all. Sorry. I know. Words."

Shania stops talking, reaches for Diego's hand, and watches as their fingers intertwine.

"And now I never want to leave. You people? You see me."

I find myself wiping at my own tears. Meagan silently hands tissues to both me and Shania.

Gil puts his hands together and stretches his arms out, fingers intertwined, and we all recognize this as his lecture stance. We're about to get our last lesson on the Camino. Unlike all the other times he's done this, I don't hear a single moan. Not a single one of us rolls our eyes. If anything, there's this imperceptible movement toward him as he prepares to speak. He has our undivided attention.

CHAPTER 40

DIEGO NELSON

It feels so right to finish this journey with Bastien at my side. Even more right that we've all stayed close together today. Though we started out as a reluctant group of eight, there's no reluctance in our expanded group of twelve—unless you count Troy's reluctance to leave Kei's side. And my reluctance to leave Bastien's. And everyone else's reluctance to leave the Camino.

We have walked all day. The last of the towns in the guidebook are being struck off the list one after the other. Through a gravel path to Rúa, on to Arca, and through a forest to O Amenal, where we crossed a river. Then we walked through more woods. It's been a day of everything, even hills.

Bastien and I walk at the back of the pack. Shania stayed with us for a while, but eventually left us to catch up with Manny and Greg.

"We must pick up twigs, Diego," Bastien says as we make our way through the woods. "This may be the last forest, no? We will need little twigs for the airport."

"Huh? Why?" I ask. But I don't wait for an answer as I scan the forest floor for twigs.

"It is no matter now. I show you."

"How much farther to the airport?"

"You will know. We will come to a marker." Bastien holds his hand up to the top of my head. "About this tall. *Diego tall*. It is to show the entrance to the municipality of Santiago. We go from there, and you see where you need these twigs, yes?"

We come to a large cement barrier wall covered in graffiti and artwork. More work of peregrinos. I recognize one of the fancy scripts near the end of the wall and I point to it.

"See that?" I say to Bastien. "Remember yesterday? The one that read *Life is Too Short*? Same graffiti artist."

This one says, *Remember to Laugh*.

"Same advice, no? Same meaning, different words," he says.

"Yeah. I guess so."

"We come soon to our monument. You kids, you'll want... what is it?" He mimes taking a picture. "The selfie?"

"Ha ha. Yeah. Selfie."

"It comes soon. We run out of forest first. You run up, tell the others to get their twigs, Diego. They will all need them."

I run ahead a bit.

"Hey, guys. Hold up," I say.

Manny and Greg turn back, and I catch up, waving my twigs. I tell everyone to start grabbing whatever small sticks they can find because we'll need them when we get to the airport.

Greg grabs the closest large tree branch he can find and starts waving it in the air. "Air traffic control?" he asks.

"Not quite. Funny." I hold my twigs up again. "Get your twigs before it's too late." Claire, Shania, Troy, and Kei are already kicking through a bit of grass along the side of the path, picking up any twigs they see.

Meagan and Gil, who had been leading the group along with Kei's sisters, come back to find out what the holdup is.

"What's up?" Meagan says.

"Bastien says we need twigs for the airport," I tell her.

"Oh, God," she says. "Yes. I completely forgot. Sorry, guys. Thank God for Bastien. Come on, Gil. We'll need to get some too."

Gil begins to pluck up sticks. Soon, we all have enough. When I look behind me, no Bastien. My heart races.

"Yo, loser," Shania says. She grabs my head and turns it in the other direction to the path ahead. "He kept walking. He's *right* there."

"Oops. Is it that obvious?"

"Yes." She takes my hand, and we start to walk.

When we catch up with Bastien, he says, "The marker. It is there."

And sure enough, it is just ahead of us. Like Bastien said, it's as tall as me. The closer we get, the more the details jump out at us. One word across the top, like a banner, announces *Santiago*. The marker has a large scallop shell swinging from a rope, all carved into the cement of the monument. Every inch of its top is covered with rocks and wilted flowers left by peregrinos.

Before we get to it, we all pick up stones. After we take turns carefully setting them atop the others on the marker, we step back and take it in.

"This, this place," Bastien spreads his arms wide to encompass all the land beyond the marker. "This is the place of Santiago. We have arrived. Soon we will hit the city limits of Santiago de Compostela. I hope you are ready for your life to begin." He winks at Becky, and she giggles.

"Pictures," Kei says. "We need pictures. All of us."

"Excuse me," Meagan says to a man walking by.

"Buen Camino," he says. He's wearing a ball cap that has the NY of the New York Yankees on it. Sweat is pouring off him, and he looks miserable, but tries to change his expression for Meagan.

"Do you think you could take our photo with this monument here? Sorry to bother you."

"Oh, no trouble. Sorry. Just in my head today. Blisters. Trying to forget them. It's a head-down, full-speed-ahead day." His New York accent is strong.

"Hey," Kei says when he hears the man speak. "A fellow New Yorker. Hi. Sorry about the blisters."

"Oh, hi. Lots of them out here. New Yorkers, I mean. But blisters too, I guess." He laughs. "Rodger. Manhattan."

"Kei. My sisters Becky and Mia. Piermont."

"Across the Hudson. Know it well."

"Nice."

"Come on then, let's get you all together and get this shot done." We all scramble to gather around the monument. After he takes a few shots, he hands Meagan's phone back and wishes us all a *Buen Camino*. We return the greeting before he's off on the path, walking away from us.

We take selfies and various group shots. I'm in one with the boys, and we're all pretending to be holding guns, all badass. And one with Shania and one with Bastien and one with both of them. As I'm about to give up the monument for someone else to have a turn, Greg steps up.

"Do you mind, bro?"

"Not at all, come on in," I say. We both snap our own shots and put away our phones. "Let's go."

The twelve of us are soon on our way, walking in mini groups but staying close together.

"The fence, the fence," Bastien says a few minutes later. I turn to my left and see the chain link fence just off the path. And intertwined in its links are an endless array of mini crosses made of twigs. The path moves closer to the fence and soon we are directly beside it.

"We have arrived. The airport. It lies beyond the fence."

A lump rises in my throat at the sight of all the crosses. Some are simple twigs stuck in the links in such ways that they form crosses. Others have decorations hanging from them and still others are wrapped in strips of bright cloth. There are even crosses on chains, store-bought ones, and wooden homemade ones on twine.

All I can think of is my abuelita and how much she would have loved this sight. Instead of forming a cross of my own with my twigs, I stop and caress a few of the ones already woven into the fence. I look around and everyone is busy building crosses and fitting them into the links. It feels so ceremonial.

"Diego," Bastien says. "You make one." I look at my twigs. They've lost their meaning to me. "Here, here."

Bastien takes them from me and removes a small spool of thread from a side pocket in his backpack. He waves it about and says, "String," to everyone present. Those who want it come running. Greg's cross is already fixed in the links of the fence.

Bastien crosses my twigs and pinches them between his thumb and forefinger. "Here, hold them like this." He passes them and takes a length of string and wraps it round and round the cross between my fingers, weaving it round and through the spaces. When he's done, he says, "Tada."

Sure enough, I have an intact cross in my hand. I walk along the fence and look for the perfect place to leave my cross for my gran. When I decide where to leave it, I bring it to my lips and kiss it before I weave it into the fence.

"Almost there, kiddos," Gil says after everyone winds down at the fence. "Next stop Santiago."

"Not quite, Gil," Bastien says. "The monument first. The pilgrims overlooking the view of the city. Come, come."

We keep walking along the fence to a small wooded area.

"Some of our last trees," Bastien says. "Soon, a highway. More hills. Lots to climb before Santiago. And then the monument."

I walk with Shania, and we hold hands. Bastien walks behind us, alone. The ever present click of his walking stick is soothing. I'm going to miss it when this is over. I sometimes hear it in my sleep.

CHAPTER 41

SHANIA REYNOLDS

Friday, July 12th – Day 14 – This Is It.

I'm not even going to write anything today. I can't hold on. The excitement that follows every step of this last day is only darkened by the absolute certainty that this amazing journey is going to end. We did this. And it was incredible. I have a movie to watch when I get home. But I know our journey is going to be so much greater than anything that could ever possibly go down in one day in a school library. We're the Camino Club. We're the real shit. I know, GILBERT!!! Words. Yep.

"Look. There," Bastien says, after we've been walking for some time in silence. We've been doing a lot of trudging. Uphill, downhill. The more they talk about how close we are, the less I believe them. It feels like the never-ending walk today.

I follow Bastien's finger and see a large group of people milling about a huge monument. I recognize it from the guidebook. "Monte do Gozo," Bastien says. "We are near Compostela now. An hour, maybe?"

"Hill of Joy," Diego says, with exactly zero joy in his voice. He doesn't even make an effort to hide his conflicted emotions.

"Yes, oui."

Manny and Greg break free of the pack. They sprint to see who gets to the monument first. It's a close race at first, but even from a block back I can see Manny beats Greg by a landslide.

Claire bursts out laughing when Manny starts this insane victory dance. He runs around the bottom of the monument and jumps up to slap his hand against its side. It almost looks like he's trying to reach the top of its base to pull himself up.

"Please, God," Gil says. "Don't let him scale that monument." He makes a show of closing his eyes and cringing, but Manny has moved on. He heads for the wide-open space just behind the monument that looks down into the small dip of valley beyond.

As we approach the cutoff that heads into the attraction, I let go of Diego's hand. "Come on," I shout to Claire as I grab on to her arm and pull her along. "Let's go see."

Kei and Troy break free, too, and soon the four of us are in a race of our own. It's not as high-octane as the first one, though. We all arrive together.

When I look back, Diego is still on the road with the others.

"Diego," I yell. "Come on. Come see."

"Nah. I'm good. We'll get there. I'm pooped."

"Come, come. There is more to see," Bastien says to Diego once they arrive. "Come. The church. It is beyond the monument, yes."

He looks up into the blue sky. "Yes, yes. Clear skies. No cloud. We maybe see the cathedral in the valley."

We all make our way beyond the monument together.

"Come, come," Bastien says. "Gather round."

Oddly enough, it's not only the eleven of us who come when he calls. Other pilgrims hear the authority in Bastien's voice and join us at the edge of the hill, by statues of two pilgrims who look off into the distance. The statues hold walking sticks in their left hands. One holds out his hat with his right hand, and the other simply holds out his hand, pointing down into the valley.

When I follow the direction of the statue's hand, I see them: the spires of the cathedral.

"These men," Bastien begins, pointing up at the statues. There are no fewer than twenty peregrinos gathered about him now and more making their way over to us. "These peregrinos of The Way. They are the statue of José María Acuña. They stand at this site to show weary pilgrims the last leg of the journey. What all of it is for, no? The cathedral in the distance. The bones of St. James, the apostle of Christ."

Others leave the monument, drawn to the constellation of Bastien... our snake charmer.

"It is tradition at this place to cry out in rapture at the first sight of what it is we seek. At this place, we also pray for the weariness in our hearts and feet, yes," Bastien says. "We take off our shoes at the statue of the pilgrims and we feel the earth where generations of peregrinos before us have walked this way."

Bastien stops talking, sits in the dirt, and removes his shoes and socks. This hits me in the same way his prayer to Diego's abuelita under the Milky Way hit me. Tears well up, and my vision blurs as they fill my eyes. I look to Diego, and he is also removing his footwear.

I can't believe what happens next; all these people drop to the ground and remove their shoes and socks. All the while, more pilgrims make their way over to us and sit in the dirt.

As I look around me, I'm guessing there are fifty of us now. When Bastien stands up, he is barefoot. And so are all of his followers, myself included.

"We feel the earth of our forefathers, no?" He walks in little circles around the statues and beyond, and all the barefoot peregrinos follow him. "We remember to be children now. Leave the rest up here on the Monte do Gozo. On the Hill of Joy. Leave your anger, your sadness, your exhaustion, your loss, your jealousy and greed. Leave it all up here in the dirt of our ancestors. We are pilgrims, peregrinos. We must walk into Santiago de Compostela as children, no?"

I'm not the only one crying. We are all mesmerized by Bastien.

"We leave these pilgrim statues behind so that they may continue to tell the others who will come after us. Peregrinos will always come. These statues, they themselves will never arrive. But they will continue to help the others as they flock to the Hill of Joy. They will point the way to the cathedral for all the weary travelers.

"Please, we put back on our socks and shoes and we bless this place. It is sacred in the way it welcomes us and ushers us forward to our Compostela. We must honor this sacredness. As I said, we leave the rest here. We walk to Compostela as children. We laugh, we dance, we skip, we play. My friends, enjoy your last walk. This incredible journey, it will stay with you. It will tell you where to begin your life. Enjoy."

Bastien turns to the valley below. He stands still beside the statues, and now he becomes the third pilgrim statue. He points into the distance, directly at a cathedral spire.

"We go." He says. As he drops to the ground to put his socks and shoes back on, a pilgrim near the back of the group starts to clap. I look at Troy and Diego, who are standing beside me. Troy shrugs and begins to clap. Diego joins him. Soon, we are all clapping for the man sitting in the sand looking for all the world like the child he has told us all to become.

CHAPTER
42

TROY SINCLAIR

THE WALK AWAY FROM THE monument at the Hill of Joy? It may be the biggest moment of magic in this weird and amazing trip filled with magic.

Bastien leads the way, with Diego and Shania on either side of him. Claire, Kei, and I walk directly behind them. She is barefoot. She stuffed her Crocs into her backpack when everyone else put their shoes on.

The weird part is, we now have a couple dozen new pilgrims in our group. Bastien is the Pied Piper of Santiago. I look behind me as we walk the hilly roadway and head down into the valley, and people are scattered all about the road.

It's up and down for a bit until we reach the highway, where we walk across an overpass.

"Oh my God," I say. "Would you look at that?"

Diego glances around, trying to find what I'm pointing at. He finally sees the piece of artwork and says, "Cool."

I grab Kei's hand, and together we run past Bastien, Shania, and Diego. We need to be first.

"A dancing star," Kei shouts. "Take my picture; take my picture."

We reach the star. It's made of rusted metal and stands as high as Kei. All its arms are slightly curled and it's askew. This makes it look like it's dancing, just like Kei said. It's so simple. It's seriously the cutest thing ever. Obviously gay Instagram is going to love it. I snap a shot of it. And then some selfie shots of Kei and me hanging from it, hugging it.

As we continue, we come to the sign that welcomes us to the city proper. Big red letters on a link fence surrounding electrical boxes spell out *Santiago de Compostela*.

"Oh my God," Greg says from somewhere behind me. "We've made it. Great God almighty, we've made it."

"Drama llama," Shania says. She laughs.

I stop at the sign, though, and grab Kei up in my arms and squeeze him. I can't stop kissing him, like this is our goodbye. Like to walk into the city is to leave him behind. This is it.

When we pull away from each other, we both try to speak at once. Then we do the *you first; no, you first* thing. We burst into laughter even as we're both doing our best not to cry.

"We will text every day. Message each other. FaceTime. Everything. Not a day goes by," I say. "Got it?"

"Yes. That's what I was going to say," Kei says. "We can do this. Long distance. Okay. Promise?"

"Of course, silly." I stand against the fence of the Santiago sign and drag him beside me. "Selfie." We take a few shots. Then Diego makes a gesture for me to hand him my phone.

"Let's get a good one, boys. With the whole sign in the background," he says. He takes my phone, steps back a few paces, and goes to snap the pic.

"Wait, wait," I say. We quickly wipe our tears away. We're a mess of laughter and tears as we rub at each other's faces with our shirt fronts. "Okay. Go."

Diego takes the shot, and I know what my next profile pic is. A picture of us—Kei and Troy—on the first day of our new compromise. The first day of the rest of our lives. Apart, but together. We can do this long distance thing.

CHAPTER 43

DIEGO NELSON

"Oh, Santiago. Santiago, Santiago, Santiago," Bastien whispers as I step away from Troy and Kei to rejoin him. There are tears in his eyes as he stares solemnly at the Santiago sign. He has his handkerchief out, swiping at his eyes. "How I love this walk. I love this walk, this walk."

He is saying goodbye to everything. I rest my hand on his shoulder and continue to walk beside him, ready to hold him if he needs me. He carried all of us here on his back. He rescued me when I fell and he rescued me when my abuelita passed away. The least I can do is be a hand on his shoulder now.

I look over, and Shania now has an arm entwined with Bastien's opposite arm. We can do this.

As we walk under a copse of trees, something makes me look up. When I do, I see four small balloons caught way up in the higher branches of one of the trees. One orange, one white, and two baby blue. All bunched together. I wonder about their story, but decide to keep them to myself. Nobody else around me looks up, so the balloons are my secret to carry.

Everything extraordinary has now become a sign that my abuelita is with me. Maybe it was she who made me look up? They are her balloons.

The city begins to open up before us as the pilgrims spread out and move in ever-growing clumps of bodies. Streets with sidewalks and buildings on either side: we have hit the city proper. The dirt pathways and trails are now behind us. Cars are everywhere, and streetlights and electrical wires. It almost feels like culture shock after the mountains, trees, and fields.

My heart pounds. I don't know what will happen when we get to the cathedral. There's a war in my brain telling my feet to speed up, telling them to slow down. The end of Bastien. The beginning of a life without Gran. The return to Moms. These things are all fighting against each other and punching my soul. I don't know how to do this. I don't know who I will become.

I return my focus to Bastien. These last footsteps have to be for him, not for me.

The buildings become more condensed, more like a city. I hear Troy tell Kei the streets are beginning to look like the streets of Paris.

"Around this corner, my friends, the first real glimpse of the cathedral. Here we go." Bastien takes a deep breath as we round the corner. "Merde," he whispers to himself as the tears begin to fall.

"There," Shania whispers as she puts a hand over her mouth. "Oh my God. There it is."

The goosebumps travel up and down my arms so quickly, I'm cold... even in this heat. When I look up, I see it for myself. Taller than all the buildings in the distance, a large, single spire reaches high into the sky. It looks slightly lost in smog or heat haze. But it is there. Larger than anything else around. Larger than all of us.

We walk on. The street narrows and becomes cobbled and on an even level with the sidewalk. We walk side by side, spreading out into the road since there are no passing cars.

It's dizzying how many corners we turn as we go deeper and deeper into the city. I have lost sight of the cathedral spire, but so many people are walking now that there's no longer a need for signs. We all just follow each other.

"It's so beautiful here," Shania says. She points above us to little wrought iron balconies over the storefronts we pass. Some are woven with plants and look so green against all the gray of the buildings.

An old woman dressed in black walks by. She's all smiles. She steps aside repeatedly, waves and bows to pilgrims. When we come up alongside her, she whispers, "Buen Camino, peregrinos. You have made The Way. Bless you, bless you."

"Buen Camino," I reply, even though I know she is from here. As we pass, I hear her say the same thing to the next pilgrim, and the next, and the next.

The buildings become bigger, more ornate, with monuments and statuary all around. Each doorway is more elaborate and beautiful than the one before. There are saints everywhere, and it feels like I'm in a Catholic place, a Vatican City in Spain. I can see why my abuelita was so happy to hear I would be coming here.

We turn one last corner and we are in a small rounded archway that connects two buildings. There are doorways on either side. A woman plays this small instrument that looks and sounds like bagpipes, and I don't remember when I first began to hear the melody.

Once we are through the arch, we walk on between the two buildings for several feet with the sky above us. Before we reach the place where the buildings end, Bastien turns to me. His eyes overflow with tears.

"We arrive at the foot of the resting place of St. James, my friends. The Cathedral of Santiago de Compostela. Shania. Diego. I give you the Plaza del Obradoiro. The greatest plaza of all."

Bastien has brought us to the edge of the opening, and a vast cobbled courtyard spreads out before us. I see a huge building across the open plaza from us. The bottom floor is lined with rounded arches. Atop the center of the building sits an enormous statue of a horse on its hind legs surrounded by warriors with arms raised. But I don't see the cathedral.

"Come, come. This way," Bastien says. I see Troy and Kei in the center of the plaza. They are hugging each other. Gil and Meagan are just behind them. I didn't see them pass us.

Bastien takes my arm and drags me farther into the plaza. I've been so busy taking everything in, I didn't realize we have been walking alongside the cathedral the whole time. It was almost within touching distance as we walked through the archway. It was the building on the left.

Bastien swings us around, and the cathedral comes into view and swallows up the presence of everything else around it. It becomes the only thing here. With Bastien on one side, and Shania on the other, I stand before it immobile. I cannot open my mouth to speak. I am mesmerized.

"We made it," Shania says. It's like a gasp escaping her lips. There is no excitement, just fact. No, there is also awe. "We made it."

She sits down on the cobbles and stares up into the face of the cathedral.

Bastien puts both hands over his face and begins to cry. And soon he is bawling inconsolably. "My lovely girls. My girls. Mes filles. Ma chère, ma chère, ma chère. We have made it. I take you now to the altar." He slowly slips to his knees.

Shania looks to me and then moves closer to Bastien and puts an arm around him.

I bend down to join them.

"Bastien," I begin. *I will not cry. I will not cry.* "Thank you. For everything. For this beautiful life you gave us. Thank you for my abuelita and my mother. My mother thanks you for taking care of me."

He removes his hands from his face and spreads his arms wide. He takes both Shania and me into an embrace, and we stay that way forever.

"Mes petits criminels doux," Bastien whispers into my ear. "My sweet little criminals."

"You made it, Bastien. You did it." I can stand it no longer. The swelling in my heart breaks free. But I am not the only one crying. Neither are the three of us. Everywhere I look, there are peregrinos hugging and crying and shouting and laughing.

"My son, my son," Bastien says as he releases us from his embrace. "You all have shown me the way. Thank you."

And it's ridiculous that this man thanks us. He has given us everything he had left inside of him. Everything.

As we scramble to our feet, the rest of the group swarms about us.

"And you were there, and you were there, and you were there!" Manny says. We all stand with the cathedral before us. Manny jumps about, circling us and shouting his mantra over and over to anyone who will listen.

"What's he talking about now?" Shania says.

"*The Wizard of Oz*," Troy says. He rolls his eyes, but they are filled with laughter. "Manny swears we just arrived in Oz and that the Camino is the yellow brick road. Everywhere he looks, he sees someone else he's seen somewhere along the way."

"Diego! From Toronto," someone says, tapping my shoulder. "Hello."

"Bill from Australia," I say. I laugh because Bill has just proven Manny's theory. Bill opens his arms, and we hug.

"Welcome to Santiago de Compostela, my friend," Bill says.

"Same to you." I turn away, distracted again by Manny. When I turn back, Bill is wandering, arms spread wide, toward someone else he recognizes.

After taking in the festive chaos of the plaza for a few minutes, I begin to feel overwhelmed. What awaits me back home now feels much closer, much more real.

"Diego. You look, how you say, heavy," Bastien says. "Yes. Very heavy. Come. We go." He points to the cathedral. "Just you and I. We go. Yes?"

"Sure, Bastien." I follow him as he begins to make his way to the steps leading up to the cathedral.

"Hey. Where're you going?" Claire asks. I turn to tell her, but Bastien beats me to it.

"We go inside. Just Diego and me for now."

"Oh, yeah. Sure," Claire says. I can tell by the look on her face she gets it. The others look on. They are all happy to let us have a private moment. "Okay. We'll wait here. We'll watch your backpacks."

"Thanks, Claire," I say before I turn back to Bastien, and we walk away.

CHAPTER
44

SHANIA REYNOLDS

Friday, July 12th – Day 14 – Santiago de Compostela and Claire

After Diego leaves with Bastien, we sit around and chill. There's so much to take in, here in the plaza. Might as well finish off this journal. I used to hate doing this, but it's okay. Maybe I'll keep one when I go home.

Gil and Meagan sit off to the side, probably going over the ups and downs of the program. They're both taking notes. But Manny and Greg? They're jumping around, talking with everyone, whether they met them on the walk or not. They're so excited, it's ridiculous. It's Claire I'm watching. She's sitting cross-legged on the cobbles, staring blankly up at the cathedral. She does not look very celebratory. I think it's time we have a talk. No doubt she's thinking about not wanting to go home.

She thinks it'll be the same. But before the Camino Club, she didn't have backup. You don't walk the Camino de Santiago with a bunch of strangers without becoming friends for life. Someone needs to remind Claire she has a support network now. Bright side? I'm sitting in front of the most beautiful cathedral in the world and my new best friends are all nearby. The bright side today is The Camino Club. I can't believe there's life after the Camino. I can't wait to begin it with my new friends.

"Hey, Claire," I say after I put my journal away in my backpack for the very last time. She looks over and smiles. "Whatcha doing? Let's walk around. Come on."

"You know, Shania." She gets up to join me. "I'm just thinking about Zoe. And how nothing's changed, and it's still going to be a nightmare back home. I don't want to go. I'm starting to panic. I *really* don't want to go."

She's worse off than I thought. She's chewing on her fingernails, and it's obvious how agitated she is. She looks like she's about to bolt into the streets of Compostela and disappear forever.

"Whoa, whoa," I say. We make our way through the throng and walk the outskirts of the plaza, where there's more room. "No. No, Claire. You're wrong. It's different. A lot different. I know we didn't hit it off right away, but we did this together. We're *all* here for you. It's not like we're going to go home and never see each other again. Come on. You know that as much as I do."

"I was thinking about that too." She finally stops eating her nails. "Wait a minute. I see what's going on here. This is like that scene in *The Breakfast Club*, isn't it? You know, where Molly Ringwald's character takes Ally Sheedy's goth character away from the group, gives her a pep talk, and then makes her pretty by scraping off the goth and making her look normal and pretty?"

"Again, I did *not* see the movie," I say. "I have zero idea what you're talking about."

"I keep forgetting that," Claire says. She laughs. "Thank God. Because in the next scene I would be hooking up with the jock. I guess that would be Manny? I know it's an old movie, Shania, but still. I can't believe you haven't seen it. It's on TV all the time."

"I don't really watch regular TV. I'm more Netflix," I say. "Anyway. You *do* realize we're friends for life now, don't you? Like it or not, you're stuck with us. And not just Greg, either. All of us. The six of us are going to be a package deal from now on."

"Greg turned out to be such a nice guy, Shan. I can't even believe it. The biggest asshole turns out to be the most sensitive cool guy in a whole group of sensitive cool guys. I feel sorry for him, though. He's having a hard time missing his little brother. And worrying about him."

"Well," I say, "Maybe we can be there for him too. We should plan something for after we get back. Just to check up on each other. I know Troy'll need it. He's gonna miss Kei like crazy. And Diego? His gran. Her funeral. We're all gonna need each other. Except maybe Manny and me. Looks like we're the lucky ones."

"Ha. Yeah."

"I know," I say. I stop and turn to her. "I have the perfect idea. Maybe you can all come to my place and we can watch *The Breakfast Club* together. You can bring Zoe if you want. You could meet Flibber."

"That sounds awesome. I like that idea."

"Good. We'll talk to the guys about it later."

"Thanks, Shania. Really."

I grab her shoulder and make sure she's looking at me. "You're not going to be alone, Claire. Okay? I promise. It'll get better."

"It already is. I mean, look at this place. Can you believe we actually made it?"

We look around at the chaos of arriving peregrinos and see celebration wherever we look. It's pretty spectacular.

"Can you believe that guy over there is with us?" she continues. "I mean, look at him."

I turn to look where she's pointing, and I see Manny dancing in a circle around Greg, Troy, Kei, and his sisters. He looks like a fool. But he's *our* fool now. Beyond them, I spot Meagan and Gil. When they see me looking, they both wave.

"Our people," I say. We both laugh.

"Come on. Let's go join them."

CHAPTER
45

TROY SINCLAIR

PART OF ME WANTS TO anchor Manny to the ground. He's taking this *Wizard of Oz* thing a little too far. I'm afraid he might just take off into the stratosphere like the wizard did in the hot-air balloon at the end of the movie. Only, Manny's so excited he doesn't need the balloon. He *is* the balloon.

I look at Kei and see he's mesmerized by Manny, watching his every move. His sisters, though, are oblivious. They're squished in together holding Becky's phone in front of their faces. They're talking with their father, telling him Kei's okay, and that they made it to the cathedral. To them, Manny is just more of the chaos and noise around them.

I get Kei's attention. He gives me this oops face, like I caught him doing something he shouldn't be doing. Guess I'm not the only one who finds himself staring at Manny.

"Come on," I say. "Let's go for a walk. I saw a few stores behind the cathedral."

"Shouldn't we wait for everyone else? Go see inside the church?" he says, once he pulls himself out of Manny's orbit.

"Nah. They're gonna be a while. We have time."

"Okay," he says. What I'm really thinking of is the row of stalls I saw on the way in. One of them sold cheap silver jewelry. I have an idea.

He grabs my hand and we head off.

"Watch our backpacks," I say to Claire as she and Shania rejoin everyone.

"Sure thing," she says.

Once we're on the street with the stalls, I try to explain my plan to Kei in a way that doesn't sound too scary.

"One of these stalls sells jewelry. I was thinking, you know, we could maybe get rings. Nothing serious. Just to remind us of each other. I know it's kind of pointless and it's probably a stupid idea, but maybe—"

"No. Stop talking, Troy. I think it's a great idea. You don't have to be like that. I like it. Let's."

"Over here." I walk him to the stall I saw on the way in. There's a bunch of black felt boxes with slots in them, and they're all filled with silver rings. The cheap kind you can find at flea markets back home. As I check them out, I realize they're mostly Camino-themed.

Kei pulls a scallop shell ring out of its slot and holds it up for me to see. "I love this one. Cool, right? Sometimes when I close my eyes, all I see are scallop shells."

I laugh. "Yeah. Cute."

I try on a ring with the Galician cross on it. The cross is red enamel, though, so it looks even cheaper than it is. Like something out of a bubble gum machine. Nope. Then I try one on with an arrow, but it's yellow enamel. It looks just as cheap. Nope.

"This one!" Kei almost screeches. He holds up a silver ring with wavy shells going all the way around it. They're carved in relief, and the indented spaces are all black. The shells really pop. I love it.

"Yes," I say, victorious. Kei tries it on, but it swims on his finger.

"Shit," he says. "Not even close."

He puts it back, but I say, "Wait. Don't give up so fast." I pick it up and try it on. It fits me perfectly.

The stall owner is talking to a girl about a necklace. I look on impatiently, waiting for them to finish bartering. When they finally finish and she buys the necklace and moves on, I hold up the ring.

"Do you have this one in any other sizes?"

"I see, I see," he says. He kneels and reaches for a large plastic tub under the table. He lifts it and digs inside. Eventually, he brings out a sandwich baggie that's swimming in a million duplicates of the exact same ring. "Aha!"

"Wow," I say. "I guess you do."

I look at Kei, and he's all smiles. We both are, because we know somewhere in that pile of rings is at least one that will fit his finger.

"Shall we?" I ask, almost a bit too ceremoniously.

"Yes," he says. "To remember the Camino we shared."

"Yeah, of course." Obviously, neither of us wants to say anything more about the significance of matching rings. About the future. I don't want to make it sound like this thing we have is more serious than it is. Even though I do. I swear, the closer we've gotten to Compostela, the more we've both tried to explain away the seriousness of what we're becoming.

The man takes a close look at Kei's finger and reaches into the baggie. He pulls out a ring with a little sticky strip on it that reads "7 ½" and hands it to Kei. "Maybe this one?"

Kei tries it on, but it's a little too snug for him. He frowns.

"No, no. Don't be sad," the man says. He jingles the bag. "Lots more."

He pulls out an eight, hands it to Kei, and takes back the other one. The new ring is a perfect fit. Kei holds up his hand and smiles.

"Aha," the man says. He drops the baggie into the container and puts that back under the table. "You match, no? Nice, nice."

"We'll take them," I say. Neither of us removes the rings. "How much?"

"For you two," the man says, smiling, "fifteen Euros each."

I begin to get all *aw, how sweet,* until I see the little cardboard sign on the table that says *Rings €15/ea.* Not so sweet. Oh well.

Kei sees the interaction play out and laughs. "How about twenty-five Euros for two?" he says.

"Yes, yes," the man says. He puts a hand to his heart. "You kill me, but yes. Okay."

"Yay," Kei says. I smile at him; we get our money out and pay for the rings. We thank the man. As we walk away, we hold our hands out to inspect the rings.

"Sweet," Kei says. "Great idea, Troy. I'm going to remember this forever."

"You always remember your first, right? That's what they say."

Oops. Too much information. I never told him he was my first. Kei just laughs. Nice.

"Don't worry. Me too," he says.

"Really?" I feel so relieved.

We head back to the plaza, admiring our new rings. Before we get there, though, Kei stops.

"Wait," he says. He begins to wiggle the stud in his nose and eventually it comes out. He passes it to me. "I want you to have this."

"Huh?" I ask, perplexed. "Why? I don't have any piercings. I can't use it."

"You dingbat. I'm attempting some grand gesture and you're killing it. Aren't you guys all about the *The Breakfast Club*?"

"Yeah, so?" I say. Even as I ask the question, though, it comes to me. "Ah! Yes! I love it. Molly Ringwald's character, at the end. She gives Judd Nelson her diamond earring. Yes!"

"I worry about you, Troy," Kei says. "You're pretty slow sometimes. You know that, don't you?"

We laugh. Kei takes my hand, puts the stud in the middle of my palm, and closes my fingers over it. I can feel the diamond press into my skin. A part of me knows this is our goodbye, even though we'll still have time together over the next day or so.

"This was amazing, Kei," I say, suddenly serious. I can tell by the look on his face he knows I don't just mean the pilgrimage or us or his nose-stud gesture. I mean everything. I pocket the stud and hold my ring finger up again. "I'll never forget this."

"Me too," he says in a near whisper. We turn the corner and we're back in the plaza.

I'm going to miss him forever.

CHAPTER 46

DIEGO NELSON

AFTER WE CLIMB THE ZIGZAGGING stairs up to the front doors of the cathedral, Bastien turns to me. His eyes glisten with unfallen tears, and his smile is everything.

"Ready, my son? To see the beauty at the end of the yellow brick road?" He winks. "Manny's wizard, he waits for us."

"Ready," I say. Yeah. There might be tears in my eyes too. I feel the weight of my grandmother inside me. And of my mother waiting at home. And of Bastien's cancer, eating away at him as we move across the threshold.

I'm not ready for what I see when we finally enter the church. It's incredibly big. Impossibly big. We stand at the back and look up the aisle toward the sanctuary where the altar is. It's by far the biggest sanctuary I've ever seen. And it's filled with gold.

"It is big, yes, Diego," Bastien says. I'm almost too overwhelmed to speak.

"Incredible," I whisper. My mouth hangs open. There's too much to look at, and I don't have words for any of it. I put my hand on the back of a pew.

We begin to walk toward the sanctuary. There are peregrinos everywhere, and the way to the altar looks impossible to navigate.

"Diego. Come, we sit. In the nave here. We wait. It's too busy, no? We sit. We talk."

I look toward the sanctuary with regret.

"No, no. We'll go. In a bit. Let's just wait. We'll sit and watch." I shrug and then nod my approval. Bastien smiles. "Good, good."

Bastien turns, makes the sign of the cross, and kneels before entering the pew. He walks midway down and sits on the hard wooden bench. I follow his lead.

"We carry with us the important women in our lives, Diego. We are so very lucky. Lucky to have known them and lucky to have this task, yes. To bring the memory of them to this beautiful cathedral."

Bastien pulls out a rosary. It's the first time I've seen it. He fidgets with the beads, but not like he's praying... just absently. I say nothing. I try to swallow the lump forming in my throat, but it doesn't work.

"My wife, she said she saw me here alone after the end of her life. And Diego, she cried. She lay in the bed in that hôpital and she cried for me. 'Alone, alone,' she say. She knows I would walk. She know me." He puts a hand over his heart and then pounds his chest for effect. "Here."

"But you're not alone, Bastien. You have us."

"This is why I say," he says. We are ignoring the beautiful cathedral around us, now. We're turned toward each other in our seats. "You say I saved you, I saved you, I saved you."

Bastien stops to search in his pocket for his handkerchief. He dabs his eyes.

"It's okay, Bastien. You did save me. Twice. You picked me up out of the mud." I laugh, and he joins me, but we're both emotional puddles. "Without you, I don't know how I would have dealt with losing my abuelita. You made everything okay."

"But no, no," he says. "What I want to say is no, I did not save you. It is the other way. I want to say to you that my wife, Diego, she would be so happy you made my last Camino so..."

He doesn't finish his sentence. He doesn't need to. I was there.

"Bastien," I say. But I can't finish either.

"I know. I know." He puts a hand on mine, which is resting on the pew between us. "The crowd, it's shifting. Maybe we go now?"

"Sure," I say. Neither of us seems capable of speech. We make our way out of the pew and begin the long walk up the aisle toward the altar and the sanctuary. Bastien continues to fiddle with his rosary beads.

"Everything is the last," Bastien says. When I look at him, I can see his pain. Along with his rosary, he's carrying a photograph and he's staring into it. "The last Camino. The last day in this cathedral. Later, the last swing of the Botafumeiro. I do it all for these beautiful ladies in my life, Diego. I do it all for them."

It's the first time I've seen their picture. His wife is behind his daughter, making a funny face and holding up a cake. His daughter is laughing so hard her eyes are almost closed. They're both beautiful. And they're carbon copies of each other. They each have long dark hair, high cheekbones, and a constellation of freckles across their faces. I think about who they were looking at when the picture was taken and I know how happy Bastien must have been in that moment.

"It is the last picture together. Cloe's last birthday. Just before she knew. That happy day. I think of what was growing inside her during this picture. I could not save her, Diego. I could not do a thing. If only we knew. If only."

"They're beautiful, Bastien." I feel so helpless. "I'm so sorry."

"Merde," he says. He stops walking and grabs on to a pew back. He holds his heart for a moment and then slips into the pew. "Sorry, Diego. I must sit again. You go. Go see St. James in the sanctuary. I wait."

"No. I won't go without you. We can wait a minute." He slides over, and I drop down beside him.

"What will I do without mes petits méchants? My little bad guys, my little criminals. What will I do? The Camino moves in magical ways, no?"

"It gave me you, Bastien," I say. I begin to cry. Have I even stopped since I entered the city? "I'll never forget you. What you did for me. For my abuelita."

"The Camino gives us what we need, my son. When we need it."

"Yes. It does."

He holds his arms open, and I allow myself to fall into them. "You are the thing that saved me on this Camino, Diego. I thank you from the bottom of my heart for falling in the mud."

We laugh but we both have tears in our eyes.

"Come, we go," he says. "We should do this. The others, they wait for us, no?"

Once again we head toward the altar. The closer it gets, the bigger it appears to be. Then it is before us, and I'm staring up at the statue of the number one pilgrim.

"St. James," Bastien says. "We give him our woes and pray to him."

We stand in silence, and I pray for my abuelita because I know she would like that. When I'm done, I peek over at Bastien. His lips are moving, and his hands are working his rosary beads in prayer. He looks incredibly fragile.

He stops and looks at me. He breaks into a smile and I can see his entire life in it. He shines. He puts his photograph away and places a hand on my cheek. I can feel the beads wrapped around his fingers.

"Your life," he says. "It begins today, Diego. Make it beautiful. Beautiful like the Camino de Santiago."

"I will, Bastien. And I'll always carry you with me."

"You're a good boy, my little criminal." He opens his arms, and we stand in front of St. James and hug. I never want to leave him.

*   *   *

AFTER OUR HUG, I LEAVE Bastien at the altar to finish his rosary. When I join the others, they are anxious to see inside the cathedral.

"You guys should go," I say after Greg moans about having waited so long to see it. "Bastien's at the altar. I saw it with him and I'll go back for Mass later."

"Sounds good," Greg says. "Are you okay, though, bud?"

"Yeah, yeah," I say. "I'm good. Better than good. Thanks, dude. You guys go. I'm just gonna walk around the plaza for a bit and check things out."

"Don't go far," Gil says. "We need to go to the Pilgrims' Office to pick up our Compostelas. Our certificates that show we finished the pilgrimage."

"Sure thing, Gil," I say.

"Have your Camino passport handy," Meagan says. "You'll need to show them your stamps to prove you walked."

"I know, Meagan. Thanks. And Bastien told me earlier I could dedicate my Compostela to my abuelita too."

"That's lovely," she says. "Yes, that's right. I hadn't thought of that. Bastien! He thinks of everything, doesn't he? What a godsend."

I feel the tears coming but I'm exhausted. "Yeah. He's the best. I'll miss him my whole life."

"Oh, I'm sorry, Diego," Meagan says when she sees the look on my face. She gives me a quick hug. "Okay. We'll go now and leave you be. I can tell you need some time alone."

"Hey, bro?" Manny says. "You cool?"

"Yeah, Man," I say. "I'm good. Gimme some."

He comes in for a high five and then we bump shoulders. The others smile and wave as they walk away in the direction of the cathedral. I hope they give Bastien the space he needs.

I walk into the center of the square. There are people everywhere. Backpacks everywhere. Shoes everywhere. Walking sticks everywhere. People are dancing. People are crying inconsolably, either alone or in groups.

I see a marker on the ground and make my way toward it. There are large stones set into the ground with words etched into them. And a scallop shell is carved into one of the stones. As I wait for my turn to see them, I think that I will never see a scallop shell anywhere in the world for the rest of my life without thinking of this Camino and everything that has happened here.

I look up at the cathedral again—this church that would blot out the sun and the moon—and I know we will all enter it together later. Either tonight or tomorrow afternoon we will see the Botafumeiro swing the length of the cathedral, pouring the smoke of incense over all of us, filling the church with its fragrant aroma. And I'll remember that scent from those times my grandmother brought me to her church. And I'll remember my abuelita, who I have carried all the way here. With the help of my friends. And my Bastien.

When I turn back to the stones, it's my turn. I take a couple photos before putting my phone away. I know it's not really a time for phones.

Not sure what else to do, I drop my backpack to the cobbles. It feels so good to be free of its weight. Like I can breathe again. As I lie down on the ground between the words and the shell, I close my eyes. I hold my breath and listen to the sounds of the plaza. A violin, the bagpipes in the distance, the clop of a horse's hooves on the cobbles. A woman nearby, softly singing "Ave Maria." People talking in every language. Every single language. Talking and laughing and crying.

I spread my arms and legs out as far as they will reach. I begin to make snow angels without the snow. I've kept the promise I made to Bastien back at Monte do Gozo, back at the Hill of Joy. I have come to the cathedral a child. Even the burden of losing my abuelita is not enough to stop my arms and legs from swinging against the cobbles as I imagine the snow angel appearing beneath me, in this square where angels are real, where angels exist all about me.

This program? This thing that Gilbert and Meagan have done? It has made warriors out of criminals. It has changed me. It has changed all of us.

Gil and Meagan will do this again. And again. Because there are others who need saving. And they will save them. No, they won't have Bastien. I am sad for them that they will not have Bastien. But I think we'll all go home with him in our hearts. As long as we live, Bastien will live. They can bring his spirit with them on their next Camino, for the next batch of criminals they hope to save.

When I finally open my eyes, Shania is standing over me, looking down on me.

"Where'd you go?" she asks as the world comes back into focus.

"Everywhere," I whisper as tears slip from my eyes and trail down the sides of my face. "Everywhere," I repeat. And I believe this to be true. It all started with fire. And it ends with fire. It's inside me and it'll burn forever.

THE END

ACKNOWLEDGMENTS

HUGE THANKS TO ANNIE HARPER, CB Messer, and Candysse Miller, the incredible team at Duet Books/Interlude Press. Thanks to Annie for doing that important and magical thing that all great editors do: make the words of their writers shine. Thanks to CB for creating a beautiful cover that far surpassed all of my wildest dreams. It perfectly captures the Camino in every way! Thanks to Candysse for being such a great hand-holder throughout the process, for finding innovative ways for authors to connect with readers, and for always being there for every little thing. Thank you all for giving *The Camino Club* a home and for being so kind to both of us.

Thanks to ALL of my first readers. I'm constantly blown away by the generosity of my corral of writing friends. Tobin Elliott, Naomi Mesbur, and Dale Long... you're all superstars! Thank you for being there for me every single time I hit you up. Thanks to Kate, Karen, Deb, Jennifer, and all the rest. You've all helped me immensely and I'm forever in your debt.

Everyone should have a stalker. Mine is Mel Cober. I adore you and the way you always have enough pins on hand to add another to the map! You're my orange.

Thanks to Michael Sue-Chuck, for being you and for constantly allowing me to be me. And thank you for your editing wisdom along the way. You're the best non-reading reader I know. I can't wait to walk more Camino paths with you!

ABOUT THE AUTHOR

KEVIN CRAIG IS A PLAYWRIGHT, poet, and short story writer who lives in Toronto with their husband, Michael. Kevin's six published novels include *Pride Must Be a Place* (MuseItUp Publishing, 2018) and *Burn Baby Burn Baby* (independently published, 2014). Kevin was a founding member of the Ontario Writers' Conference Board of Directors, and sat on the Writers' Community of Durham Region's (WCDR) Board of Directors as Membership Coordinator.

CONNECT WITH KEVIN ONLINE

🌐 ktcraig.com
🐦 KevinTCraig
📷 kevinthomascraig

an imprint of interlude **press**

🌐 duetbooks.com
🐦 @DuetBooks
ⓣ duetbooks
🛒 store.interludepress.com

also from duet.

The Summer of Everything by Julian Winters

Wes Hudson's summer has gotten complicated. His job at the local indie bookstore is threatened by a coffeeshop franchise looking to buy it. His family is pestering him about college majors. And he can't stop pining over his best friend, Nico. When all three problems converge, Wes comes face-to-face with the thing he fears most— adulthood.

ISBN (print) 978-1-945053-91-7 | (eBook) 978-1-945053-92-4

Short Stuff edited by Alysia Constantine

It could start anywhere... At a summer vacation at the lake, just before heading off to college. In a coffee shop, when the whole world is new. In a dragon's cave, surrounded by gold. At a swim club, with the future in sight. In *Short Stuff*, bestselling and award-winning authors dial down the angst in four meet-cute LGBTQ young adult romances.

ISBN (print) 978-1-945053-89-4 | (eBook) 978-1-945053-90-0

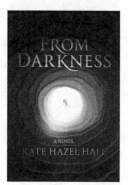

From Darkness by Kate Hazel Hall

When sixteen-year-old Ari Wyndham's life is tragically cut short, a strangely familiar young woman sent to summon Ari's soul to the underworld chooses to save her instead. Doing so upsets the balance of life and death in Ari's remote coastal village, and a rift opens from the underworld, unleashing dark magic. Together, they battle to prove that their bond is strong enough to defy the Fates and save the world from darkness.

ISBN (print) 978-1-945053-98-6 | (eBook) 978-1-945053-73-3